ABOUT THE AUTHOR

Emme DeWitt lives in the Chicagoland area with a mostly blind rescue beagle and a healthy stash of hoodies and mismatched coffee mugs. HARBINGER is her debut novel. Emme is also abysmal at describing herself, her various writing projects, and how she manages not to burn down her apartment with her culinary "genius."

To find out more about Emme and keep up to date on the latest Dawn of Eight releases, check out her website.

www.emmedewitt.com

A DAWN OF EIGHT NOVEL

HARBINGER

EMME DeWITT

For Caroline and Dena, whose strength and wisdom breathed life into Noah from the very beginning

ISBN-13 978-0692715765
ISBN-10 0692715762

Published by Iron Sparrow Media
www.ironsparrowmedia.com

ONE

The sting of Adele's quick backhand broke through the barrier of my thick moto jacket, jarring me from my reverie. My hand instinctively crossed my chest to rub away the pins and needles. I sighed in annoyance.

"Gah, rings. Really?" I grumbled, tenderly touching my arm for any signs of injury. "Now I'm going to bruise."

"Shhh," Adele hissed. Her head continued to whip around, trying to find the perfect position to eavesdrop on the muttering leaking through the closed office door without leaving the confines of her seat.

I sat up straighter in my chair to ward off another reprimand, but my fingers continued their search for tender spots. My eyes focused instead on the salt residue my boots had left on the once pristine oaken desk in front of me when I'd tried to reposition my long legs earlier. The pins and needles in my arm now matched those in my entire right leg, which had fallen asleep in its uncomfortable position.

Adele was unsympathetic. Tension rolled off her in waves, filling the spacious office in minutes.

Another sigh escaped as I checked my phone for the time. This time, I got a cut eye.

"We've been sitting here for twenty minutes," I said.

"And?" Adele's head snapped around again at a lull in the conversation outside.

"And," I replied, trying to choose words that would not merit another hit, "I'd rather wait in the car."

My eyes had already scanned the walls lined with books to exhaustion. I tried to make out the titles, but they were far enough away in small enough letters to force me to give up after a few minutes. Nothing else held my interest in the room, which was first and foremost functional, not stacked with bobbles, knickknacks, and other design magazine worthy clutter that one typically found in an administrative office. Someone had been taking leadership advice to heart.

"You can't wait in the car," Adele said without hesitation.

"Because—" I bit my lips a little too late.

Adele's head swiveled around to face me. Her silence dragged on as her eyes ceased to blink.

"It's rude?" I finished uncertainly.

She sighed, breaking her glare only to roll her eyes at me. "Bingo," she said, her attention refocusing on the door.

"Isn't it also rude to keep us waiting?" I asked, picking at a loose thread at the end of my frayed sweatshirt sleeve.

Adele hummed at me. Suddenly, she whipped around to face the desk, crossing her legs and readjusting them to seem comfortable and unassuming.

The doorknob clicked, and a head popped into the room. Adele turned slowly in her chair at the noise, feigning mild expectation.

"So sorry for the delay," the secretary said. "The dean was waylaid by a sudden emergency. She should be in shortly."

"No problem," Adele chirped, her smile so wide it came off as maniacal instead of sincere. Even I could tell the difference.

The secretary bowed out, and the door shut with a crisp snap. I blinked, and Adele's crazy face was gone.

"See?" Adele said. "An emergency." She smacked her leg in satisfaction.

"At least we know it wasn't me this time," I muttered darkly.

"What?" Adele said.

"Nothing," I replied. I wrapped the length of loose string around my finger, pulling it tightly to break it off.

"Listen, Noah," Adele said, her full attention honed in on me.

I glanced toward the murmurs that punctuated the silence from the other side of the door, hoping Adele would remain distracted so we could avoid this conversation. Again.

"Your father left very explicit instructions in your trust," Adele said as she always did. By now, we had a script.

"I must be enrolled in school until I'm 18, at which time I will graduate. Continued support is only offered if I graduate with honors. No arrests. No convictions. No fuss. Or no money," I chanted, the words burned into my brain better than my times tables.

"Of course, but," Adele said, pausing for a deep

breath.

I frowned, turning to face her. There was never a "but."

"This is the last stop." Adele's posture braced for my response.

"Okay." I twisted the freed string into a tight ball between my fingertips as I strategized where to discard it. Likely, I would have to return it to a pocket somewhere to be forgotten about. I hadn't seen a trash bin in the office, at least not one easily accessible to guests.

"No, Noah, I'm serious," Adele said. "The board got you this slot through some serious connections. No one else would take you."

"There's always public school," I said dismissively. "Federally, I think they're required to take me."

Adele shook her head. Her fingers pinched the bridge of her nose as she sighed. "You have to make this work for the next two years. No...incidents," Adele said.

"It's not like I purposefully get in trouble," I argued. "It just happens." My fingers continued to work at the tiny ball of string, and I watched my long fingers flex with the movement. My nail beds were a wreck, the length bitten raw to the quick. I wondered if painting them would accentuate the damage.

"Well, it can't happen here," Adele said. "You're cut off if you get expelled."

My fingers froze.

"We've survived before." I shrugged, redirecting my attention to the smudges on my boots. I rubbed at them, worried the salt might damage the leather.

Adele cleared her throat. Her jaw moved without sound as she tried to find the words she wanted.

After a few moments, it clicked. "You're leaving if I mess up," I said. My words were fact, but a lump grew in my throat.

"It's been the arrangement from the start that I would watch over you until you graduated—"

"Or until the checks stop," I said coldly. I continued to rub purposefully on the heel of my boot.

"That is not true," Adele snapped.

"You're just following the contract. It's fine." I was already done with the conversation. Mentally I wiped it away, swallowing hard to clear the lump as well. "It's not like you're my mother anyway."

"Seriously?" Adele said. "You're going to say that to me?"

"It's the truth." I shrugged, focusing on the greying smudges on my boots.

"Even so, I did my best." Adele crossed her arms and legs angrily. "Not like you made it easy."

The blanket of silence stifled the room, replacing Adele's nervous energy with muted anger.

"Do me a favor." Adele broke the silence after I'd moved from cleaning one boot to the other, the ball of string lost on the paisley carpet below. "Count to three before you say anything factual. Really consider if it's necessary. If it's kind. It should help reduce any misunderstandings with people who don't know you're not as much of an asshole as you come off."

I snorted. "Oh, I'm more of an asshole the more you get to know me." A slight smile pulled at my lips.

"Yeah, but just fake it a little until they're in too deep." Adele's hand talked nervously for her in the air. "You don't need a ton of friends, but having at least one or two people in your corner is important."

"Not too many people jockeying for those

spots." I snorted.

"Well, you've got one, but she's old and lame and calls you No-no to embarrass you in public." Adele picked the fuzzies off her suede booties. Our heads were now level to one another and the desk.

"Lame? I mean, your slang could use some updating, but you're the most fashionable hacker I know." I brushed imaginary dust from my now immaculate boots.

"I code," Adele said. "That does not make me a hacker."

"I see the support checks. I'm aware of the cost of living. I can even do math," I said in mock surprise. My wide eyes met Adele's.

She mirrored my shocked expression. "Really?" Adele said in mock admiration. "Since when?"

"I can even do differential equations," I replied. "You can be impressed any time now."

I slouched back down in my chair, crossing my arms over my stomach. My butt was now asleep from the hard, unforgiving wooden torture device known as a Windsor chair. Adele's leg bounced in mild agitation next to me as she returned upright as well.

"I'll be impressed when you graduate." Adele's eyes finally took in the office. "It would be nice to stick it to the board. Bunch of grumpy old biddies."

"I'm sure they're not used to being so involved with their investments," I mumbled through my collar, which had crept up to cover the bottom half of my face. Even in such an uncomfortable position, I was happy the small rift with Adele was already smoothed over. I didn't like it when we were on bad terms.

"If they weren't so cloak and dagger about everything, I'm sure it would be less work, too," Adele grumbled. "You're a teenager, not a mobster."

"At least I got to keep my name." I sighed.

"There is that," Adele said. "You don't really look like an Ashley or a Jennifer anyway."

"Those were my options?" I asked.

"Or the ever popular Mary." Adele was unable to contain her smile. "We could even smooth it together and make it Mary Ashley or Mary Jennifer."

"I hate you," I mumbled.

"I have strong feelings for you also." Adele's smile shook with quiet laughter.

The door flew open, catching both Adele and me by surprise. The secretary stood sentry holding the door handle.

Adele leapt out of her seat, hauling me up by the arm.

She rapidly fired into my ear. "Try not to say anything. Yes ma'am or no ma'am if you have to reply. Don't make faces. Don't check your phone. Don't do anything remotely considered insulting or offensive. Got it?" Her face was obscured by my long kinky hair that had fallen off my shoulder as I stooped to her level. Even with her wedge booties, Adele was a good six inches shorter than I was.

I nodded, my eyes on the door. I nudged her with my elbow as soon as I saw a blur, allowing her to step back to her place as if our pep talk had never happened. I shoved my hands in my pockets, doing my best to school my face so I wouldn't get kicked out before I even started.

TWO

A woman strode into the office, the air from her movements fluffing her cropped grey hair with each step. Her hand was extended out to Adele even from several feet away. The dean and Adele plastered on the requisite polite smile, showing just enough teeth. I didn't attempt to mimic them, citing instruction number three about remaining inoffensive.

"Ms. Kincaide, my apologies for your wait." The dean used both her hands to clasp Adele's hand. "I do appreciate your patience."

"Not a problem." Adele's voice was pitched higher than normal. "We're happy to squeeze into your busy schedule."

"Ah, Ms. Young." The dean released Adele's hand for a few good pumps of my own. Even in her black power suit and heels, she seemed to be mildly perplexed at my looming height. The hesitation was evident only for a moment before her smile widened and her posture returned to its power pose. "Please, have a seat."

The dean settled herself behind the large desk, and I took extra care to avoid kicking the desk as I crossed my legs. I squinted at the marks from earlier, realizing belatedly I should have wiped those off when I was cleaning up my boots. Oh well.

"So," the dean said, "the good news is that most of the paperwork has already been taken care of by the trustees, as they sent your files ahead."

"We do appreciate you accepting Noah so late into the school year," Adele said. "I'm glad it hasn't been too much of a burden."

So far, I thought to myself.

"Of course! How could we not accept her? Legacy students are always such a joy to have." The dean's smile didn't reach her eyes. "We take great pride in our alumni community. And both parents, no less!"

I stiffened in my seat.

Both parents? My eyes slid to Adele, and she gave me the most imperceptible head shake. The message was clear. Not now.

"And of course, we can't forget you, Ms. Kincaide." The dean's hands were clasped in front of her on the desk. "It's been such a treat to see you as well. Fifteen years flies by, doesn't it?"

Adele laughed, the tinkling tone sounding off in the austere room. Adele's nerves from earlier now made perfect sense. Even after all these years, sitting in the principal's office still affected even the most confident adult.

"Absolutely. It's so great to see Noah will be benefiting from the same strong leadership as I did. And her parents, of course. A lot of great memories," Adele babbled, nodding her head.

"I certainly hope so," the dean said. "We've prepared both her schedule and her dorm room, so as soon as her tour guide arrives, we can get her started."

"Dorm room?" Adele's smile faltered.

"Yes, residency rules are still the same from when you were a student," the dean said with an oblivious smile. "You remember."

"Ah, yes, but the board should have included some additional paperwork and explanation." Adele's smile was growing more forceful by the minute. "Noah needs special accommodations, so she'll be residing with me off campus."

"We did receive the recommendations; however, residency is a requirement for admission. That was made clear to the board, and they accepted. I assume this won't be a problem." The dean's voice was missing the hitch of a question.

I bit the inside of my cheek.

"No, ma'am," I replied, noticing Adele's tongue stuck behind her teeth in shock.

Her eyelids fluttered a little, and I wondered how long it would take her to reboot from the shock to her system. Adele had been half confident I could succeed using our old standby routine, but now that I was forced to do it on my own, I could tell she was preparing for instant failure. A knot formed in my stomach.

"Wonderful," the dean said. "Your student guide should be waiting for you outside. Thank you both for your time. We'll see you for Parent's Weekend, right, Ms. Kincaide? You shouldn't miss it."

The dean's expectant smile was our cue. I stood, inclining my head slightly in thanks before turning for the door. I grabbed Adele lightly by the arm, and she stood up obediently. We were already at the door before she finally reacted.

"See you next month," Adele said cheerily as her goodbye.

"Looking forward to it," the dean said indulgently, already half focused on some files splayed across her desk.

We ducked out the door, and I shut it before the secretary could jump from her seat. Luckily, the phone rang just then, and the secretary was otherwise occupied.

I still held Adele's arm, and I squeezed it tightly to get her attention.

"Ouch." She frowned at me.

"Hello." I waved my hand in front of her face.

"What?" She dropped her voice so the secretary's one-sided conversation covered our own.

"I'll be fine," I said. "What is with you?"

Adele shook her head. "I'm fine," she countered. "But you're screwed."

"Thanks for the vote of confidence," I muttered darkly.

Adele let out a big breath, steadying herself. "Plan B." Her eyes squinted in concentration. "Scope out campus. Find a place you can use when you need to get away. Text me if you have problems. I'll come get you."

I tugged my phone out of my pocket, glancing briefly at the screen before presenting it to Adele.

"Zero bars. I didn't even know that was a thing." I flicked through my settings to check out the internet access options. No phone calls I could deal with. No internet? No thank you.

"Fine, use the Wi-Fi and the old chat app. I'll keep it up at home. I emailed you the new address if you need it." Adele pinched the bridge of her nose.

"If residency is a requirement, I'm pretty sure they'll get pissed if I sneak off campus," I argued. "I thought you said I had to stick it out. It's a year and a half until graduation."

"Then you figure it out," Adele said rapidly since the secretary was almost ready to hang up her phone conversation. "You keep me updated though. I'm in your corner, remember?"

"Got it, Coach," I said just as the secretary set the receiver back in the desk phone.

"Ms. Young?" she said. "We will transfer your things to your dorm room. Your guide is in the hall. She'll..."

The secretary was cut off by another phone call, which she answered promptly with a reserved NPR voice.

"Good luck." Adele stood on her tiptoes to give me a quick hug. "Behave?"

I snorted. I headed toward the doors the secretary had indicated, but a noise prompted me to turn around. The secretary was holding out a manila envelope, shaking it at me while she tried to remain impassive on the phone. Her face seemed desperate, so I went back to grab it. I lifted it in salute to both Adele and the secretary, bursting through the door into the narrow hallway before the lump in my throat would make things awkward.

Immediately, I met resistance. I looked around and realized I'd knocked down someone with the door.

"Whoa, sorry." I crouched down to the fallen student.

Her long dark hair shielded her face, but she waved me off as I tried to help her back up.

"You okay?"

"Relatively." She smoothed her uniform back into place. Without hesitation, she walked toward the illuminated exit sign in quick strides.

"Wait up." I trotted after her.

Her hair flew behind her shoulder as she looked back at me in confusion. She didn't slow her pace and was through the exit doors and out of sight by the time I reached them. I wasn't used to having to keep up with someone a foot shorter than me, and the slick tiles made me wary of jogging.

The air compressors on the doors hissed at me as I looked around for the girl. The doors finally snapped shut with a thud, and I was alone. I tapped the manila envelope on my thigh as I thought about what to do next. Nothing much I could do if my guide abandoned me. A metallic noise came from the envelope, and I slowly walked down the brick archways toward a stone fountain I could see in the distance. Self-guided tour it was.

THREE

As I walked, I ripped open the envelope, dumping its loose contents onto my open palm. I peered inside, noting several pieces of paper and some brochures. I'd check my class schedule later, and the map might be useful, but my attention was drawn to the keys I held in my hand. The first ring held a few discolored brass keys with a leather tab embossed with an insignia. I dropped those keys into my pocket and palmed the other key ring, holding it up to the light. The key was much older in style, but it shone brightly even in the cloudy fall air. It didn't quite suit the ring or the thin metal snowflake-shaped disc it was stuck on.

Immediately, I twisted the key off the ring with its cheesy decal. I tossed the snowflake ring back into the envelope and put the older key in an inside pocket, not wanting to lose it now that it was on its own.

Looking up, I found myself already at the fountain. I scanned the buildings bordering the courtyard, noticing the archways behind me led to a similarly sterile old brick building. The facade from the parking lot looked much fancier with sculpted columns and molding, but on this side, it was all spare lines and narrow windows with very little fanfare. Definitely felt institutional.

I sighed and sat down on the edge of the fountain. The lip was wide enough for me to fold my legs underneath me in my favorite position. All tucked under, no one could tell how freakishly tall I was, and I could pretend to fit in for a little while. My hands rested on my knees in a meditation pose, and I soaked up the fading afternoon sun as the impact of the past half hour finally sunk in. As much as I always tried to fly under the radar, this time was different. Adele had talked about getting people in my corner, but as I sat with the cold concrete sandwiching me with the minimal warmth on my face, I knew staying the loner would be my safest, trouble-free option.

The manila envelope protested in my hand when I flexed my fingers unconsciously. I pulled out the brochures, noting the white faces and blues eyes staring back at me. The brown of my hand laughed against the bright sheen of the paper it held, and I sighed. The wind had blown my hair into my line of sight, and I carefully tucked it behind my ear. The curls sprang free almost immediately. No, fitting in would not be an option. The key was trying not to stand out too much. I just had to figure out exactly what that looked like.

My fingers had made their way to my lips, and by the end of the brochure, any nail that had dared to grow past the bed had been cut back ruthlessly to the root. I stopped the moment I tasted blood and scowled at my traitorous fingers. I rummaged through my satchel for the balm Adele had gotten me for my last birthday. Just thinking about Adele made the lump in my throat surge back to life, and I muttered angrily at all the obstacles between me and the soothing peppermint oil that would at least heal my cracking nail beds.

"Oh my God, your hair is so beautiful!" a voice shrieked in my ear.

My gut clenched about the same time I felt an unwelcome hand on my head. Instinctively, I blocked the hand and pushed its owner aside. My head whipped up to find the offender, my eyes blazing with anger.

In front of me stood a triad of brochure clones, all pale skin, light eyes, and blue tartan uniforms. The girl in front still had her hand outstretched, while the two clones behind her clutched their backpack straps nervously. Realizing I must look like a crazed animal, I worked hard to stifle the snarl curling my lips and purse them against the venom I was ready to let loose.

"Excuse me?" I said through clenched teeth. I tried to take deep breaths, but the hairs on the back of my neck and arms remained charged from the intrusion. The thing I hated more than anything else was someone touching my hair. The thought alone kept my rage fully intact.

"Sorry, I just couldn't help myself!" The girl gave a childish laugh. "I've never seen hair like yours before. It's just so luxurious. Like in a magazine. My hand just reached out on its own."

The girls flanking the bold girl laughed at her bold behavior.

My eyes squinted to slits, but I managed a smile back. "Well, now you have." I bit the inside of my cheek to keep my response to just that.

"Are those extensions? Mine never look that good." The girl's hand was outstretched for another round while her lip turned her smile into a pout.

I pulled my head back and out of reach. "Nope, all my own," I said. "Unfortunately."

"My hair could never get that much volume." The girl pouted, her friends sympathetically patting her back. "This weather makes it so lank and stringy. I'm so jealous!"

"Yeah, weather can be a real bummer." I let my elbows rest on my crossed legs. Might as well get comfortable if this awkward conversation was going to continue.

"You'll have to show me some tricks." The girl took a seat next to me on the fountain.

The clones—twins I now realized from their identical features—stood clustered near the girl but didn't sit.

"I'm pretty sure genetics has more to do with it than styling," I said defensively. "Sorry I can't help."

"That's okay." The girl patted my leg in what I assumed was meant to be reassuring.

My body tensed again at the intrusion, but I didn't say anything.

Under the radar. Under the radar. Under the damn radar, I chanted to myself.

"Oh my goodness, where are my manners?" the girl said.

I was thinking the same thing.

"My name is Aileen. Aileen O'Rourke." Her eyes were looking at me expectantly.

I didn't recognize the name, but her face made it seem like I should have. "Nice to meet you," I said simply.

Aileen fidgeted at my apparent lack of appreciation of her name. "My family owns the biggest construction firm in all of New England," she said through gritted teeth, keeping her sunny smile in place.

"Sorry, I just moved here from the West Coast." I shrugged. "I don't know much about the area."

A tinkling laugh escaped from Aileen, and her friends joined her. She patted my leg again.

"No worries, you'll learn pretty quickly," she said. "This is Honore and Grace. Don't try and tell them apart. I barely do."

Another laugh escaped Aileen, but the laugh seemed a little more forced from the twins. They shared a look, and I had to bite my lip to mangle the smile creeping in.

"So," Aileen said expectantly. "What's your name?"

"Oh, right." I sighed internally that I couldn't escape sooner. "Noah Young."

The triad's eyes all widened simultaneously, and I leaned back a little from the impact.

"What?"

"Young, like Nathaniel Young of Young, Pruwitt, and Shaw?" Aileen gasped.

The color drained from my face. Of all the people with my common last name, how did she know my father right off the bat?

I cocked my head to the side to hide my surprise. "Who?" Were there no other famous Youngs in the Boston area? Maybe I was being too paranoid and showing my hand.

Aileen huffed, pulling up a picture from a quick search on her phone. She shoved the headshot into my face, and I stared into my father's eyes for the first time in many, many years.

"He's only, like, the youngest, most badass corporate lawyer in all of Boston. You're not anybody if you can't get him to represent you. He still visits on young alumni weekends." A fangirl sigh escaped from Aileen's half-daydream state as she took her phone back from under my nose.

"Wouldn't he be too young to have a kid our age?" I deflected, trying my hardest to sound doubtful. "We were probably already walking when he graduated from here."

Aileen frowned. Honore and Grace bent their heads together for a brief moment and nodded their agreement.

"I guess you're right. It would have been quite scandalous if he had a daughter your age." Aileen giggled. "Plus, you know, he's..." Aileen's hand bounced in the air, as if gesturing to my whole being.

My bronze skin and textured hair against his luminous skin and light eyes. How could we possibly be related?

"White?" I let a bark of a laugh escape.

The girls joined me in my laughter, although only one of ours was fake.

"I know, right?" Aileen said. "What was I thinking?"

"I'm just a nobody," I assured Aileen. "No big, important connections here."

"Hmmmmm." She squinted as she surveyed me. "I'm not so sure of that. Not just anybody can walk in here, especially midyear. Are you sure you're not related to anybody?"

"Nobody worth bragging about," I said confidently. "Trust me on that."

Aileen looped her arm through mine, and I blanched as she tugged me in close.

"Don't you worry about a thing, Noah," Aileen said. "I'll make sure you're a somebody around here. I have my ways." Aileen gave me an assertive nod, and the twins mirrored her own confidence behind her.

I let out a nervous chuckle. "That's okay. I'm more of a wallflower, behind-the-scenes kind of girl," I admitted, trying to disengage from Aileen's tightening grip.

"Nonsense! I can tell you're one of a kind. We'll have you ruling campus in no time." Aileen gestured wildly with her arm.

Just then, a bell tolled, signaling the end of classes. Students trickled out from the buildings surrounding the square, and I kicked myself for not ducking away sooner.

"Just in time for free period! Perfect." Aileen stood and brushed imaginary dirt off her tartan skirt. "I can introduce you to everyone before dinner."

"That's really not necessary." I remained seated on the fountain's ledge. The triad gave me a triple frown, and I scrambled to find a good enough excuse that didn't directly insult them. All my favorite possibilities were varying levels of verbal and physical offense, and I had to discard them one after another after Adele's voice echoed in my conscience.

"Oh, don't be so shy!" Aileen crowed. "I promise I'll make the best introductions. There's people worth knowing around here, and then there's everybody else."

"I wonder where you fit in," a raspy voice cut in.

Aileen's sunny disposition dimmed, and the twins crossed their arms in tandem, sending out laser beams from their tiny, doll-like eyes.

"I hardly consider you someone worth knowing, Hag, unless it's to know to avoid you," Aileen said, her tone prickly.

Aileen's big blonde head blocked my view of the aggressor, so I couldn't see the source of the voice. The twins acted as another sort of shield, but the girl ducked easily through their defenses to stand directly in front of me, her eyes level with my seated gaze.

"Here you are," the girl said to me. "Thought you might have tried escaping through the woods."

I leaned back again, this time not because of close inappropriate physical contact like with Aileen, but because I needed a little more space to analyze the person who stood before me.

As pristine as Aileen and her twin minions were, that's how disorderly the newcomer was. Where glossy, pin-straight blonde hair should have been, bright red and maroon pieces lay in haphazard chunks of varying lengths. The look could have been from a graphic novel or a high fashion magazine, but it was off-putting all the same. One of the maroon chunks lay across one eye, so the only one I could see was a vibrant green that looked almost like a fake contact. I was mesmerized.

"I'd run to the woods if I saw you coming, too," Aileen hissed. "Could you not scare the new girl before she even gives the rest of us a shot?"

"She doesn't look scared to me." The girl's green eye squinted in equal scrutiny. "At least not of me. Maybe of the three of you cyborgs, but not me."

"You kind of look like a cyborg though," I said to the girl without thinking. I bit the inside of my cheek again, trying to silence any more thoughts from strolling unpoliced out of my mouth.

She laughed, the unruly mass of hair fluttering with the movement and revealing a milky blue eye.

"I'll take that as a compliment," she said. The merriment on her face faltered a little when she looked over at Aileen. "What are you looking at?"

"Are you seriously asking me that question? Have you even looked at yourself in a mirror lately?" Aileen said with disgust.

"Yes, actually. It takes a lot of work to get these fabulous eyebrows." The girl winked in my direction.

Aileen snorted. She must have been so disgusted, she'd run out of comebacks.

"Whatever," Aileen said. She turned to me, ignoring the girl beside her. "Noah, once you've settled in, come by the quad. We always hang out there when we're not in class. Or maybe we'll see you at dinner. If she doesn't scare you away first."

"Thanks," I said, not wanting to commit to anything.

The girl in front of me waggled her fingers in a taunting goodbye. "See you at dinner, Bestie!" she called after Aileen, causing the twins to shuffle closer behind their leader. "Don't forget to save me a seat!"

The girl chuckled. "I can't help myself. It's just too fun," she said, half to herself. She sighed before facing me again.

"Ah, sorry about that. Also, slight miscommunication on the timing of your tour. Hope you weren't super inconvenienced." She bent slightly to follow the triad out of sight. "I can't believe they let the animals out of the zoo unattended."

"It's fine," I said. "No lasting damage done. At least not by you."

"Oh, you might be able to get away with murder with that bunch. Aileen's already planned out her future wedding with you as her maid of honor. It's all for the pictures, you know. She'll keep you even if it kills her," the girl said dismissively.

She caught me staring at her after a moment of silence. "What?"

23

"Sorry, what's your name?" I said directly, realizing belatedly my phrasing was off.

"Margaret O'Brien, affectionately known around campus as Mags the Hag." She offered me her hand. When I stood to receive it, her green eye bulged. "I really only use the Hag part for special occasions."

"Noah," I replied.

She nodded as she took me in from head to toe. "Naturally," Mags said.

We both took a moment to openly stare at one another, until Mags broke out in a huge grin.

"I like you. You're going to be great fun." She marched off to the corner of the square.

I quickly fell into step beside her. "You think so? I guess so long as it's not a tragedy, I can deal." I shifted my bag to my hip.

"All the best comedies are," Mags quipped back. "Especially ones set in high school. Ugh."

"Yeah, not looking good so far," I muttered darkly.

"Eh," Mags said. "Still a little early to tell. How do you feel about food first and tour later?"

Our walk took us directly into the shadow of a large cathedral-like building. The setting sun was playing tricks on the stained glass windows, and I could see a steady stream of students heading toward the entrance like worker bees to a hive.

"Works for me," I said.

"Plus," she said, her hand coming up to feign an aside to her sole audience member, "you seem smart enough to read a map."

I laughed.

"Something like that," I said.

"Good," Mags said. "I can't do the tour without an immense amount of sarcasm and disdain anyway. It's probably better I don't ruin your first impression of campus with my commentary. You'll learn to hate it in your own time."

"Comforting," I said.

"I do aim to be very nurturing in my delivery," Mags said. "It's a skill."

The final archway between us and our destination loomed overhead, and I careened my head to check out the patchwork of stone and brick. Something about architecture and masonry really intrigued me. I could entertain myself for hours with old buildings. I had a feeling Windermere would be no different. The noise of a scuffle brought me back to the present.

Mags had launched her arm into the air, clipping a boy at his neck and proceeding to flip him off his feet and onto the walkway in one fluid motion. He lay there coughing and rolling around in pain as Mags straightened herself.

"We've been over this, Adair," Mags said affectionately to the boy on the ground. "You can't sneak up on me. My ninja skills are too much for you."

Adair groaned in response.

I stood impassively to the side, wondering if I should try to help the kid up. I didn't want to get in the middle of anything. My eyebrows rose to meet my hairline as I took in an obvious detail of Mags' current opponent.

Adair sat up, trying to brush himself off while simultaneously catching his breath. His hand loosened the tie and undid the first button to clear his airway. Instead of worrying about his health, my eyes fixated on the darkness of his hand against the formerly pristine shirt and jacket, now smudged with dirt. A sense of déjà vu came over me. Our eyes met, and a weird kinship connected the two of us.

"You all right?" I finally managed.

Adair nodded at me in response.

"There go my manners again," Mags chided herself. "Adair Reid, Noah Young. Lest you get any funny ideas, Adair and I really do get along well when he's not trying to scare the living daylights out of me."

"Trying?" I asked.

"My success rate could use some improvement," Adair said with a chuckle and bright smile. "If someone didn't have an eerie sense of the future, I'm pretty sure I could get away with a lot more."

Mags rolled her eyes. "If you didn't breathe like a moose in heat, I'm fairly certain you could sneak up on people better," Mags retorted, holding out a hand to Adair.

He sprang up quickly, brushing himself off and seeming in good spirits. "Next time," he warned Mags.

"Yeah, okay." Mags closed the distance between our group and the food mecca before us. "Good luck with that."

"I don't need luck," Adair bristled.

"You need lasagna," Mags said sagely, turning to face us at the top of the stairs. "Which smells like what's for dinner."

"You can smell that all the way out here?" I sniffed the air and came up dry.

"Ninja skills." Mags waggled her fingers and looked at me with her kooky eyes.

Adair just shook his head. "Don't encourage her," he said to me. "It'll only get worse."

"May I present to you the dining hall," Mags said with a flourish, opening the thick wooden doors to a downdraft of garlic and aged cheese. She took a deep breath and hummed happily.

"Don't say it." Adair sighed and shook his head.

I followed them into the din of the dining room wrapped in the comforting smell of Italian food.

FOUR

The weight of one hundred gazes rested on my skin as I moved my fork from plate to mouth. The intense scrutiny only made me hyper aware of the buzz of hushed whispering collectively dissecting my table manners. I felt like I was the sole performer in an arena, with spotlights and several angled projector screens.

"So have people never seen a girl eat lasagna before, or do I have something on my face?" I said finally to Mags and Adair, who were merrily shoving food into their mouths across from me.

"Maybe not two pieces, but you're a giant, so you're putting it somewhere," Mags said in between mouthfuls, wielding her spoon like a laser pointer. "They probably can't decide where to stare first. There's your hair, your skin, your badass clothing, which I must say looks way cooler against the sea of tartan than usual. Or I guess we could count your freakish height."

"I'm sitting down," I countered, eliciting a snort from Mags.

Adair shrugged. "They'll calm down. Took them a whole year not to do double takes on me," he muttered around a mouthful of garlic bread.

"Comforting." I sighed. As predicted, the not standing out part was going to be a challenge.

"Actually." Mags leaned closer toward my face.

I met her gaze evenly, refusing to blink until she did.

"Eyes. You should definitely add your eye color to that list. What color is that?" Mags' neck was bent at a disturbing angle, making me rub mine in sympathy.

"All of them." I cleared my throat. "Sometimes they change color with the light. The brown on the inside sometimes make them look green, but technically they're like a grey blue color."

Mags nodded her head in appreciation.

"There's also the possibility they are staring at me, which is still extremely common. Or Adair." Mags weighed the options in the air with her fork. "The three of us together must really be a sight."

"We should start charging admission fees," Adair said before shoving another piece of garlic bread in his mouth. "We should get some benefit for being the freak squad around here."

"You can't put a price on this face," Mags said in mock dismay, indicating her whole face, which she'd contorted into a horrifically funny visage.

Adair choked on his food, and a snort escaped from me, breaking the thread of anxious thought agitating me.

I shook my head, causing my hair to fall from its perch behind my ear. Sighing in frustration, I pulled a hairband from my wrist and sloppily secured the majority of its weight at the nape of my neck. A few pieces remained free, but I let them fall where they would.

A lone round of applause erupted from across the table, and I looked up in confusion.

"That was beautiful," Mags said. She elbowed Adair. "Don't you think so?"

"Mags has some serious hair envy," Adair said to me.

"Not feeling the maroon and fuchsia anymore?" I asked her. I squinted to survey her multicolored mane again and was mesmerized by the prismatic effect of the two bold colors. "It suits you."

"I wish I didn't have to spend so much time and money on it though. Natural hair is the best." Mags sighed.

"Yeah, well, the breakage from this quick lapse in judgement will haunt me for months." I indicated my secured hair. "Agree to disagree on whose hair is more enviable."

Mags cocked her head to the side again, but her green eye was unfocused. I looked behind me, trying to figure out what she was looking at.

Mags jerked herself upright, snatched the remaining piece of garlic bread from Adair's plate, and launched it across the room. Two rows down, it collided with a brown head of hair nearly imperceptible among the empty wooden chairs and tables.

A silence exploded in the air, the gaping lack of conversation pressing on my ears. Adair stopped mid chew, vacating his seat to track down the victim of Mags' ire.

"What just happened?" I said aloud, not expecting an answer.

Slowly, the buzz of hesitant whispers built back up, rushing the silent air out in a vacuum. Mags uncrossed her legs and stood to receive her escorted guest.

Adair hauled the boy by the back of his shirt, high enough that the kid was scrambling to touch his toes to the ground. As soon as he landed in front of Mags, he tried to bolt, running quickly into Adair's chest.

"Apologize," Mags said to the kid. "And hand it over."

Her palm hung in the air expectantly, and the boy paused only long enough as if realizing his escape routes were nonexistent.

"I wasn't doing anything!" he crowed, crossing his arms.

Adair cleared his throat behind the kid, and the boy jumped out of his skin.

"Don't make me repeat myself," Mags warned. "Just give it up. Come on." Her fingers waved impatiently at him.

My eyes pinged in quick rotation between the three, and I could tell from the halting buzz that other commentators were glued to the spectacle as well.

"I don't know what you're talking about." The boy sniffed. "You should be the one apologizing for throwing food at me."

"If you do not give up your phone immediately," Mags said, slowly pressuring the boy as she stepped closer and closer into his personal space, "I will upend you and your entire backpack right here, right now. I will then toss you in the fountain in only your unmentionables and see how quickly you can scurry back to whatever hole you came from."

The boy paled but did not move.

"Adair," Mags said, cueing the madness.

In the blink of an eye, the boy was upended, his pockets turned out by gravity and some vigorous shaking by Adair, the dining hall audience lost their minds, and Mags smiled triumphantly with a smart phone in her hand. Just as quickly, the boy was right-side up, Adair looked unruffled, and I stood up to bus the dishes.

Sneaking silently out of the focal point of the action, I dropped the dishes at the bus station while keeping an eye on the madness. I cringed when I realized my bag was still at the table. Any thoughts I had of a quiet retreat had been lost at my oversight.

"Yikes," Mags narrated, scrolling through the phone. "I suppose I'd be a ponce, too, if my mother named me Llewellyn. Too bad your passcode wasn't as impressive as your name."

"Hey, give that back." The kid squirmed, his shoulder bumping recklessly against Adair.

Adair's eyes narrowed, and the kid crossed his arms, his face contorting in rapid flickers trying to hold back tears.

"Here we go," Mags said finally. "Several photos. A video? Seriously?" Mags snorted in disgust.

I'd slowly inched back center stage to grab my bag. My whole body stiffened at the mention of a video.

"You recorded us?" I asked, my anger focused squarely on the eyes of the little kid.

He balked at my intensity. His mouth moved up and down like a guppy out of water fighting for oxygen.

"Why would you do that?"

"They told me to," he said in a rush, his words now accompanied by the tears he'd been holding back. "I didn't want to, but I didn't have a choice. Please, just let me go. I won't do it again, I promise."

"Not us." Mags twisted her mouth in a bitter smile. "You."

FIVE

My mind went completely blank with anger. Instantly, the phone was in my hand, and I flicked through the pictures, coming across several video clips as well. Without bothering to consult anyone else, I ripped the case off the phone, tearing out the battery and jamming my thumb savagely into the factory reset button behind the SIM card. The boy squealed, but shut up after one nudge from Adair.

The cold anger in my gut flipped into a molten sea of acid. The warm feeling snaked up to my throat, but instead of worrying about throwing up, I knew what that meant. I had to leave. Now.

"Find out who," I ground out loudly enough for only Mags to catch.

Her green eye slid to me with a slight frown, but she nodded in understanding.

I slammed the miscellaneous pieces of the snitch's phone into his chest, checking his shoulder as I shoved past him with my bag. The entire dining room hushed again as I marched away from the epicenter of the evening's drama. The eyes were back in full force, so I strode confidently toward the glowing exit sign, hoping I could find some sort of broom closet to freak out in.

The warmth in my throat surged, and I had to clench my jaw shut so the noise would not escape. Lines of melody wound around in my head, poking and jabbing their way through my consciousness in any effort to escape. I had to get away from as many people as possible before I erupted. Causing an incident my first day was a personal record I was not willing to achieve.

The cold metal of the door brought me back in check a little, and I was able take a deep breath once the thunderous snap of the exit door bolted home behind me.

The staircase gave me pause. It was clear this was an addition, with one wall of brick and the remaining a horribly painted cinderblock medley. My eyes locked on the rusted metal of the staircase, the imprinted metal bringing up memories of fire escape staircases from my brief stint in New York. I took one cautious step down to test the weight.

Realizing I wouldn't die immediately, I trotted down one flight of stairs, flinching at the raucous noise that echoed up the stairwell with each step. I paused at the landing, but it only mentioned classrooms and miscellaneous halls. I poked my head through the door, noticing the well-lit hall and the far-off echo of laughter from one of the distant rooms.

My throat still burned, but the intensity was retreating. My nostrils flared with the deep breathing exercises I was running through in my head. The immediate need for a quiet place faded slowly, but I decided to play it safe for next time.

I continued down the next flight, finding it noticeably dimmer than the previous landing. Motion-activated lights buzzed, lazily flickering to life as I stepped into a much smaller hallway filled with about four times as many doors. Each new stride brought a new pair of doors.

My hands were cupped against the small panes of glass. I was close enough for my nose to leave fog fields on the glass as it pressed against the cool surface. The whole level was filled with practice rooms. Whether they had a piano in them or just a music stand and chair, the soundproof tiles gave them all identical layouts. I tried to estimate the number but gave up as more sub hallways branched out, leaving me lost in a labyrinth of identical rooms.

Occasionally, I checked a door, and it would be locked. This happened more often with the piano rooms than the empty ones, but some locked rooms had individual instruments in them as well. They must be private rooms for individual students. I was sure the specs were in the packet full of brochures I'd shoved in my bag, and my fingers itched to unearth it to satisfy my curiosity. I mentally slapped myself to refocus. Knowing a little detail like that was not a priority right now. Figuring out which one of these rooms would be the best emergency safe room was the priority.

Just had to figure out how to figure that out.

I sighed into the hall, trying to remember the layout of the halls in my head. The only way out was the stairwell I'd entered from. I couldn't see the glow of an orange exit sign, and I didn't have enough time to check for a sneakier back staircase. Keeping that in mind, I didn't want to be trapped too far down a dead-end hall, but I also didn't want to be easily accessible from the entrance. I needed to find a door I could get in whenever I needed and lock from the inside.

The nearest room was empty, so I opened the door quickly, checking the lock. I jogged down the hall, checking a few more to make sure I was correct. Only private rooms had locks of any sort. I was going to have to break into a private room.

Day One: Noah Breaks School Property Prompting Immediate Suspension

Such a cute headline.

I pinched the bridge of my nose, leaning against the frame of a vacant room to restrategize. I rifled through my bag to get the set of keys I'd been given. I quickly discarded all my options, finding the size or the teeth to be completely unmatchable to the locks on the private room doors. I exhaled and crossed my arms in frustration. How was this going to work?

I felt something poke my ribs. I shifted my arm uncomfortably, but the pain didn't go away. Realization hit me with brute force, and I fished the old snowflake key out of my inner jacket pocket. It, too, was the wrong shape and style.

"Hey," a voice called out.

I jumped in surprise, hitting my head on the low fake ceiling tiles above me.

"Ow," I groaned, rubbing the tender spot on my head. I turned around to find the owner of the voice. "No need to shout."

"What are you doing?" the voice said.

I squinted, but the timed lights had gone out, and I could only see a shadow.

"Sorry." I waved a fistful of keys in the air. "Just trying to figure out which one's mine."

The lie burned my throat a little, but my face was smooth and emotionless.

"Do you even know which room you're looking for?" the voice continued. "All those are already rented out."

"Got me again," I said with a nervous chuckle. I pulled the manila envelope out enough for him to see the new student badge of ignorance. "They just gave me a set of keys and told me to get on with it."

"Let me see." The kid finally stepped into the light. He spoke with a sense of authority and confidence, so I handed over the keys without a fight. He frowned at each of them in turn and discarded them almost as quickly as I had done. "Are these all you have? This ring is all dorm stuff."

"Just this," I said impassively, opening my palm to display the old skeleton key.

He shook his head.

"Might be a library room key, but not a conservatory key. Are you sure you have a practice room? Like I said, all these are assigned already." He looked at me skeptically.

"You might be right." I shrugged. "I requested one, and they didn't say anything to the contrary. Maybe I don't have one after all."

"You play?" he asked, his head nodding at the guitar behind the glass of the private room I was attempting to break into.

"A little," I said. "Some piano, some guitar. Mostly self-taught, but I think I got into the guitar elective here."

"Impressive," the boy said. "Not too many girls want to tackle that class."

"Oh," I said, not sure if he was implying the difficulty of guitar or some other reason.

"It's kind of known as a boys' club," he explained. His eyes looked me up and down. "You'll do fine."

"Thanks." I frowned.

"So do you need a piano room then since you'll be using the class guitars?" he asked, his eyes still squinted at me, feeling me out.

"Yeah, actually. That would be great. An upright

if it's an option," I said. "Is there a public room maybe I could use?"

"None of the public rooms have pianos. Some have keyboards, but..." The boy snorted. "Hardly worth it."

I nodded, keeping my silence. I was going to see if he would take the bait.

He walked back toward the room he'd exited, the lights finally catching his movement and turning on. Before he made it to his room, however, he paused, looking to the room on his right.

"Actually." He looked back at me and jerked his head.

I trotted over to join him. "What?" My eyes were darting back and forth between the boy and the room he was frozen in front of.

"There's only one room I can think of that could use some attention. You wouldn't run into anyone. It's already paid for, so no one's going to snatch it away," he said.

He seemed to be convincing himself, so I stayed quiet. I was willing to wait for however long it would take to convince this kid to help me.

"I don't know how much you know about campus lore yet. You might have heard already, but there was an incident at the beginning of the summer. A football player had an accident at practice. Been in a coma ever since." The kid paused. "Good guy, really. He was also into music, even though practice conflicted with a lot of the band stuff. Anyway, he has a practice room. This one."

My eyes darted to the darkened glass where the boy seemed to be staring.

"Coma, huh? That's horrible," I said, a knife going through my gut. Something told me his ousting and my entry was not just convenient, but maybe a little too fortuitous.

"Right?" He sighed, his lips moving as if weighing something in his mind.

"You seem all right, too," he finally said.

My eyebrows rose. "Oh, thanks," I said in surprise.

He brushed past me, ducking quickly into his room. I waited, unsure if my patience had paid off or not.

He reappeared, a pair of keys in his hand.

"I'm down here all the time, so I look after the rooms. Here's one of the spare keys to his room. Use it whenever you need it." The boy offered the key to me.

"Really? You don't think it'll be a problem?" I asked, a little wowed the room was so freely given.

"Just don't trash the place, and I'll look the other way," he said. "I'd much rather the room get used anyway. Seems like such a shame to just let it get dusty."

"Thank you," I said again. "Uh, sorry, I didn't catch your name."

"Sean." He offered a hand.

"Noah." I pumped his hand firmly.

"Yeah, you'll do fine in guitar lab," Sean said with a dry chuckle. "Just try not to bring the drama down here. I like it quiet."

"Yes, sir." I winked. "I'll do my best."

Sean waved at me, retreating back into his practice room. The lights dimmed, leaving me in the dark with only the light of my phone to use to jiggle the key home in the lock in front of me. I made it into the room without too much struggle, but I caught the door so it wouldn't slam shut and disturb my already disgruntled neighbor.

Having such a close neighbor around at all times was not ideal, unless I could convince him to play lookout for me. Sean let me in easily enough, and I couldn't decide if that was more of a pro than a con. Either his judgement was impeccable, or he was apathetic to everything but the instruments getting occasional love.

My hand pounded the textured wall tile for the light switch, and I nearly lost a nail when I finally did catch it. It wasn't so much of a switch as it was a dimmer. Looking up, I snorted at the HGTV approved recessed can lighting in an otherwise poorly carpeted glorified closet. The contrast amused me, allowing me to finally relax enough to breathe fully.

I rolled my shoulders one at a time, allowing my head to fall into a deep rotation. The kinks and knots in my muscles were unwinding as my fingers drifted toward the slightly discolored keys. My fingers ran through a few quick scales, and I was happy to hear clear notes roll back toward me instead of the off tune buzzing I was bracing myself to hear. My cheeks pulled up in a sardonic smile, attributing the tuning to the grumpy practice room guardian across the hall.

The warmth that had disappeared temporarily raged back full force, burning my throat painfully. My partially open mouth was not prepared, and suddenly, I was singing. The song came from somewhere deep inside, the melody haunting and destructive. It grated against my tight throat as I attempted to control it. It raged on, twisting my tongue with foreign lyrics in a language I never understood.

I could feel the tears streaming down my cheeks as my inner self battled with this unknown traitor for control over my voice and body. Calling this hellish noise singing was too polite, but I had no other words for it. The euphemism had stuck ever since it had begun. I felt like I was screaming. The volume was so powerful, as if the projection of the song to as many ears as possible was more important than its dynamic. My fingers trailed along with the melody, and I cursed myself to stop. I did not want to fuel this monster any more.

And then with one last note, it was gone.

I collapsed onto the keys, making them clang in dismay. My breathing came in raged pants, which only tore my sore throat even more. I swallowed hard over and over, trying to center myself.

At least it was over now.

At least it had happened here.

At least no one heard me. I hoped.

SIX

As soon as I opened my eyes, I groaned. After years of going to sleep and waking up in the same spot, you'd think I would've accepted it by now. Some shred of hope survived every night, only to be dashed when I woke up stuck in the same recurring nightmare.

My eyes adjusted, as they always did, to the dusky evensong of the forest around me. Compared to Washington, these trees were downright scrawny. I couldn't tell you the type, but they stood like weeds, blocking my view of the sky and the horizon with their presence. Their numbers seemed to have grown lately, or at least to me they seemed closer together. It was getting harder and harder to remain here in the evenings and watch the same horrors on extended loop.

Although the trees and the foggy atmosphere blocked my view of ground and sky, they accommodated my night visitors without complaint. Steadying myself against a nearby tree, I paused to decide my strategy for this evening.

I was trapped in this dreamscape until at least dawn. It worried me that I couldn't seem to wake myself of my own accord, nor postpone these evening walks if I wanted to stay up late. Not sleeping was not an option, no matter how many

Red Bulls I drank. Adele hoped in time the dream would be something I could control, but I was skeptical. Nothing seemed to be in my control anymore.

But I could at least decide what I was going to do tonight. I could walk toward the horizon all evening, like I did when we lived in Arizona, maybe even long enough to loop around to my nightly origin point. All it did was tire me out and cause me to eat like an Olympic swimmer. Based on the food situation here, eating like a horse would only draw attention to myself, and I attempted to stay under the radar as much as possible. Jury was still out if that could even be a possibility here.

So I wasn't going to walk all night, but I didn't particularly feel in the mood to make rounds of the night visitors. I'm sure some new ones had popped up, but I much preferred thinking back to my daytime reality than finding some new horror show episode to queue up.

I looked down at my hands, willing paper and pen to magically appear. Sometimes I just needed to make lists or diagrams to sort out my thoughts. Not having the ability to do that in my dreamscape was frustrating. Not like it would stay here or magically transfer into the real world with me. It was just as well.

I decided to face the inevitable and seek the nearest night visitor to get it over with. When I pushed off the tree, my fingers didn't make a sound as they scratched against the jagged surface of the bark. The eeriest part, I thought as I trudged toward contestant number one, was the silence.

Nothing made a sound here. My footsteps were silent. The wisps of atmosphere that clung at my ankles moved slowly in a hypnotic dance. Nothing else moved—no wind blew, no whispers in the heavy air, no white noise. Just complete silence. The night visitors, caught in a closed loop of agony in their final moments, also didn't make a sound. Their faces contorted, and I knew they must be screaming until their throats were raw, but not even I could hear them. I wondered if they could hear themselves, or if part of the reason why they screamed was because they couldn't.

I tried not to think about them too much, which was a feat for me. Something told me that once I figured out the why of their existence, I'd be forced to act. This twisted dream world had to exist for a reason. I just wasn't informed directly what that reason was.

To be honest, I treated myself like a ticking time bomb. I didn't think I was especially equipped to run into the flames and save people. In those darker moments when I tried to rationalize how I couldn't help my dreamscape neighbors, I wondered if the point was that I shouldn't. That even if there were a way, they were there for a reason, and that reason was that death was inevitable. Entropy. You couldn't stop it, and if you got in its way, you too would find out exactly how fragile life could be.

Sometimes too much thinking led you down a dark, dark path.

It took me only moments to reach the closest night visitor. I used to call them mirages, like the things your mind made up under extreme duress, but I knew in my gut that my mind didn't make these images out of nothing. They were real somewhere. They had to exist. Also, I couldn't help but think that if our roles were reversed, I would want someone to think I was real. To take me seriously.

I shuddered as soon as the night visitor came into view.

I called this one Harry. No reason I could think of, but the middle-aged gentleman kind of looked like he could be called Harry.

Harry's particular agony was one of the most disturbing to watch, and I couldn't help but sigh when I saw he would be my first of many tonight. Harry was a little on the pudgy side, and his closed loop visual allowed me to slowly watch him collapse in on himself. It became quite gruesome in the three minutes it took for his loop to close. At first the indents started in his chest and stomach but quickly turned to his limbs and finally his head. His eyes always locked on mine no matter where I stood, and his silent screams rattled inside my head as I watched what would be his death.

Collapsing in on himself was not going to make the coroner's report in the case of Harry's eventual death. None of the closed loop death scenes were ever true in blow-by-blow action. Elliott, a small freckle-faced night visitor, had looked like he was drowning in his death loop. I ended up saving him from an asthma attack in the first grade and haven't seen him since—dreamscape or otherwise.

I kept Elliott on my mind because I was curious if I would ever see him again. Would he reappear in the dreamscape as soon as his next cause of death was imminent? If I saw him again, did that mean I should intervene?

Elliott was why I thought I was meant to save them, even though I realized at some point, we all have to die. Something about such a young child dying didn't seem right to me, and I'd acted without fully realizing the consequences of my actions. But I was young, too, and my instinct had been to save him.

It would be so much more helpful to know the rules behind the dreamscape. I could be content not worrying about them if they all were meant for death. The life cycle didn't exist without death and regeneration. It went against nature. But if there was such a thing as a right death. If that existed, and I existed, didn't that mean I should intervene?

Adele hadn't quite seen it that way, so it was no surprise that the second I saw a night visitor walking around in real life, we fled. Most times we went to a different state, but occasionally we hopped a time zone or two. Never to New England, at least not until now.

I'd gotten some pings in the dining hall. More than a few were around, but I'd decided to ignore them and try to focus on being unnoticed. That had clearly failed, but I didn't want to give in so easily. Adele had said last stop, so night visitors or not, I would have to deal. Imagining Adele's response to my first day distracted me for a moment.

A smile couldn't quite make it to my lips, though, because Harry was folding in on himself again. Harry was not one of the folks I'd met today, so his fate was still firmly on track toward this death, whatever it manifested as in real life. I thought it might be a car accident, with all the indents, but I also thought it could be something like a heart attack. I was still playing around with some of the symbolism and whether it was more abstract in manifestation or more directly related. As much as I tried to parse out the possibilities based on the appearance and content of a visitor's death loop, I was still stabbing wildly in the dark for the conclusion.

I sighed heavily and said a silent goodbye to Harry as he entered the loop again. I averted my eyes and walked away. Tonight I had no new information. No new thoughts. Harry was stuck in his loop, and I was stuck in mine.

There was so much I didn't know. About this place. What it meant. What it was for. Why I had to be the one to witness these horrible deaths night after night, unable to change anything and unable to escape. Sometimes Adele and I talked frankly about it, and she used to say it was a gift. At least some of my talents. We hadn't spoken about it in a while, both of us too exhausted from running away from it to really call it a blessing anymore.

I continued on, checking on all my visitors. No new inhabitants popped up in my walk, and none disappeared. We stayed in limbo together until I felt the warm rays of dawn tingle on my skin, and I seemed to dissolve into the mist, reawakening in my own body.

SEVEN

The dreamscape spit me out around 4:30 in the morning, which was a little earlier than usual. Clouds covered what little attempt the morning autumn sun made in streaming through my seventh story window. Even the birds were quiet.

I'd crawled up an ungodly number of stairs on my own last night after I lost my voice in the practice room. Clearing my froggy throat, I could tell today would be a tea with honey day. I stretched my limbs in a final fight to find a comfortable position and snooze.

For once, my feet didn't dangle over the end of the bed.

I rolled off the side with a graceless thump. Dragging myself to the closet, I surveyed the uniform wardrobe while rubbing the sleep from my eyes. I flicked through the hangers, my fingers moving purposefully among the sea of blue and green. Holding the jacket up against my baggy hoodie, I saw the length seemed right on target. I grabbed a few skirts and pants and found they were actually the proper length for my long limbs. It seemed I would not be turning too many heads today.

I sighed in relief.

My sleepy limbs took their time climbing through the pressed wool pants and blazer. The rumor was that New England winters were brutal, but I was barely keeping ahead of a mild chill in the morning half darkness. I was taking no chances.

I tiptoed out of my bedroom with my schoolbag, finding a note pinned to the outer door. I shared a suite with someone, and the common area boasted two desks, a couch, and a modest entertainment system. I hadn't even noticed them when I stumbled in last night. The room looked as picturesque as the brochures had promised.

Apparently I'd scored the penthouse and hadn't realized it.

I pulled on the note, and it came away from the door easily.

Heard you come in last night. Glad you found it okay. I won't see you until X's lecture, so try and keep out of trouble until then. Use the school email if you need an SOS. Later, roomie. Mags

My eyebrows shot up at the final line. So the kooky tour guide was my suitemate.

I grabbed for the doorknob and found an additional note stuck to the handle. I had to uncrumple it to read what it said.

P.S. Beware the feline librarian. It may look cute, but just don't look it in the eye. You'll thank me later.

I carried my frown down the narrow hallway, trudging down the stairs with one eye on the railing and the other on the pair of notes. My hand slid down the rails smoothly, only catching on the occasional corner post at each landing. Although the staircase looked rickety, it seemed like the old wood had grown more stubborn over the years and dared anyone to doubt its efficacy. It reminded me of a funhouse staircase built to make you question perspective and the rules of gravity. I patted the final post once my foot hit the ground floor.

The ground floor also held an echo of places I had been before. Its age was showing in the uneven plaster walls, warped floor boards, and howling window panes, but it felt like an old man full of stories instead of a dilapidated old lean-to that had been used beyond its years. My hands trailed along the walls as I took in the silent great room. One student was passed out in an armchair, but otherwise the cavernous room was empty.

I wandered around to find the kitchen and hopefully a box of tea. Exploring could wait until I was a little more fortified. I didn't plan to do much talking today, but making a cup of tea would kill some time until the rest of the world woke up.

The cupboards were well worn and screeched loudly in protest as I searched for the communal mugs and tea. The feeling felt familiar, and a shiver tingled up my spine.

I whirled around in the kitchen, searching for the disturbance that put my body on edge. The kitchen was empty. Still, the niggling feeling in my gut caused the rest of the hairs on my body to stand at attention. If it wasn't a person, was it déjà vu?

I abandoned my quest for tea in favor of a scouting mission. I walked the entire first floor, searching for the cause of the feeling so I could put an end to it and move on with my day.

"You've really gone off the deep end this time, Noah," I mumbled aloud, checking the shadows behind armchairs and between table legs. Something just needed to jump out at me already. It was like I was living a scene in a horror movie that just wouldn't end. The tension was petering out into annoyance.

I sighed when I completed the circular route back to the kitchen and found it, too, was devoid of any bumps in the night. The feeling remained, leaving me in a dark mood. The mug I'd found lay abandoned on the countertop, but I didn't feel like tea anymore.

My eye caught the antique porcelain crocks that lined the counter, thoughtfully labeled in winding script. I popped the lid to the smallest one and grabbed a handful of honey packets. Adele had promised to stock the new house with my favorite cough drops but hadn't foreseen my alternate arrangements. The honey packets would have to do for now.

I made a beeline for the front door, pausing in the blustery mudroom at the amusing sight that caught my attention.

In front of me, a gloved hand stuck out. Another, this one a bright yellow sport glove extended far enough to nearly touch my cheek, waved from behind the first. All along the wall, various coat hooks and knobs stuck out. Several were occupied by gloves, some by hats, and many by an army of jackets. Woven throughout all these were scarves, linking various items in a psychedelic traffic system. Clearly, what had been intended only for practical use had been repurposed into a living protest piece by the students who lived in the dorms. Even the boots were stacked to mimic the waves of the sea instead of using the orderly, symmetric slots as they had been intended.

If this was how people dealt with winter up here, I was going to need some serious amendments to my wardrobe. Snowshoes perhaps.

Thinking back to my brief encounter with the brochure doll trio, I was glad I was in the rickety old dorm. I had a feeling they wouldn't be visiting much, and even though the thought of winter annoyed me, I much preferred mismatched gloves and Nordic headwear. Practicality over style would get my vote any day.

I strode confidently out into the brisk morning air but had to buckle into myself against the temperature.

"Absolutely ungodly," I howled through chattering teeth, wincing as every pass of wind cut through my clothes. I jogged down the dirt path, happy for any shelter. Half-frozen tears stuck to my eyes and blurred the path in front of me. I vaguely recalled having a map in my bag but dismissed the idea as soon as I realized I would have to unearth my bare hands from their pocket sanctuary to retrieve it. Not worth it.

I reached a fork in the path, which had finally joined the cobblestones of the academic quad. My body careened left and up the stairs, finding myself coming from the opposite side of the dining hall than I had the day before. Good to know.

The heavy doors were no match for my desperation to escape the elements. I lunged inside, uncharacteristically twisting behind me to close the door before the wind could get any other ideas. I braced against the gloss-stained wood as the feeling returned to my fingers and nose.

For a moment, I thought about emailing Mags to bring a coat for me to class, but I balked. Once the sun was higher, it would warm up. I just had to make it in between buildings for the most part, and my entire morning would be relegated to the library anyway.

Anything to avoid going back out in the cold air too soon.

I stood up straight, shaking off the momentary lapse in judgement and the remaining shivers that had attached themselves all the way down my spine. I fished my phone out of my jacket pocket, finding the time to be an amazing 5:15. I wasn't sure when breakfast started, but I had a feeling I wouldn't have to fight any other students for a good spot in line.

Something moved in my peripheral vision. Just a quick flash as I scrolled mindlessly through my email and notifications. My head snapped up, but my eyes couldn't lock on the target. I scanned the entire hall. Not a soul was there. Save me.

I sighed, pinching the bridge of my nose but making sure not to smudge what little eye makeup I'd managed to slap on. Coffee. Forget tea, I needed coffee.

I shouldered my way through the assembly line door. The trays were out for the cold options while the burners simmered pools of water, readying for the hot options. Bangs and shouts from the kitchen crew filled the small space, but the noise was comforting. It reminded me of family dinners in Chicago when I was a kid and my aunts and uncles shouted at each other over smoky pans of oil and mountains of chopped vegetables.

My eyes caught the percolator in the corner, and I busied myself with making as black a coffee as I could manage. The semi-automatic machine had too many options, so I ended up hitting the espresso button until the cup was half full before hitting the black coffee button. Belatedly, I realized the caffeine content might cause me to see other imaginary objects, but I was in too deep by that point. I promised myself I would have a nice big carb load to fill the hole in my stomach lining this caffeine bomb would create, but I hadn't seen any bagels on my brief survey of the breakfast smorgasbord.

I turned quickly on my heel, determined to find bread of some sort among the sea of half-filled trays since the heat of the poorly insulated disposable cup had seeped through to my palms. I looked up in enough time to register the hit before I joined my newly brewed coffee on the floor.

EIGHT

"Dammit." The heap sighed next to me.

I looked forlornly at the coffee spilled all over the floor, tarnishing the pristine glimmer of the marble. Who puts marble in a school kitchen anyway? One of the bobby pins in my hair was stabbing my scalp, but no other serious injury registered in my brain. Way too early to deal with blood loss anyway.

The grumbles continued from the heap of a person next to me as I sat up and checked my uniform for stains. My nose crinkled at the thought of having to venture back through the cold to change clothes so soon after I regained feeling in my extremities.

"Who has any business moving that fast at this hour of the morning?" the mass grumbled.

My eyes squinted briefly, trying to place the voice.

"Good morning to you, too, Sean." I straightened before the pool of coffee could soak my butt. The disposable cup lay off to the side, and I thanked whatever luck I had that it wasn't a ceramic mug that had broken.

I wasn't superstitious, but enough bad omens

before lunchtime and a person might get a complex.

"Noah?" Sean finally hauled his torso upright to confront his opponent. He rubbed his ears delicately, and I could see the tangle of earbuds in his jacket and blazer combo. I felt a slight ping of guilt, but it was gone before I could blink. "What the hell are you doing up this early?"

I offered my hand, and he hopped up gratefully.

"I could ask the same." I left him to adjust his haphazard layers so I could pick up the empty cup from the pool of coffee at our feet. I waved it in his face. "Should I make it a double this time?"

"Seriously." Sean rubbed his whole face with his hands. "I'll take five of whatever you're having."

I tossed the cup in the open can next to the beverage bar and began the process again, this time making sure not to move too quickly and spook Sean again.

"Long night?" I asked, pausing only to hand him the first coffee.

He accepted it with a brief sheepish smile, lifting it in cheers before he took a long pull. I nodded in understanding and resumed making my own coffee.

"Easy to lose track of time down there," Sean said as I finally took a sip of my new coffee.

I turned around to face him, leaning back onto the counter as I nursed my drink. "Working or playing?" I asked.

Sean shrugged in response.

"Just practicing. I have some auditions coming up, so I have to memorize a lot of new pieces. Pretty stiff competition out there." He shrugged again. "Same old, same old."

"You a Landing kid?" I asked him.

His eyebrows shot up in surprise. "Are you asking if I really need to practice if mommy or daddy can buy me a spot?" Sean shot back.

I waited him out, taking another sip of my coffee.

He bristled at my lack of response. "It doesn't work like that in music conservatories. You actually have to have talent. Talent comes from practice," Sean said, "Scholarship kids don't have a monopoly on that, last time I checked."

I took another sip of my coffee. Sean fidgeted with his earbuds.

"Anyway," he said, "I have to get back to practice."

He turned to storm out the door, but I grabbed him by the arm.

"Hey." I caught his heated gaze. "I didn't mean it like that."

"Of course not," Sean threw back at me, his shoulder stiff as I held on.

"I really didn't, okay?" I said. "I'm not trying to say anything about your work ethic or whether you should need it or not. I don't know your story. I'm just not good at giving context sometimes."

Sean brushed my hand off his arm, but his body seemed to relax a little at my half apology.

"I forget you're new here," Sean said. "You'll find out soon enough. You'll know everyone's story by the end of the week. And they'll know yours."

"Doubtful," I said, "but thanks for the warning."

Sean frowned at me and took a long time to look away. I wasn't sure what he was searching for, but he must have found whatever it was. He scratched his jaw, looking through dead air for a while.

"I'm not really sure what's going on at this school, but I don't think it's possible for you to stay out of it," Sean said, finally breaking his pensive silence.

"What do you mean?" I asked.

"I can't put my finger on it. Weird things have been happening, and everyone just seems to go along with it. I'm not really attached to the gossip network around here, but it all started right about the time of Colm's accident." Sean crushed his cup and tossed it in the trash can.

"Your friend? The one whose practice room I'm using?" I felt the hairs on the back of my neck rise slowly in apprehension.

"Friend might be a strong word, but okay," Sean replied. "Everyone's turned into this crazy hive mind. It's the creepiest thing." He shook his head.

"High schools are always like that," I dismissed. "Especially private schools."

He shrugged. "You'll have to see it for yourself. Like I said, I can't really explain it." He absentmindedly looped his earbuds around his fingers. "Just try to keep to yourself. And stay the hell away from Aileen and her crew."

"Oh?" My eyebrows raised in interest.

"Every hive needs a queen bee." Sean shrugged.

"What about the Landing kids?" I asked. "Do they follow her, too?"

Sean snorted, breaking the spell of his nervous fidgeting.

"Hardly," he replied. "I'm not even sure they register on the food chain around here."

"That's good," I said. I mentally kicked myself when I realized I'd shared that sentiment out loud.

"You're in the Landing?" Sean said in surprise. His cheeks colored, and the white of his earbud wires flashed against his dark uniform as they resumed their nervous dance.

"Mmmm." I gave him a good-natured shrug. "Maybe it's better to be there and off the radar than be in the middle of the hive."

"Landing kids are their own problem. Like a weird secret society that polices themselves." Sean's forehead creased with worry. "I don't know which is worse."

"Well, on that cheery note," I crumpled my own coffee cup and tossed it to join Sean's in the bin, "I should probably get going."

"Yeah, I should get back to practicing, too." Sean hesitated in front of the door.

I walked past him to the line of trays, which had filled out somewhat in our brief time together. I found a basket of bagels and grabbed two still warm to the touch.

"Listen," Sean called across the room. "I'm down in the practice rooms most of the time when I don't have class. Don't be a stranger, okay? Maybe let me know you're around next time so I don't crap my pants."

"You spill my coffee one more time and you'll be wishing you could see me coming," I called back to him.

He smiled and saluted before backing out the door.

I tore off a huge chunk of warm bagel, letting my teeth keep time to the churning thoughts running through my head. The hairs on the back of my neck hadn't calmed down any, which gave my skin an itchy feeling. The warring sensations were driving me crazy, so I decided the only logical option bordered on the insane.

Go back outside.

I checked my shoulder through the entry door into the food assembly, promptly bumping into someone attempting to come in. With my mouth full of bagel, I mumbled an apology as incoherent as my cloud of thoughts.

I choked when I recognized the face.

Sandy haired with a line of freckles across his face, the boy scowling at me was normally bursting into flames in my dreamscape. He stayed in the quadrant with the drowning young woman with a birthmark on her cheek and the angry man whose wrinkles cracked and shattered into a thousand pieces.

"Could you just move, please?" He snarled, trying to shove past my frozen body toward the door.

I choked on the bagel in my mouth, pounding at my chest as the coughing rattled a small piece loose from the wrong pipe. The boy finally shoved past me, and I was alone to greet a slowly growing trickle of students coming in for breakfast.

I shoved the rest of the bagel into my bag next to its brother for safe keeping.

This was a new record. A new night visitor sighting in under twenty-four hours? My hand was shaking as I tried to smooth back a strand of hair. I was dying to message Adele, but I knew the harsh truth before I even thought of what I would say.

I had to make it work. I had to deal with it until graduation.

I took a stream of steadying breaths, in through my nose, out slowly through my mouth. The students were more and more cognizant when I looked up. Their frowns and chatter in pairs made me realize I was causing a slight scene. It was too early to start the rumor mill going. Way, way too early.

So you saw a night visitor, I narrated to myself as I took self-assured strides to the door. No big deal. They don't bite. They don't even recognize you.

In through my nose. Out through my mouth.

You don't know who they are either, a voice in my head argued. So, really, what's there to worry about.

I'd made it under the archway in the atrium. Less than ten steps and I was outside in the bracing chill of the early morning sky. Plenty of room to think outside.

I looked up to meet a pair of heavily lined eyes, framed by a mass of chin-length curls.

My mind flashed to the field next to where Elliott had been prior to my intervention almost ten years ago. Those eyes. Those curls. The death loop played in my mind as I stared through this girl, who dodged around me, continuing on into the dining hall with her arm carelessly thrown around her friend's shoulder. Their tinkling laugh echoed in the enlivened hall, and my stomach twisted.

Two. Two night visitors in under twenty-four hours. This time, minutes apart.

I could feel the cold sweat seeping into the collar of my shirt, and I tugged at it savagely. The door loomed in front of me, and I left before it could shut behind the next entering student. Someone called out after me as I bumped them in my haste. I didn't care.

My eyes scanned the horizon, finding a good number of students filtering in from the athletic quad and dormitories on their way to breakfast. I trotted hastily across the courtyard, aiming for the academic buildings. Fewer students were in that direction, but my eyes were glued to the streams of blue and green funneling to the dining hall.

A shock of blonde hair. A wry smile. Amber brown eyes.

Each new sighting sent a lightning bolt through my frame. The fear was overwhelming me as I lost count of the number of night visitors in my field of vision. My hand tightened in a vise grip around my phone, and I hid behind the column Adair had used as a hiding spot the night before.

My ragged breathing echoed against the brick wall and the concrete of the pristine columns identical to the one sucking all the heat from my back. I squeezed my eyes shut, willing the parade of death loop images to stop crowding my field of vision. One by one, they popped up, just as I'd seen them in real life, but this time superimposed against their death loop. Each one was dizzying in its familiarity. I'd been watching some for years, and then they appeared in real life.

"Get it together, Noah," I reminded myself. "You can't have them catch you being crazy. Not today. Not ever."

What does it mean? I screamed at myself. I had so many pieces of the puzzle, but it was like starting with no edge pieces. No boundary to work inward from, just so many differently shaped pieces of sky that I couldn't seem to connect.

I felt a tear trickle down my cheek, and I wiped at it angrily. Resolved, I took several deep breaths, directing all the anxiety out with each exhale. I kicked off from the column, standing straight without any assistance. Once I found sure footing, I rubbed my face, checked that my unruly curls were still pinned back and contained, and brushed off my clothes. Slowly, the hairs on the back of my neck and arms seemed to lower, making me feel less like a porcupine and more like a rational human being.

I looked around, finding no witnesses to my first mini meltdown of the day. I unearthed the map in my bag to find out exactly where I should be going. A bark of a laugh escaped me, and I clapped my frozen hand over my lips before anything else could escape. The brick wall looming in front of me had been my destination after all.

I noted the side entrance but decided for orientation's sake I should go the usual route. My feet found their way back to the cobblestones, and the buckles on my boots jingled merrily as I struck the ground with each step.

In no time, the front entry greeted me, and I trotted up the small staircase to the main door. Just as I neared the top, however, a flash of green caught my eye. I froze, teetering inside my boots to find balance from the halted forward momentum.

P.S. Beware the feline librarian. It may look cute, but just don't look it in the eye.

You'll thank me later.

NINE

I'd never lost a staring contest to a cat before, but as my eyelid twitched in protest, I realized this would be the first.

The chemical green orbs hung suspended on a black face and shimmered with every minuscule twitch of my traitorous muscles. It was like watching myself through a tinted mirror. Even trying to stand completely still, my feet wavered to correct my balance, and my boots creaked in protest as I swayed imperceptibly back and forth. I squinted my eyes at the guard cat, its tail flicking in laughter.

"If you're looking for a password, I don't have one," I said, breaking the silence of the deserted academic quad. The cat's ears flicked forward, responding to my voice.

We waited it out for several more minutes.

Then, the cat sneezed.

I took the momentary lapse to leap over it and through the front door, pulling it shut behind me before the little dragon could get in. I leaned against the door, shaking my head loose of its ridiculous thoughts.

"If this is keeping it together, I'm a little worried what berserk looks like," I scolded myself in the warm entryway. Unlike the dining hall, the small room was lined with tapestries and oil paintings, softening the clatter of my boots on the marble floor. It seemed much homier than the former cathedral and less institutional than the administration building. I noticed the old smell of books still hanging in the air as I trotted up the small staircase to the next landing, my footsteps muffled by plush carpet.

As I took in the details of the library, my boots scuffed softly on the carpet and my head rolled back and forth trying to take note of the ceilings, exit signs, and general signage. The information desk sat empty, and my class schedule mentioned only a study carrel number. The maps I'd been given were not for the interiors of buildings, only the nicely painted aerial view of campus proper.

I found a side staircase, but my only option was up.

Easily enough, I made my way to the second floor. Only part of this floor was filled with book stacks. Much more furniture squeezed its way between the stacks, slowly thinning the books and taking over the remaining floor plan. An odd line formed where the carpets changed from a plush cherry red to a flat muted crosshatch, and I stood under a large plate glass skylight. In front of me, the smell of plaster still hung in the air, crowding out the slight moldiness of aging paper.

The floor dropped away in the middle, allowing the distorted beams of the skylight to break the barrier to the first floor as well. The small lanes created by this opening allowed enough space for three students to walk abreast. A series of doors with numbers like the ones on my schedule lined the walls. So these were the study carrels.

I walked slowly past the dark rooms, finding all of them encased in glass, completely open to the view of any passerby. Great. I would be stuck in a glass cage for students to stare at me while I navigated my calculus homework.

I snorted, shoving my hands deeper into my jacket pockets.

The hallway stretched even further, so I followed it to see what else the library had in store.

The glass cages ended after I counted ten. I would be curious to see how filled they were throughout the day, or if I was blessed to be one of the few caged students with the privilege of private study.

At the end was a large observatory. The ceiling domed high above me, making the space seem much bigger than it was. The bookshelves in this room seemed to be the same as the others in the library, but they looked child's height under the expansive ceiling. The floor was covered with round tables of various sizes ranging from a coffee table barely able to hold my book bag to a table that could seat twelve.

I scoffed again, thinking of King Arthur.

A sneeze greeted me.

My head swung around but not fast enough for my scanning eyes. I didn't see a single soul in the entire room. I strode quickly to the end of the room, where a door was set into the wood paneling. If I hadn't placed my hand on the wall, I might have missed it. My fingers caught on an elaborate sun carved into the wall.

I stepped back, surveying where the door melted into the background of the wood. Now that I was looking for it, I could see a barely defined outline a little thicker than the other panels. My fingers reached out automatically to trace it again.

This time, I kept my hand on the wall, dragging my fingers against the smooth grain and the steady bumps of the vertical boards. I paused when they hooked on another design.

An ornate maple leaf came to life under my searching fingertips.

On a hunch, I quickly moved along, following the tight hug of the circular room until I stood in front of the final carving.

A snowflake.

My hand instinctively went to my chest and the inner pocket where I'd tucked the old ornate key. I was itching to open it, but the sneeze came again and my hand snapped back to my side.

The sneeze had been much closer this time. My left hand was still touching the snowflake, and I was torn. Investigate what was behind the door, or investigate the allergy-ridden snoop?

I felt a bump on my shin.

I looked down, my reverie broken by the odd feeling.

And found myself staring into a pair of green lanterns.

I jumped in belated surprise, letting out a yell that echoed back at me with unexpected force in the carpeted room. The cat snorted at me, licking its paw and proceeding to clean its face. I grabbed the shoulder strap of my bag, frowning at the tricky little cat.

Just like at the library entrance, it seemed to be guarding the door, expecting some sort of password. After taking a moment to clean both sides of its face, the cat put its front paw down resolutely, looking at me with those unblinking eyes.

"Open sesame," I said with a head nod toward the door. The cat scooted its butt to block the door, blinking once slowly at me. I crossed my arms.

"What's your issue?" I asked the cat, whose only response was a flick of its tail. "I see."

My eyes narrowed at the cat as I wondered if it would be worth it to try to move the darn thing so I could check out whatever was behind the door. If it had its own guardian, I had a hunch it would be something worth looking at.

I reached slowly into my jacket pocket, and the cat's eyes followed my every move. I pulled the key out of its hiding spot, holding it up in front of the cat's face.

It sneezed at me, pulling its hind leg up and proceeding to clean its undercarriage.

"Seriously?" I said, my voice rising higher than I'd intended. "Could you just move, please?"

The cat continued to clean itself.

"I'm giving you fair warning. Then I'll move you however I like." I gave the cat a pointed look.

It paused briefly in cleaning itself, as if contemplating my threat. Clearly I had not been harsh enough because after very little consideration, furry little Satan continued its morning bath.

A growl escaped me, and I could feel the warmth tickle my throat. I slapped my hand on my throat, scolding myself for my rashness. I couldn't afford to break out into song right now.

The cat finally paused its cleaning, choosing to stand and shake out the tufts of hair that had raised after my growl. Finding my threat empty, it sat down again and resumed its favorite pastime—staring me down.

A loud sneeze broke the tension.

Both the cat and I jumped at the unexpected

sound.

Another sneeze erupted right next to us, this time accompanied by its owner. A curtain of long dark hair hung around the girl's face, obscuring it from my view. With a pang of recognition, I realized she looked like the ghosts in Japanese horror movies, which just made me want to laugh. The girl walked directly in front of me, making a beeline for the cat.

In less than a second, the cat was upended in her arms, its legs stuck up indignantly as she cradled him like a baby. She turned to me, part of her face peeking out from the dark hair.

"He's the worst when meeting new people," she said, her voice warm and friendly as if we had been friends for years.

I nodded, as if I knew exactly what she meant. Something else itched in the back of my head, another familiarity.

"Hey, have we met before?" I asked her, trying to get a better look at her obscured face. "Didn't I see you at the administration office yesterday?"

"Oh, yeah, sorry about that," she said with a sheepish grin. She lifted up her cat-filled arms. "I'll get him out of your way for a while."

The girl turned to go, but I grabbed her arm. She froze, her neck disappearing beneath her tightened shoulders.

"Sorry." I released my hold on her arm. I'd only meant to ask her name, but I was taken aback at how my light touch had made her flinch. I let her scurry away with the crazy cat before I could fight against the instinct I had felt. It didn't quite feel like me, but after another few thoughts, it seemed something Adele would scold me about. I'm sure no one really likes to be grabbed randomly.

I lost myself in thought, my thumb stroking the ornate key I still held in my palm. Even without the guard cat, now didn't feel like the right time to go in. If that girl was here, that meant more students would be coming shortly. I might as well get a head start on my pile of self study work.

With one last touch of the carved snowflake, I pushed off the wall, darting through the bookshelves and tables to my assigned glass box. Now seemed the perfect time for calculus. I needed to clear my head and think about concrete equations with definite right and wrong answers. Something told me it would be one of the few times this place made any sense.

TEN

Adair found me collapsed on top of my Latin text with my curls splayed out across the various marked-up pages of translation footnotes.

"Hey," Adair said, knocking politely on the open door.

I'd tried working with the door shut, but something about my breathing bouncing back at me in the vacuous room was driving me insane. After about twenty minutes, I'd propped it open.

My head popped up from its uncomfortable pillow of glossy bound paper.

"Hey," I said, my voice froggy from disuse.

"Sorry to wake you. Time for class." His brow furrowed in thought.

I flicked my eyes down to my nest of notebooks and texts, quickly putting them back in order and ready for their home in my bag.

"No worries." I laughed inwardly about his worry. He couldn't wake me from sleeping. Even during the day, I couldn't nap. I honestly couldn't remember the last time I'd actually slept.

"How's your first day?" Adair asked as we trotted down the stairs and out into the quad.

I shrugged, happy to match my long stride with his. The sun had broken from the cloud cover, letting a few rays warm my face on our brief walk.

"Riveting," I said dryly.

Adair chuckled. "Yeah, private study can do that to a person. How many hours do you have back to back?" he asked politely.

"The whole morning," I said.

He grimaced in sympathy. "Mine are spaced out, so I don't mind it. If your tutor doesn't come, though, you can always go back to the dorm," Adair offered. "Mine comes about once a week like clockwork, so I get away with not being in the study rooms much if I can help it."

"Good to know," I said as we jogged up the stairs. I whipped out my phone, noticing how close we were cutting it. "Sorry, we're almost late."

"We'll live," he said as he pushed through the door.

I ran into his back. We both grunted at the unexpected impact.

"What gives?" I asked, unable to see past his shoulder. He turned to face me briefly.

"Mags and Aileen are at it again." Adair sighed.

He managed to weave through the wall of student bodies that had clogged the hallway outside the lecture hall. I followed close behind, trying to get an idea of what was going on before I entered the fray.

Adair had made it ahead of me to the center, but I hung back to witness what looked like the showdown of the week. Students near me were already speculating on what had set them off this time.

Mags and Aileen faced off against one another. The murmuring of the students distorted what they were saying, but the body language was close to a fistfight. Aileen was flanked by the twins, and as much as they tried to look haughty and strong, they kept sharing nervous glances. Aileen's cheeks were flushed, and she kept trading verbal spars with Mags.

Based on Aileen's agitation, I would put money on Mags being the winner of this particular battle. She seemed self-assured, her eyes dancing with glee as she flung insult after insult at her favorite opponent. Adair walked up to Mags and spoke a few words in her ear. She seemed to pout momentarily before nodding in agreement.

I pushed through the crowd again, finally breaking the inner circle.

"Jeez, Aileen, I was just trying to be friendly," Mags said with a wicked grin.

Aileen looked like she'd been slapped in the face. This must have been a complete one eighty from their previous exchange of words, and Aileen was not prepared. Her lips spluttered as if she couldn't find any words to fling back.

Aileen's eyes caught mine as soon as I broke free from the circle. I walked up between the two girls, sharing a quick glance with Adair, who gave me a slight shrug.

"Hey guys." I ignored the huge crowd surrounding us. "Aren't we going to be late to class?"

Aileen stomped her foot, letting out a very unladylike growl. Mags replied with a too sweet honey smile.

"You're right, Noah. We should really get to class." Mags turned on her heel and walked directly into the lecture hall. Adair followed like a shadow, and I turned to go after them.

Someone grabbed my wrist.

My eyebrows rose high on my forehead for

whoever had grabbed me. Aileen's desperate face searched mine.

"You need to stay far away from her." Aileen's wild eyes watched Mags' back going into the hall.

"We're roommates. That's going to be kind of hard." I shrugged.

"You're in the Landing?" Aileen's voice broke. She released my arm like it had burned her. The twins gasped. "How?"

I replied with a shrug. "No idea. I just go where they tell me. And right now, they're telling me to go to class." I took another step, but Aileen's voice made me pause again.

"Something's not right. This used to be a safe place. That witch has ruined everything," Aileen said, the venom in her voice making the hairs on the back of my neck stand up. "All you Landing kids are bringing this school down with you. I'm not going to stand for it."

Aileen shoved past me into the classroom. I cocked my head to the side as her words ran on extended loop in my brain. I had no idea what she was referring to, but it made me pause. Both Sean and Aileen felt like something was going on, and I couldn't lie and say I hadn't felt a little off center since I got here.

I realized belatedly that the hall had cleared, and I was the only one not in the lecture hall. The bell tolled for class, and I lunged for the door, shutting it behind me.

As I turned, I felt like I'd been punched in the stomach. Below me sat a bowl-like amphitheater with almost a hundred students in rickety wooden fold-down seats. My eyes scanned the rows of students, and almost every other student pinged my memory. One after another, death loops came to mind, and the hole in my stomach grew. It was like this morning, only way, way worse. I stopped counting once I hit fifty.

I squeezed my eyes shut, taking a deep breath. I could feel multiple eyes on me, and my feet moved of their own accord. I slid into an empty seat just before the side door opened and the teacher walked in. The loud echo of the door slamming shut brought me back to my senses a little, and I was able to grab a notebook and pen from my bag. I set my pen down firmly on my notebook before my shaking hand could drop it. I clenched my hands together in my lap to the point of pain. Anything to keep me grounded.

"Good morning, class," the teacher said.

A booming echo of staggered good mornings replied, and I flinched, biting the inside of my cheek hard. Facing forward, I put all my energy into focusing on the teacher.

The name Ms. Xavier was scrawled on the chalkboard in the corner along with the homework and reading for the next day. I did my best to neatly copy the information into my notebook as Ms. Xavier lectured. Once I was done, I attempted to follow the lecture and take notes. I could hear the scurrying of pens across paper around me in the hall, but my pen barely moved.

The weight of the stares was like a suffocating blanket around me. I couldn't even be sure they were actually looking at me, but every time my eyes flicked up from my notebook to find the professor, they crossed the path of no less than five night visitors. The death loops assaulted me, and I closed my eyes again.

"Are you okay?" I thought I heard a voice say. Suddenly, I couldn't feel the weight of my pen in my hand any more. The hinge of the desk platform in front of me squeaked. Magically I had a little more space to breath.

"Put your head between your legs," the voice said. "Breathe deeply. You'll be okay."

I did as I was instructed, my clammy forehead resting on the slightly itchy fabric covering my knees. And then, for the first time since I'd been little, I passed out.

ELEVEN

I woke up with a start.

Looking around, my eyes registered something vaguely familiar, yet simultaneously horrifying. The trees crowded around me, but I could still see slivers of the midday sky above them. Even the dips in the uneven ground felt like they came from a distant memory. Then it hit me.

I was in my dreamscape.

But it was daytime.

I twisted around, the ground clear of the usual silent fog. Instead, I was grabbing at grass below my fingertips. The rustling alone made me freak out even more.

I leapt up from my seat on the ground, and the scuffle of my feet against the slightly dusty ground assaulted my ears. I groaned.

"Oh, this is so not good," I said pathetically. My hands shot to my temples, shielding my eyes from the vast periphery of the day-lit dreamscape. "How the hell did I even get here?"

"I always wonder the same thing," a guy's voice said behind me.

I spun around, my fist ready to strike. I lashed out first, panicking at the loud noise in a place that used to drive me insane from its stillness.

A warm hand grabbed my fist, easily deflecting my attack but holding on. My eyes focused on the hand first, verifying it was in fact human. Normal. Alive.

My eyes followed the arm attached to the hand, which thankfully was also attached to a set of shoulders, a chest, and a very amused face. Not a translucent image on repeat, but an actual human being. Or the closest proximity to one that could exist here.

"Who are you?" I growled at my captor. Even after he'd clearly sidestepped my assault, he still held onto my hand. My free hand flexed in agitation, but I held back from surrendering my other hand to the stranger.

My eyes surveyed the rest of the owner of the hand pressing my fist firmly in place. A boy about my age, with broad shoulders and only an inch or two on me, which was still impressive considering I nearly cleared six feet. His blue eyes matched the color of the sky in the daytime dreamscape, making the color drain from my face. Was he like me? Did he get stuck here every day, like I did every night?

"Say something before my fist does the talking for me," I growled, my free hand clenching in solidarity.

The boy laughed, letting my hand go. He took a step back, raising his hands in surrender. "I'm sure I could take you, but just in case I can't, I'd rather keep the peace and my pride intact," he said with a wide grin. His shoulders shook with contained laughter, which just made me want to punch him even harder.

"What are you doing here?" My words were laced with steel.

"What are you doing here?" he replied, his good nature twisting the words from a demand to a curious request.

"I asked first," I argued.

"I was here first." He shrugged.

"Hardly," I said. "I've been visiting this place since I was ten."

"I've never seen you before," he said. "And I've been here for what seems like forever."

"It's not like this when I'm usually here." I crossed my arms violently against my torso.

"Oh?" His eyes glittered with curiosity. "It's always like this for me. How does it normally look for you?"

I squinted my eyes at him, trying to determine if he was messing with me. Was the dreamscape different depending on who visited it first? Or when it was visited? How many people had access to it?

My feet circled around the boy as I surveyed him from all sides. The questions circling my brain fueled my physical circuit, and I made it around two times before he broke in.

"Anything I can help with?" He tried unsuccessfully to keep a smile off his face.

"I already asked you who you are and what your business is here, but since you're being uncooperative, I'll have to figure it out myself." I paused in front of him.

"You haven't offered any of that information either," he argued. He stuck his hand out to me. "Nice to meet you, fair lady. My name is Colm. And if you can figure out what I'm doing here, I'd like to know, too."

I shook his hand, a deep wrinkle creasing my forehead.

"Noah," I replied. "How long did you say you've

been coming here?"

Colm shrugged.

"It's been almost all the time lately. If I'm not here, it's just blackness. Before that, I think I went to school." Colm scratched the back of his head. "That's where things get fuzzy. It's, like, almost in my grasp, but then it slips away. You know what I mean?"

"Hmmmm." I stared at his face again. I got on my tiptoes, placing my hands on his shoulders. I stared into his clear blue eyes, searching for something. Some hint of recognition. Colm stiffened.

I finally stepped back and crossed my arms.

"I don't think you're a night visitor," I said haltingly. "But I'm not sure that's true either."

"Okay," Colm said.

A heavy silence dragged on, and I could hear the wind in the trees around us. As I shifted my weight, the grass crinkled beneath me. I brushed my ear against my shoulder in agitation. The noise was deafening.

"You said it's different when you come here," Colm prompted me. "What do you mean?"

"Well, you're sure as hell not here," I said, the noise around me causing my tone to come out more prickly than I intended. I sighed. "It's dark. There's fog along the ground. No noise. And the people..."

Colm's eyebrows rose in surprise.

"Well." I paused to search for the best words to describe them. "They're not as lively. Not in the traditional sense."

"What does that mean?" Colm asked, his eyes innocent of the weight of his innocuous question.

"They're like holograms," I said. "You know, like in space movies?"

"Yeah, sure," Colm said. "That seems kind of weird."

"Yeah," I said with a dry chuckle. "Kind of."

I shoved my hands in my pockets, shocked to find my uniform had transferred with me into the dreamscape. Normally at night, I was dressed in the same black clothes regardless of what I wore to bed. I frowned at the wool blend pants, demanding they answer for their presence.

I felt Colm's presence enter my personal space bubble.

I looked up, and his face was only inches from mine. I stiffened, wondering what his play was.

Instead of coming any closer, his hand reached out. His thumb traced the insignia on my lapel, and a ghost of a smile flickered across his face.

"Do you recognize it?" I asked softly, not wanting to spook him.

Colm's eyes flicked up to meet mine. He seemed surprised at our sudden close proximity. I didn't blink, holding his gaze. The air between us sizzled with energy, and Colm held his breath.

I stepped back, creating an arm's length distance between us, leaving Colm to bounce up on his toes. He shook his head, as if he'd been in a trance. My heart was pounding as well, but I tried to calm my breathing imperceptibly. My eyes were locked on Colm.

Who was this kid?

"You said you probably went to school, right?" I asked him, giving him something tangible to focus on. Colm's eyes met mine again, this time with his head cocked in confusion. I tapped my lapel and the Windermere crest he'd latched onto only moments before. "Did you go to Windermere?"

"Windermere," Colm repeated softly to himself. Slowly he nodded his head. "Yeah, that sounds familiar."

The realization hit me like a sack of bricks.

My mind flashed back to my conversation with Sean earlier this morning. His sort-of friend in the coma. The one whose practice room I was using. Because the kid was in a coma.

I took a deep breath in, walking away from Colm and into the trees. My hands reflexively shot to my temples as I worked out the timeline of events again. Plugging in all the details, I could come to only one conclusion.

"Noah," Colm called after me, his feet making soft landfalls in the grass as he tried to catch up to my quick pace. "What is it?"

"I need to think." I waved him away.

He caught my wrist instead, jerking me to a stop. He pulled me around to face him, his eyes darker in concern.

"Tell me what's going on in there." Colm softly tapped my temple.

I turned my head away from his touch, but his grip on my wrist was firm. I held it up in my line of sight.

"Let me go, Colm," I said in a low voice, the heat of my anger leaking through my vocal cords. Even here, it burned.

I counted primes in my head to calm down. The anger had to go down, or I was going to lose control in front of Colm. If I threw a tantrum in the dreamscape at night, no one was there to get hurt. I could let it all out with no consequences. Now that I was in the daytime version along with Colm, I couldn't be so sure my voice wouldn't hurt him more than in real life.

Colm let my wrist fall to my side, but he moved to block the direction I'd been moving in.

"Talk to me," he demanded. "What is it?"

"I don't even know. Not for sure." I tried to walk around him. He blocked me easily, and I didn't try to move him. "I don't know enough yet to know for sure."

"Then what's your best guess," Colm pressed.

"I hate guessing," I muttered aloud to myself.

"Humor me," Colm said. "Hypothesize. Best educated inference."

His play on words made me take a step back, but he closed the gap, pressuring me with his presence. I could feel the desperate energy rolling off him, and it made me flinch.

"Fine, but could you just," I put my hands out in front of me, "give me some breathing room?"

He obliged, but I could tell he wasn't happy about it. His eyes scanned me continuously, as if trying to figure out if I was about to run or not.

"I've heard your name," I admitted. "At school."

"And?"

"And." I took a deep breath. A voice in my head warned that telling him he was in a coma would probably be the worst thing I could do. I didn't know how he would take the news. "You've been in a coma since the beginning of the summer. It's October now."

"October?" Colm stepped back at the news.

"You've been unconscious for almost six months," I said slowly.

"I don't remember you." Colm shook his head.

"I just transferred in." My hands rose slowly in front of me. I felt like I was trying to placate a bear. I could tell Colm was one step away from losing his tenuous hold on reality. "I've been using your practice room. Your friend Sean told me about you."

"Sean?" Colm said. "Sean let you use my room? He hates everyone. He would never do that." Colm frowned at me.

"He said he would rather have it used than let it sit and gather dust. I promised not to be a bother, which is the only reason he let me." I spoke softly. I took a tentative step toward Colm, but he seemed to be back on the downward spiral of panic.

Panic I had caused.

I closed the gap I'd created for myself as I saw the light in Colm's eyes darken and almost extinguish. I kicked myself mentally for opening my big, dumb mouth.

"Colm." I laid my hands gently on his chest. The waffle texture of his thermal shirt was warm to the touch, but the light pressure of my hands didn't seem to register to him.

"Hey." I moved his chin down to meet my gaze.

Colm's eyes snapped into focus once he saw my eyes.

"Hey," Colm said, the laugh lines near his eyes crinkling a little as a tightlipped smile forced its way onto his face.

"We're going to figure this out, okay?" I moved his head up and down in a nod with my grip on his chin.

A flash of a toothy smile broke through the fog of panic, and Colm grabbed my hand, keeping it on his face.

"Deal," Colm said just as a cold knife stabbed through my gut.

I doubled over in pain, but it was over as suddenly as it came. My breath came out in ragged pants, and I could hear Colm calling my name behind the ringing in my ears.

"Noah!" Colm crouched next to me on the ground, my hands still in his. "Noah! Are you okay?"

"I don't know," I said through clenched teeth. Another shot of pain lanced through my stomach, and I screamed.

Not a normal scream. A banshee scream.

My throat was on fire, and I shut my eyes against everything. I could feel tears trickling down my face, and I crumpled to the ground as another stab joined the others, this time in rapid succession.

"No!" I screamed, my voice raw with power. I could still feel the warmth of Colm's hands cradling mine.

Finally, I opened my eyes, determined to see the harm I'd caused Colm with my voice. I had to learn. I had to get better.

But Colm's clear blue eyes were staring at mine. Somehow, he had thunderstorms in his, I thought idly to myself. He seemed otherwise unharmed, which sent me reeling in surprise. I wasn't allowed very long, however, before another lance broke through.

"Noah," Colm said softly. "Just give in to it. Fighting it isn't helping you. I'll be here. You have to go. Now."

I screamed again. All the anguish and the pain I'd bottled up from the past day of continuous torture finally came out. As soon as I ran out of breath, though, another shot of pain came. This time, I opened myself up to it, letting it swallow me whole.

The warmth of Colm's hands seeped through my consciousness as I was dragged back into consciousness.

Once again, I could feel the hard wooden seat beneath me, my sweaty forehead still pressed to my wool-clad knees. I took a steadying breath, praying silently none of the screams I'd let loose in the dreamscape had filtered through to this side. I prepared for the padded van and the hug-me jacket.

I felt a hand on my back. Something cold and inky was leaking through the barrier of my jacket, and my stomach dropped. In one movement, I grabbed the arm, moving it into a locked position before I launched the heel of my free palm into the solar plexus of whoever had been touching me and felt a satisfying sting on the palm of my hand.

TWELVE

"Well, she's sure awake now," Mags' voice said above me. "Remind me never to try and wake her up if she oversleeps again. I don't think I can take the hit."

Adair groaned next to me, his body curled up on itself. I had to give it to him though. He didn't even take a knee.

"You all right?" Mags whispered to Adair, peering over his head. "Ms. X is still down there."

"It's fine," Adair gasped, his lip warbling into a grimace. "Just gotta walk it off."

Mags snorted. "You should probably go to the nurse to make sure she didn't break a rib," Mags whispered back.

"Should have warned me," Adair grunted, turning toward the exit.

With his vacancy, the huddled circle barrier was broken and I could see the lecture hall was empty.

"What happened?" I muttered under my breath, rubbing my temples delicately.

"You passed out in class," a soft voice said next to me. I jumped when I saw the dark-haired girl from the library. Her large brown eyes looked at me unblinkingly, waiting for me to ask something else.

My eyes narrowed a little.

"You've been here the whole time?" I half asked. She nodded once.

"Thankfully or you would have caused a bigger scene," Mags said brusquely. She seemed leery of the dark-haired girl but was somehow begrudgingly grateful.

"Scenes are no good," I agreed.

"We've got to stick together." Mags sighed heavily. "It's my fault. I should have filled you in last night."

"You'd think your foresight would be better attuned," the doe-eyed girl muttered.

My head bounced back and forth between the two, who were now locked in a glaring contest.

"About what?" I said. My head felt like it was filled with cotton, and I pinched the bridge of my nose to try to calm the growing headache that was about to make my ears pop.

"Little this, little that," Mags said simply, sticking her tongue out at the other girl. "You okay to walk?"

"Yeah." I grabbed my bag but stood up too fast. I reached for the armrest, and someone caught my elbow. I looked over to thank the girl once again, but she was already waving off the thought before I could open up my mouth. After a deep breath, I managed to shuffle to the aisle unassisted.

"Ms. Young," Ms. Xavier called from the base of the amphitheater.

I grimaced before turning on my heels to face her. I schooled my face before I got into trouble for that, too.

"Yes, ma'am," I replied, feeling the air being sucked in on either side of me. Great. Clearly a teacher I wanted to upset.

"To make up for your nap during my class, I hope you'll join me for some one-on-one tutoring every Saturday for the rest of the semester. Don't let it happen again." Ms. Xavier looked down her nose at me above her sharp black frames.

I swallowed hard, trying to force away the indignant backtalk about to spew out of my mouth. How was an hour of passing out worth six weeks of Saturday detention?

"Yes, ma'am," I said again, biting the inside of my cheek hard until the air compressor of the side door hissed shut.

"Wow," Mags said, her mouth slightly agape. "That was harsh."

"It was good you didn't argue with her," the girl said. "I'm sure it won't be that bad."

Both Mags and I peered at the girl as if she'd grown horns from her head.

"You go then," Mags said in my defense.

The girl shrugged.

"So." I tried to think about anything else other than my doomed Saturdays for the coming eternity. "What were you saying before? About filling me in?"

"Right." Mags checked her phone for the time. "Now's as good a time as any. Scurry along, I've got this." Mags dismissed the dark-haired girl, who looked mildly put off.

"Enjoy getting the party line," the girl muttered only loudly enough for me to hear before she ghosted through the nearest door. She left so quietly, I had to watch her go to make sure she really had left.

"Weird, that one." Mags blew a stray chunk of fuchsia out of the way of her clouded eye.

"Bunch of June Cleavers you've got here," I said dryly back. "Who's she anyway?"

"Little Mouse?" Mags leaned against the nearest row of chairs. "That's Evangeline. The only time she comes out of hiding is for this class. You've seen her?"

"Yeah, couple of times." I frowned at the door Evangeline had just exited through.

"She's got extreme social anxiety. Keeps to herself. She's in the library more than the librarians." Mags shook her head. "It's gotten bad lately. I don't even see her at the Landing or at meals."

"So she's Landing, too?" I asked. "Is there anyone normal in the Landing?"

"Scholarship Landing, aka Cavanaugh House, has been home to the weird, the poor, and the too brilliant for their own good since the school started. I doubt your quote unquote normal brethren would dare step foot in that tradition." Mags snorted and crossed her arms. "Plus, the new dorms have been new for ten years and they still smell like plaster and new paint. It's toxic."

I crinkled my nose, and Mags followed suit.

"Exactly." Mags let out another sigh. "It's not like Landing kids have always had a target on their backs. That's been more recent. Some weird things have happened on campus in the past year, and they always point the blame at the black sheep." Mags shrugged.

"I've heard. Vaguely." I surveyed Mags. Her narrative was dancing around the true topic. I could tell she was leading me in slowly, but I felt impatient. My headache was not getting any better, and I honestly wanted to go hide in my room for the rest of the day.

"Yeah, they don't even bother whispering anymore." Mags cleared her throat. "The Landing has another legacy. It's housed, shall we say, particularly gifted students since the inception of the school."

"Gifted." I latched onto her euphemism. Finally, we were getting somewhere.

"As I'm sure you're aware, people are not always as they seem." Mags paused long enough to point a huge nonverbal finger in my face. "They can see things others can't. Or can feel things."

"Or do things, yeah I got you." I tried not to sound too blasé about it.

"Right." Mags shrugged again. "Most of those gifted kids get it from their parents, so they know a little something about it as they grow up. Then there's always the ones who are the first in their families to show the talents or who don't have family around to teach them how to handle their gifts."

"And which category do you fall into?" I asked, pushing to the heart of the conversation.

Mags chuckled. "Little bit of all of those categories, like yourself." Mags held my gaze.

My eyebrows floated up lazily as I tried to conceal my absolute shock. Of course, I couldn't hide everything one hundred percent, but I thought I'd done a little better job than that.

Unless Mags had a way to get that sort of information from my entry papers. It wouldn't take a big leap to read my psychiatric files, my school records, and even the letters from the board to piece the puzzle together. That is, if you were looking for that sort of puzzle.

"The thing about families, even if they fall on the gifted side, is that a lot of times they aren't able to help you learn and grow into your own. They're a little too close to it, you know?" Mags moved her hands to grip the sides of the armrest she was perched upon.

"What, is the Landing some secret training ground for the next generation of so-called gifted kids?" A derisive snort escaped me before I could pull it back.

"Elevated," Mags said, "is the technical term."

"Elevated," I repeated. "And is it normal for so many Elevated kids to be clustered in one school? Isn't that kind of dangerous?"

"It's not like we rip a hole in the universe if we're in the same time zone." Mags waved away my concern. "It's better we're all together and can help one another. It sucks trying to get a handle on your Elevated senses when you're too busy trying to remain hidden. We look out for one another, like today in class. Evangeline saw you needed help and stepped up without hesitating. Dodged a real bullet today. Could you say the same if you were all on your own?"

"So you and Evangeline are Elevated." I ticked people off on my fingers. "I'm going to go out on a limb and say Adair." I paused for confirmation, and Mags gave a quick nod.

"Who else?"

"Well," Mags said. "That's where it gets tricky. Not everyone is as community minded as you or I. The ones I know about tally to just over a dozen. Some are more advanced than others. Some probably won't ever really come into their senses like you and I already are."

"What does that even mean?" I pushed, demanding more. Mags seemed to be showing more and more of her hand, and I was going to get the whole story, even if it took all day. If she wanted to pretend we were on the same side, I wouldn't dissuade her. Not until I knew what was really going on around here.

"So everyone in the world has basic senses, right? Sight, hearing, touch, taste, smell, sense of time, and so on," Mags said. "But those of us who are Elevated are able to transcend the different planes of existence in one way or another. Each plane has its own balance. For instance, what we call the vitality plane deals with the life cycle. Creation and entropy. Some Elevated people who are more on the life end of that spectrum can heal, or revitalize, while others can hasten a person to their death. Those are only some examples of how those energies get manifested. There's as many different versions as there are flavors of Ben and Jerry's."

"How many planes are we talking?" I asked, both guilt and curiosity warring in my mind for so desperately wanting to hear the answers.

"Eight." Mags took in a deep breath and held it. She looked up, seemingly lost in thought for a moment as her eyes lost their focus.

"Mags?" I prompted after several minutes of silence.

She was frozen across from me, her arms losing their grip as she slipped farther down the rabbit hole.

I lunged forward, grabbing her shoulders just before she keeled over face first onto the floor. Her body didn't want to balance itself, and I didn't know how long she would be out of it. Slowly, I let her legs fold under her and eased her to the ground. I pulled her legs out in front, leaning her against the row of seats.

Crouched down at her eye level, I surveyed her slack face. Her posture and open eyes reminded me of a creepy life-size doll. I squinted at her eyes, noticing the green one had dulled slightly, remaining out of focus. The clouded blue eye, however, had brightened considerably, and I thought I could see a flickering of light shining through it. The fluorescent lights above us caused a sickly glare, though, so I wasn't sure if something really was going on in Mags' dead eye or if I'd imagined it.

Mags gasped for air, her arms jerking at her sides in surprise.

"Damn," Mags whispered, shaking her head clear. "Hate it when that happens."

"You all right?" I asked, still crouched over her protectively.

"Yeah, fine." Mags waved me off. "Happens all the time."

"I see what you mean, about the helping each other out part." I indicated her spot on the floor. Mags looked down in surprise. "You went a little Raggedy Anne on me."

"Oh, creepy." Mags shivered. "I hate dolls. Ugh, sorry to do that to you."

"Hey, now we're even." I shrugged, retreating to grab my bag.

"We'll pick this up later, okay?" Mags said, her mind already elsewhere again.

"You okay?" I asked again. My gut was telling me something had shifted, but not having any idea what had really just happened, I didn't have any real evidence of a problem.

"Yeah, I just can't be late." Mags checked her phone again pointedly.

I knew a lie when I heard one. Not wanting to press her, I let her off the hook. I doubted she would tell me the truth right now anyway.

I walked up the shallow steps toward the exit, hoping the dining hall still had some food available for a quick lunch. I'd dawdled too long with Mags and her weird Intro to the Elevated Life lecture. A niggling thought itched in the corner of my mind, and I couldn't stop myself from asking.

"Hey, real quick." I turned to face Mags, who was messaging someone on her phone. She glanced up, still distracted by the unfinished message in her hands. "What's Adair's gift or whatever?"

My mind recalled the searing pain I'd felt in the dreamscape. Whatever it was, I wanted to stay as far away from it as possible.

"Adair?" Mags asked, returning to her phone. "He's Elevated in the Unconscious. He can manipulate dreams, like the Sandman. I think the technical term is a dream walker." Mags' mouth muddied the words at the end, as if she was talking to herself. Her attention was so focused, she let slip more detail than I'd expected.

A cold sensation pooled in the bottom of my stomach. Someone who could influence your dreams. What did that mean for my dreamscape? Was Colm safe?

"And me? What's my gift?" I asked, waving my hand in front of my slack-jawed roommate.

"Elevated in Entropy. Very rare. You're a Harbinger, more specifically a banshee. That's just speculation though, since no one's witnessed you firsthand," Mags muttered again, frowning at the keyboard beneath her fingertips.

"And what's the square root of 144?" I asked, testing the boundary of the odd psychic encyclopedia that had temporarily possessed Mags.

"Twelve," Mags replied, her reverie broken. She sneezed, making me jump back out of the way. "Whew, that was a good one." Mags shook her head, and the fogginess that had taken over when she'd been messaging had finally been lifted.

"Ready to go?" I asked innocently, inclining my head toward the door.

"Yeah, let's jet." Mags trotted ahead of me and out of the lecture hall. "I'll find you during free period. You can borrow today's notes."

"Sounds good." I watched her run off across the quad toward the administrative building. I paused in the archway of the lecture hall entryway and surveyed the cloudy afternoon sky.

Even knowing I wasn't the only weirdo around wasn't the comfort I always thought it would be. Something had been going on at Windermere before I'd arrived, and I felt late to the party. It would take a lot more digging to find the rest of the story. Between Colm stuck in my daytime dreamscape, the warnings from both Sean and Aileen, and the odd feeling I got from the pauses and unspoken words between Mags and the other Elevated students, I was seriously considering myself at the greatest disadvantage I'd ever experienced in my life.

And to think, only three and a half more semesters until graduation.

THIRTEEN

On Saturday, in the doorway of a dusty converted broom closet that doubled as Ms. Xavier's office, I waited for either my punishment or the dust mites to kill me. What little space the built-in bookshelves saved was overtaken by the piles of books balanced precariously on virtually every other surface. It definitely felt more like a storage closet than an office, but it didn't really matter where I was. I was stuck for the next eight hours.

I'd knocked politely on the outer door, waiting the requisite count of three before entering anyway. A note with instructions greeted me on one of the many towers of books. I recognized the handwriting from the chalkboard, even though the note was unsigned.

Please catalogue the volumes on the desk. You'll find a fresh pack of notecards and several pens in the desk drawer. As soon as you're done, please categorize them according to relevance.

I flipped the note over, looking for a postscript. According to relevance? Relevance to what?

With a heavy sigh, I dropped my bag on the floor, my dreams of completing my homework dashed. I was impressed Ms. Xavier didn't even show up to her own detention to make sure I was there. Based on how the students reacted to her, I could only assume her reputation for being a strict teacher had some ground. No one must dare skip out on her detentions.

I eyeballed the stacks of books piled almost to my height on the desk and tried to estimate how many volumes I was working with. After I surveyed the stacks, I grabbed my phone and earbuds. No other rules expressly prohibited them, and I didn't want to lose my mind alphabetizing ancient texts to the soundtrack of my own breathing.

The books multiplied the more I pulled them off the two desks and onto the floor. More and more seemed to come from every corner, even squeezing themselves spine up between other towering piles. I popped my head out into the empty hallway, checking both ways before deciding on my working strategy.

I piled the books according to alphabet grouping along the wall outside the small office.

Systematically, I grabbed a pile of books, hauling them back into the office to refine their alphabetizing, fill out a card with the basic information, and lug them back out into the hallway for the next batch. After several piles, I started to enjoy the monotony. My arms ached from the abuse, but I could visibly see my progress. It felt like meditation.

In the middle of writing a card, my fingers spazzed, making me drop my pen. It rolled under the desk to the point that even my long leg couldn't retrieve it. I got on all fours, reminding myself on loop not to hit my head on the low-hanging desk.

A pair of green orbs greeted me, and I forgot my chant.

My head struck the underside of the desk hard. I howled in pain, cursing nothing in particular. My hand found the pen, and I snatched it up. The eyes followed my every move. Even in the darkness of the closet, I could see the cat's tail flicking back and forth merrily.

"Laugh all you want, Little Satan," I growled at it. "You'll get yours soon enough."

The tail paused. The eyes disappeared slowly, only to reappear just as slowly.

Yet again, I was getting out-sassed by a cat.

"Blink blink to you, too," I muttered darkly, crawling out from underneath the desk. I brushed myself off and plopped back into the chair, trying to recoup the zen focus I'd been practicing before the cat threw me off my game.

"How's it going?" a soft voice spoke behind me.

I jumped again, this time hitting my knee on the underside of the desk. Without even seeing the cat, I could feel it laughing at me as I bit back another string of curse words.

"Gah, who doesn't knock?" I howled, rubbing the pain away from my bruised kneecap. I swung my rage around to find Evangeline in the doorway, holding a coffee in each hand.

The smell reached me about the same time I recognized the dining hall disposable cups.

"I come in peace." She lifted the coffees emphatically.

"I didn't know I needed a coffee so badly until just now," I murmured.

Evangeline walked over, setting the cups down before fishing into her pockets for a handful of granola bars.

"Here, figured you could use a break." Evangeline handed over a granola bar before I could grab the coffee. "Food first. Your hand will keep seizing up if you don't eat something."

"It's just from overuse. It's been a while since I've had to handwrite this much," I said.

"Yeah, I can tell." Evangeline peered over my shoulder at my growing mountain of notecards.

"My handwriting is beautiful," I argued, trying to hide the messier ones. "Or it was in the beginning."

"Mmhmm," Evangeline hummed, taking a sip of her own coffee.

"Shut up," I said dismissively. I lifted the coffee. "Thanks for this, by the way. Perfect timing."

"It's a gift," Evangeline said with a grin. It faltered as I stiffened at the word.

She sighed heavily, sitting down on a pile of hardcover encyclopedia volumes I'd been working through. Her petite frame left her leaning more than sitting so her feet wouldn't hang off the ground. I wouldn't have trusted the Dr. Seuss constructed pile with my whole weight either.

"Mags needs to keep her mouth shut about other people's business," Evangeline said. "And she definitely needs to work on her speech. Using the term gifted is just stupid and confusing."

"You don't have to tell me if you don't want," I said, desperate to continue the normal charade a little longer. I cradled my coffee protectively, not wanting it to be un-gifted.

"And I'm not going to pretend like I know you or your situation any better than you do either, unlike some people." Evangeline rolled her eyes. "But if it makes you feel better, I'm not the one who can see the future. I will throw Mags under the bus on that one though. That's all her."

"So when she goes all limp?" I asked, picturing Mags' limp doll posture in the lecture hall a few days before.

"She's getting a vision, yeah." Evangeline gave a dismissive wave. "Hers is so textbook, it's almost boring. Nearly every Elevated sap on the temporal plane is an oracle one way or another."

"You sound like you know a lot about this Elevated thing," I hedged, taking a long pull of my coffee.

"Little bit," she admitted with a shrug. "And at the same time, very little at all."

I nursed my coffee, taking a long look at Evangeline. Something seemed very off-putting about our conversation. It was almost too comfortable. This was not the girl who ran away from me on my first day. Even when it had just been Mags, Adair, and me, Evangeline had clammed up and spoken very little. For having such intense social anxiety, she seemed too normal to me right now.

"About that," Evangeline said. "It's a little more complicated. That's why I don't like Mags speaking for me. I like to do it in my own way on my own time."

"What?" I asked, pressing the coffee cup to my pursed lips. Had I said that out loud?

"This," Evangeline waved at herself, "is my natural personality. When I'm by myself, this is one hundred percent me. It's when I'm around a lot of people that I freak out and bolt. If I can't run, I sit tighter than an oyster making a pearl."

A laugh escaped me as I thought how ridiculous the analogy was.

"Thought you'd enjoy that one." Evangeline smiled into her coffee.

"I know I said I wouldn't pry into your business

earlier, but—"

"You need to know if I can read minds. Or if I'm like one of those mentalists who is really good at reading body language," Evangeline said, taking the thought directly from my mind.

I crossed my legs, letting my agitation out in the bouncing of my foot. "Something like that, yeah." I cleared my throat.

"The answer is a little more complicated. Like I said, I don't know everything either. I'm still figuring myself out. Beyond knowing the plane I'm on and how I experience the world, that's about all I know definitively," Evangeline admitted. "Here."

She reached over and grabbed a blank note card and my pen. She drew a square, then rotated the card and repeated another square. It looked like an oddly geometric eight sided star.

"Did you just draw a sun?" I asked, peering at the symbol in front of me.

"This is the symbol of the Elevated. It has to do with some lost prophecy about the Eight, who are the embodiment of the planes in perfect balance. I haven't heard what the exact prophecy is, but I'm more self-taught than a lot of other Elevated kids. That's a story for another day," Evangeline said. "Possibly more like a week. It's kind of messed up."

A dark chuckle escaped Evangeline, but I remained silent. My fingers traced the pattern.

"So these are the planes?" I asked, nudging her back on track.

"Yeah," she said, "they're always written as equals, but in real life, there's a bit of hierarchy that goes on. Like high school, but it'll follow you 'til you're dead." She flung a wicked grin at me.

I laughed in surprise. "Yay," I said with as little enthusiasm as possible. "Where do I sign up?"

"Vitality and Sentient planes are the cheerleaders and quarterbacks." Evangeline marked them on the diagram. "Relative and Temporal are like the student body president and the valedictorian. Still important, not too useless, but can be more helpful later in life on resumes rather than being the golden boys and girls."

"But it's not a hard and fast rule," I argued.

"Exactly. That's based on the perception of which Elevated abilities are more valuable. And history. The movers and shakers and power play makers typically come from Vitality and Sentient planes, but that doesn't knock anyone else out of the running." Evangeline took a breath but hesitated.

The faucet of information shut off, and I checked to see if she was okay.

People had a bad habit of losing consciousness around me.

"I'm fine." Evangeline shook herself from her freeze frame. "Just deciding how much of an info dump you are ready for."

"You were talking about power play makers. You said it's like high school," I said, leading her back to the topic I really wanted to know about. While Adele and I were on the run, it felt like things got fixed a little too easily. As I grew older, I thought maybe someone was making the right things happen at the right time. I needed to know if my hunch had been right.

"Well, you get a bunch of powerful people together, and they think they can rule their own little kingdoms. Just like the ultra rich feel untouchable and play by their own rules, that's kind of what's happened among the Elevated. At least our parents' generation," Evangeline admitted. "I don't know much before that. Not like there's an Elevated 101 class we could take. Although I'd sign up for that in a heartbeat."

"Right?" I let out another heavy sigh. I looked at the diagram, my fingers tracing it instinctively.

"Noah," Evangeline said quietly again, making my head snap up. Now that I was so used to her being herself, any retreat back into her protective shell made my stomach turn.

"What?" I asked.

"I did have some ulterior motives for coming here today." A slight blush bled through her tanned skin.

"Complete strangers don't just bring you coffee?" I replied. "Weird."

Evangeline smiled, nodding in understanding.

"Honestly, I know your plan is to stay as low profile as possible," she said, "but I have to say from experience, it's not going to work. You're going to get dragged back into it, and I just thought you ought to know what you're up against."

"Go on." I waited for the band-aid to be ripped off.

"Firstly, we're going to keep this between you and me," Evangeline said, her eyes searching mine. "I've been able to stay below the radar because they think I'm a dud. I don't think that'll keep me hidden for very much longer, but I have to try."

"Not a problem," I agreed. "Secondly?"

"Don't trust Mags," Evangeline blurted out.

Our eyes met, and I could only hear my own heartbeat in my ears. Her words had been so sure, I was taken aback.

"Why shouldn't I?" I asked, my foot stilling finally in anticipation.

"I'm not saying she's on the wrong team." Evangeline pursed her lips as she tried to choose the best words. "Do you know anything about major league baseball?"

The question took me by surprise.

"Not really," I said. "What does Mags have to do with baseball?"

"Some major league teams have several teams below them so they can choose and develop talent. If a major player gets injured, they have a back stock of potential replacement players they're already familiar with who are loyal to the team," Evangeline said. "Make sense?"

"I'm following," I said.

"As a reward for getting better, players can move up the levels to get closer to the major league team. The teams below them are known as a farm team," she pressed. "Do you understand?"

"Windermere is a farm team, isn't it?" I said, dread weighing down my words. "It's like boot camp for Elevated kids."

"The Landing has always functioned like that for as far back as the school has been around. In all of the school's history, though, this many Elevated or Elevated potential kids have never been at the school at one time. Something's not right," Evangeline said. "I've tried to stay out of it, but it's a magnetic field. I can't help but feel the pull."

"How does Mags fit into this whole farm team concept?" I asked.

"She's a scout. Numero uno in recruitment. You can't fault her charisma, and she's very good at bringing people into the fold. She's going to try and reel you in, but you've got to resist," Evangeline said.

"Why?"

"It's not just Mags you have to worry about. It's who she's recruiting for." Evangeline's head snapped up in surprise.

"What is it?" I asked.

"I gotta go." Evangeline hopped off her perch. She tossed her cup, dropping to the floor on all fours. A yowl echoed from under the desk, and Evangeline returned with the cat in her arms. Yet again, the cat looked absolutely horrified at being manhandled, and I couldn't keep the grin off my face.

"Just trust me." Evangeline inched out the door. "I'll try and explain better later. Or maybe you'll find out yourself." She squinted at me. "Yeah, you'll figure it out. Anyway, I'll take Ig with me so you can get back to work."

"Ick?" I asked, amused that a cat would be named Ick.

"No, Ig, short for Ignatius," said Evangeline, burying her face in his black fur. "Just ignore him. He has a little too much fun messing with the students sometimes."

"Thanks again for the coffee," I called after Evangeline as she disappeared around the doorframe into the hallway.

No problem, I heard in my head.

I dropped my cup, scooping it up before the last mouthful of coffee could splash onto the floor.

In the distance, I could hear a couple of students talking loudly in the hall. I stashed the Elevated diagram in my back pocket. Launching myself into the hallway, I grabbed the remaining few stacks still in progress and took them back into the safety of the office.

On my way out the door, I shut off the lights and slung my bag over my shoulder opposite the side I was used to. A sharp pain pressed against my collarbone, and I grimaced as I dug around for the source. My fingers tightened around the old key from the snowflake keychain, and the imprint of the carved door in the library floated up in my mind.

I shut the door of Ms. Xavier's office behind me, gauging where the loud students were in relation to me. I turned on my heels, heading the opposite direction. Too many mysteries were piling up in my head. Gripping the key tightly in the palm of my hand, I resolved to answer at least one of those questions today.

FOURTEEN

The bright afternoon sun surprised me after being in Ms. Xavier's office for so long. The clouds had parted and seemed to be giving the students one last hoorah before the blanket of winter fully smothered any hopes of a bearable escape outside.

I passed several gaggles of girls, dressed in a variety of plain clothes on their day off. The flow of student traffic coming from the athletic quad and newer dorms was more stocked than a salmon run and about as daunting.

My phone buzzed in my pocket, and I had to move the key to my other hand to answer. The phone attempted to sink into the imprint the key had left, but the mental imprint left me distracted when I answered the video chat.

"Hey." I stuck my phone against my cheek as I tried to find a safe place to shove the key without drawing any attention to myself. I could feel eyes following me across the quad, but I pretended I didn't. Somehow making eye contact with the social aggressors would label me the freak, and I was too tired for that nonsense today.

"Whoa, what am I looking at?" Adele's voice rang out into the air in front of me.

"Sorry, give me a second," I muttered, trying to free my hands so I could face the screen. Finally, I hauled the phone in front of me, glancing up occasionally and trying not to run into any decorative pillars or planter boxes. "Better?"

"Is this a bad time?" Adele asked, her mouth half full of red licorice.

"I dunno, am I interrupting your," I paused to check the time, "breakfast?"

"Har har," Adele garbled around the candied ropes. "Ladies and gentlemen, the girl's got jokes!"

"My life's a joke," I muttered to myself, dodging out of the way of a statue.

"Going that well, huh?" Adele asked. "How's everything? Making any friends?"

"Well, this is my first real look at the outside world today. Just broke out of Saturday detention a little early, but I'm sure I'll make up for it later," I said briskly, trying to breeze over the bad news so Adele had a better shot at missing it.

"Detention? Excuse me? Back up." A half-eaten licorice rope fell from her mouth in surprise. She was perched on top of her favorite stool with a worn out hoodie and faded pajama pants wrinkling beneath her contorted posture. The webcam on her large monitor gave me my first look at our new house.

"Ooo, is that a bay window?" I said, noticing the curtains drawn behind Adele to reduce any glare.

"Ooo, is that an attempt to dodge the question? Poor attempt. I thought I raised you better." Adele waggled a fresh rope at me in admonishment.

"Sorry, I'm a little distracted," I admitted, rubbing my face. "Lots going on."

"You okay over there?" Adele asked, her frowning face ready for my best lie.

"You might not remember high school since it's been at least three centuries since you've been, but there's a lot of school work, not to mention all the social drama," I said, trying to couch my problem in the standard whiny teenager narrative.

Adele's face deadpanned, and I knew she'd seen through the attempt.

"Do I look that old?" Adele pulled on her cheeks in mock horror. "I just got a new wrinkle cream!"

"Yeah, so old." I sighed.

Adele stopped aping at me, her lip jutting out in sympathy. "No-no," she said, finally dropping her voice to a more serious tenor. "What on earth happened? I just dropped you off a few days ago."

"You know how quickly I turn good situations to ash." I waved my fingers at her through the phone. "It's one of my many special skills."

Adele snorted.

I gave up on walking, worried I would eventually wander into the bordering forest and get lost forever. Glancing up, I realized I was outside the library by the side entrance I'd noticed the other day. A fire escape ladder crawled up the side of the building, ending just short of the roof. I frowned at it, taking a seat on one of the bottommost steps.

"What got you detention? Did you hit someone?" Adele said, her tone unamused.

"I wish," I replied. "You would not believe the number of people I've come across I'd like to hit."

"Noah!"

"I was joking," I lied. "I, uh, fell asleep in class."

Adele's jaw snapped shut. I glanced around, wondering how private my conversation really was. I couldn't see anyone, and the echoes of cheering students through the quad told me some sort of game was happening and was likely the center of everyone else's attention at the moment. I crossed my fingers and my toes that my hunch was correct.

"And how did you manage that?" Adele squeaked out.

"You know how overwhelming new schools can be. Lots of new people. That odd sense you've seen those faces before. Like it wasn't the first time you've met them." I raised an eyebrow at my lame explanation.

"Like that time you had déjà vu in Washington?" Adele asked, her fingers already typing furiously on her keyboard. She was distracted, looking at another monitor.

"Worse. Like, fifty times worse," I muttered.

Her fingers froze over the keys, and she gave me the most horrified look I'd ever seen on her. "All right, I'll come get you," Adele quipped, hopping down from her stool to search for her purse. "Damn the contract."

I sighed.

"This is too much. You can't handle it. I'm coming to get you right now. The dean and the Board can eat my shorts," Adele called from out of frame. "Where the hell did I put my keys?"

"What did I tell you about keeping your purse and your keys in the same spot?" I whined to the abandoned video call. "How am I supposed to help you find your crap if I haven't even been there?"

"Found it!" Adele called triumphantly, hurrying back into frame.

I sighed again. This time, Adele looked up, abandoning her search for her keys within her newly located purse. She frowned at me.

"What?"

"Thanks, but I'm fine," I said miserably.

"Did you ask for a breath mint? I'm sure they're in here somewhere," Adele babbled, rummaging through her purse again.

"Addy!" I called out to Adele as I had when I was a child. Before the dreamscape came and ruined both our lives.

She dropped her purse in surprise. "What!" Adele hollered back.

"You're not coming to get me," I said simply.

"Yes, I am."

"No, you're not." I shook my head. "I'll figure things out. I promise."

"You can't stay there," Adele said simply. "Fifty times today. A hundred times tomorrow. No. Absolutely not. Give me twenty minutes, and I'll be out front."

"Adele," I barked at her, pointing at the screen. "No."

"Don't you take that adult tone with me!" Adele shot back. "Luckily your voodoo doesn't work on the other side of technology."

"That's a poor example. A, you're never affected anyway, and B, we have not fully tested my range to be able to say that definitively," I argued.

"Well, I don't like it." Adele plopped herself back down on her stool with her newly found purse to her chest.

"Noted and appreciated," I said, "but you're going to have to let me figure this out on my own. In my own time. Where have I heard that before?" I asked myself, shaking my head at the disjointed thoughts that were pulling my attention in all directions.

"Fine, I'll leave you alone, but you have to promise to text me updates. None of this whoops I got detention forever and ever, but it's fine, I'm only one sass back away from juvenile detention, okay?" Adele gnawed nervously on another licorice rope.

"Can I text you my care package demands?" I asked, my hand falling subconsciously on my throat. "I could use some throat lozenges."

"Lozenges, huh?" Adele raised her eyebrow. "I'll see what I can do."

"And stop messing around on those message boards," I said, eliciting a guilty pout from Adele, whose eyes flickered to another monitor.

"I'm a grown lady." Adele straightened her posture against my barb.

"Yes, and you should be ashamed." I stuck my tongue out at her. She returned the favor, and I felt a smile tug at my lips.

"Chin up." Adele punched the air in solidarity.

"Talk to you later," I said, signing off. I tucked the phone back in my pocket, letting the cold bite of the fire escape on my backside tie me down to reality. I stared up at the clouds running across the sky, wishing Adele could just whisk me away from my problems like she had in the past.

Starting over new was easy. Leaving no lasting marks on a landscape, on people, or on a school was easy. I could float in a crowd unnoticed. Deep down, I hated having to be the first to run. Just once, I wanted to be able to stand my ground and claim the space as mine.

I stood up from my uncomfortable seat, shoved my hands deeper into my pockets and exhaled. This time around would be different. I would stay, but I would stay on my own terms. The old skeleton key clanked against my nails in my jacket pocket. My fingers closed around it tightly.

The first step was always the hardest.

FIFTEEN

The library was as deserted as it had been my first morning here. I passed row upon row of empty tables and silent stacks and had an eerie sense that maybe even the librarians were playing hooky. I kept a lookout for Ig, but he didn't materialize either.

With zero witnesses, I wasn't even sneaky when I walked back to the dark lacquered wooden panels of the domed conservatory room. I careened right, walking straight up to the snowflake door.

I frowned at the door, unable to find a keyhole or any door handle.

How was I supposed to open it?

I flipped the key around in my nimble fingers, scanning the seams of the door for any weak points or secret push points. After finding nothing along the seams, my fingers reached out to the snowflake emblem carved into the door. I traced it idly, appreciating the level of detail in such a deceptively simple design.

The design was perfectly circular, just like the sun and the maple leaf had been. They were all about the same size. The secret to opening this door would also open the others. I glanced down the curved wall, making sure I was still alone. The shelves behind me gave decent cover, but if someone else knew about these doors, they would know exactly where to look.

I dragged my fingers heavily down the outward curve of the carving, finding it had a little give.

My head snapped back to stare at the carving. I stepped forward, my nose nearly touching the door. My fingers pushed gently around the edges of the design, feeling the wood give slightly. As I pressed more toward the center, I had to use more pressure to feel the give in the wood.

An idea struck me.

I placed my palm fully on the snowflake, pressing hard inward and then twisting it like a combination lock.

The snowflake sprang back in my hand, opening a small hatch. Peering behind it, I found a slightly tarnished metal-plated keyhole for an old-fashioned key. I fished the key out of my jacket pocket, sliding it home into the lock and twisting it.

Something jabbed me in the hip, and I jumped back in surprise.

A handle had sprung from one of the panels in the dark wood. If it hadn't practically impaled me, I wondered if I would have noticed it against the dark-stained wood. I tested the handle but found the door just as shut as ever. I grabbed the key with one hand and the handle with the other. Twisting the key again, I pushed the handle and felt it give slightly.

I shoved the door with my shoulder, barreling into the room. The door snapped shut cleanly behind me, with the key safely back in my left hand. Scowling at the door, I stepped back to see if I could find the mechanism from this side of the door. My fingers traced where the snowflake had been on the opposite side but met only smooth, cool wood.

"I'll be damned," I said aloud, tapping the spot with my nail-bitten fingertips.

I moved away from the door into the room proper. The scattered plush furniture, several decades out of date, and the star pattern on the evening blue walls made it seem like a secret hideout the Lost Boys might enjoy. Part of the plate glass of the domed ceiling created an overhang before brick took over. The odd ceiling dimensions pointed to the secrecy of the rooms. Even from the outside, you wouldn't be able to tell they were here.

Where the fort atmosphere left off, an old-time study took over. It was an odd pairing, but it worked well for the space. The walls, carpet, and furniture were all deep shades of blue, blending into the near black of the stained wood continuing from the outer door.

A large desk sat sentry at the end of the room in front of a series of lead-lined stained glass windows. The natural light filtered through, throwing just enough brightness onto the desk to illuminate a neat pile of books stacked to the side. I moved them a millimeter to better read the spines and noticed the dark imprint of where they had protected the desk from dust. A thin film coated the rest of the desk's surface, and I drew the Elevated sign absentmindedly in the fine powder.

It sat there taunting me before I wiped it away with a swipe of my palm.

"Ludicrous," I scolded myself. "This whole situation is absolutely ridiculous."

I sighed, forgetting about the cloud of dust I'd stirred up by disturbing the desk. A series of sneezes attacked me, and I rubbed my nose violently to discourage any more from popping up. Leaning against the desk, I looked up at the stained glass of the windows.

The style was similar to the windows in the dining hall, and I realized belatedly that the school had likely hired the same architect when they first built the campus. The library had undergone some renovations, but the old section and the conservatory dorm was too old fashioned to be anything other than original. It still had the soul old buildings have.

My thumb found its way to my lips, and I gnawed thoughtfully at the sliver of nail that had dared to grow past the nail bed. I let the images in the stained glass wash over me, imprinting them to memory.

Several of the texts I'd been categorizing for Ms. Xavier dealt with the history of campus. They were stuck in the middle of *Mythology: A Beginner's Guide* and *Herbal Remedies for the Highly Attuned*. While copying names and titles, I'd taken note of the topics of each book, hoping if I bookmarked them from the beginning, sorting them into categories would take less time.

I remembered some architecture books in the mix, and I'd taken advantage of the time given to me. Several of those design books had glossy printed pictures stuck in the middle of tissue paper thin pages. Something about the stained glass window in front of me niggled the back of my mind. I'd seen something similar; I just couldn't place which book it had been or if it was just the dining hall stained glass impairing my memory.

I dared to sigh again, this time bracing for a series of sneezes. When none came, I pushed off the edge of the desk, my eye catching on the pile of books I'd moved earlier. I tapped them back in place before exaggerating the angle the other way. The spines seemed innocuous, except for the emblem at the bottom.

It was the Elevated symbol.

I pulled the pile of books to me, searching the front matter, searching for some connection. The titles and topics varied, with one of the books even being a work of fiction. They all had the same publisher, though. The publisher with the double square signature.

On a hunch, I marched over to the wall of bookshelves, which had to hold a thousand books. My fingers plucked through the many volumes, pulling out the marked books one by one. By the time I was done, my back ached from the awkward exercise.

I stood back, surveying my handiwork.

Almost a hundred individual texts were pulled out, creating a floating staircase maze throughout the sea of books along the wall. I switched to my other thumb, tearing savagely at the overhanging quick.

"What is going on around here?" I interrogated the books. "What are you doing here?"

A series of bangs came from the door, and I jumped out of my skin. I managed to cover my mouth, however, and no sound escaped.

I could hear voices on the opposite side of the door, but I was too far in to distinguish individual words or speakers. With a leery glance at the bookshelves, I moved toward the door, leaning my face as close to the door as I dared.

"Someone's in there, I know it," the first voice said. Since it was muffled through the door, I wasn't sure if I knew the speaker.

"Don't be an idiot," the second voice scolded. "No one's been in Winter for twenty years."

"That's nice. There's still someone in there right now," the first voice said. "I swear."

"Not everyone can easily locate a needle in a haystack like you, but I'm telling you you're wrong. No one is in there," the second voice said. "Besides, how are you going to prove it?"

"Prove it?"

"Yeah, no one gets in without the key. No backup either. If the key is gone, it's gone for good," the second voice said. "You know how these rooms work. Don't make a fuss."

"Just because you can't prove I'm wrong doesn't mean you're right," voice one said, followed by quick, heavy footsteps.

I heard a sigh through the door and soft footfalls follow the first speaker away from the door. I looked behind me at the wall of books. Could they hear me through the wall?

The books called me back to the shelves, and my curiosity overruled my sense to stay away from the common wall that had drawn attention to me in the first place. I crossed my arms, slowly going down the rows one after another and reading the titles of the mysterious publisher. No particular common topic or time period seemed to pigeon hole the marked books. Fiction books were interspersed among them and transcended genre categorization.

I leaned against the back of the couch, falling onto it into my favorite thinking position. All the blood rushed to my head, and my hair escaped its loose tie to splay around my flushed face in a large halo. The softness of my curls on my cheek comforted me as I crossed my legs over the back of the couch, letting them dangle in the air.

Resting my hands on my stomach, I let my mind wander. All the little bits and bobs I'd picked up today floated through my brain, sometimes branching down further into sub-thoughts and ideas. I let my mind play with the possibilities, allowing the logic to speak up for itself. If I put enough data points in a graph, I was bound to come up with a correlation. I just wasn't sure what would come of all these seemingly disparate facts.

My phone buzzed. I fought with gravity to unearth it from my pocket, amused to find I could connect to the school Wi-Fi in this super-secret lair.

It was an email from Mags asking if I was coming to dinner. Not likely. I checked the time, finding it early even for grandma dinner.

My daydreaming time interrupted, I sighed heavily, coughing in response to the cloud of who knows what I'd kicked up in my collapse onto the couch. Checking my landing spot, I flung my legs over my head, tucking them in with just enough clearance not to annihilate the coffee table also covered with books.

I stuck the landing, hopping upright with my curls cascading not far behind. I needed a guitar in my hands as soon as humanly possible, I decided.

Taking one last look at the puzzle I'd left myself in the bookcase, I grabbed my bag from its neglected spot on the floor and pressed my ear to the door.

I was greeted with silence. After a quick count to three, I yanked the door open, sticking my head out to check if the coast was clear. Finding an empty hall greeting me, I slid out the door, closing it as quietly as I could behind me. I lunged around a stack of books, making it seem like I'd been searching for fourteenth-century religious texts instead of discovering my new favorite hideout.

A pair of green eyes waited for me at the end of the stack. I spooked, nearly letting a loud curse escape me.

"Ig!" I scolded the cat. He waved his tail at me, and I imagined the finger waggling he was trying to give me. "I will get a bell for your collar. Try me one more time."

Ig sneezed at me, getting up and wandering away. His disinterest annoyed me, but he somehow managed to turn his dramatic exit into my escort to the stairs. He sat at the top of the stairs and waited, racing me down to the ground level and out the side door.

Our paths forked as soon as our faces hit outside air. Ig dodged into the bushes as I made a beeline for the practice rooms. I shook my head, hoping some owl didn't feel like an early evening snack.

I stopped, realizing I was worrying about a cat. I shook my head, trotting in the cooling evening air to get back into the safety of a heated building before anyone came looking for me again.

SIXTEEN

I ghosted through the empty dining hall without being seen. Even the distant banging of the kitchen staff barely registered as I strode through the cavernous room. The buckles on my boots echoed loudly in the open space, and it occurred to me that I might need a change of footwear if I was going to beat Ig at his own game. Being able to move imperceptibly across campus would be preferable to the catwalk I'd endured earlier. Self-consciousness and cobblestones were a dangerous mix.

The raucous noise of my boots only got worse as I barreled down the indoor-outdoor staircase that led to the practice rooms. I made it to the subbasement floor in record time, walking into a brightly lit hallway.

It took me a second too long to register the lights in the hall. The time sensitive lights were handy for more than energy conservation. I walked into the unwelcoming arms of Sean.

"Could you make any more noise?" Sean grumbled, his arms crossed outside his practice room.

"I could always try," I offered sincerely as I pulled out Colm's spare key. "At least it's just me and not some other hooligan."

"Yes, thank God." Sean threw his arms in the air. "And here I thought I could practice in peace."

"Oh, speaking of that." I wedged my bag between the door and its frame. "Can I ask a favor?"

"Other than mooching off a prepaid practice room?" Sean asked. "What is it now?"

I placed my hands together in front of me, adopting the closest thing I had to puppy dog eyes. I even went so far as to stick out my lip in a little pout.

"Can I borrow a guitar?" I asked, adding a helpless sniff for good measure.

Sean sighed, rolling his eyes.

"There's only a piano in here, and I don't want to pilfer one from the classroom upstairs."

"Do I look like someone who cares?" Sean turned to retreat back into his room now that his scolding was done.

"Pretty please?" I asked, grabbing his sleeve playfully. "You know I'll take the best care of it. Plus, it'll only be fifty feet away from you at all times. Scout's honor." I placed my hand over my heart for added effect. Sean turned around to scowl at me.

"You really push the boundaries of neighborly etiquette, you know?" Sean disappeared into his room and reappeared with a beautiful cherry red acoustic guitar.

"It's so beautiful," I said in a hushed tone, stroking the firm neck and fret decals with reverence.

"Don't make me regret it," Sean said in a warning tone.

"Never." I gave him my broadest smile. "I really appreciate it. Having a really shitty week, and the piano isn't quite cutting it."

Sean waved me off.

"I don't need to know the personal details. No crying on my guitar," Sean pointed at me in all seriousness.

"I'll do my best." I tried to stifle a laugh.

"I'm dead serious. You cry and you never see that guitar ever again." Sean was holding the doorknob to his room.

"No," I whispered in horror, clutching the guitar tightly to me. "I promise I'll be good."

Sean waved me off again, this time the sharp smack of his door slam reactivating some lights that had dimmed. I punched the air in delight, careful not to bump the guitar on the doorframe as I retreated into my own little room.

As soon as the door shut behind me, I pressed the button to lock it.

A sigh escaped me, and I felt my shoulders relax again. I pulled out the piano bench, folding one of my legs beneath me as I settled down onto it. A quick pluck at the guitar strings determined the guitar was in perfect tune. Of course it was, I thought to myself with a dry chuckle.

My fingers drifted from chord to chord, the other hand picking the notes lazily. The tone wasn't particularly clean with my thumbnail now nonexistent and my pride too fragile to go across the hall and request a pick. Even so, I found myself humming along to the nonsense I was creating along the fretboard.

Slowly, my humming brought about its sibling tone and my hands stilled against the strings. I sighed, feeling the heat grate against my vocal cords. I couldn't even sing along to my own compositions without slipping into a song.

I checked the time, figuring everyone was at dinner by now. If I was going to let loose, now would be the time.

My fingers resumed their place on the neck, and I followed through on some scales before going into the chord progression I'd been messing with for a while. As I hummed along, my voice picked up on dissonant tones. After a few runs of clashing notes, my fingers slid into the chords that would harmonize against what I was singing. The warmth in my throat slowly trickled down to my stomach, and I could feel the power growing as the volume increased.

As quickly as I dared, I pushed the edge of my voice, hoping to burn through the song so I could go back to my peaceful practice of my own original work. The song, as powerful as it was, was annoying me today, and I wished it would go away.

I coughed, my throat cutting off the tone as soon as my tongue stuck back against the roof of my mouth. It was as if I'd swallowed a mouthful of molasses. Nothing I did cleared the blockage, and I was having trouble breathing.

My eyes watered as I clawed at my throat, pressing in random places to see if I could dislodge whatever was blocking both my airway and my voice. Then, the bottom half of my vision blacked out. I felt like I was floating. I had enough sense to fall to my knees and rest the guitar against the wall. Whatever was happening, if I survived and the guitar didn't, I wasn't counting on Sean to be very forgiving.

And just like that, I blacked out.

The field of black was new for me. I was either awake or in my dreamscape. I never transitioned into an intermission screen. It was like an extended blink, and then bam, bedroom. Bam. Dreamscape.

I was getting more nervous the longer the darkness remained. Was I dead? Or was this sleeping?

On a scale of apathetic to blood-curdling scream, how freaked out should I be?

Before I had any longer to think about it, my dreamscape blinked into existence. But it was the daytime kind, and a pair of blue eyes greeted me.

"Hey, stranger." Colm smiled. "I was wondering when you would come visit."

I sat up, my hands gripping the dry grass that cushioned my fall. If I'd fallen. I wasn't sure that's how this whole thing worked, having just experienced materializing myself.

"Do I just appear?" I searched the landscape for any other indication of my impact. "When I show up. Is it like, poof, I'm here or like I fall?"

I hated the desperation in my voice, but I needed something concrete to analyze. I needed a question and an answer. Something had to make sense, or I was worried I would really lose my mind.

Colm sat cross-legged next to me, resting his arms comfortably on his knees.

"Does it matter?" he asked, his face hovering near mine to try to catch my eyes. For some reason, I couldn't look him in the eye. Not when I was freaking out about possibly dying.

"Can you just answer my question, please?" I said, the edge of panic slipping through my fragile facade.

"I can tell you're coming, but you do just kind of appear. I knew where to look for you, and by the time I got here, so were you." Colm reached out for my hand in the grass.

His warmth remained, and my body flinched at the contact. He didn't recoil, though, but kept his steady hand on mine.

"Okay." I nodded. "Good to know."

"Noah," Colm said, his voice softened. "You're okay."

My eyes couldn't help it. They shifted directly into his line of sight as soon as I stopped telling myself to avoid it.

"Are you sure? Because I'm not so sure," I admitted, a lump forming in my throat. "I'm not sure I'm not dead right now."

"You're definitely not dead," Colm assured me with a pat of his hand. "If you were dead, I wouldn't be talking to you right now."

"How do you know?"

"A very smart girl told me I wasn't dead, just sleeping. Your consciousness is here, but you're definitely still breathing on the other side. If that logic works for me, it's gotta work for you, too, right?"

"That very smart girl doesn't know everything," I muttered darkly. "If she did, she would know how to get out of here."

Colm squeezed my hand, bounding up and dragging me with him. "Come on, let me show you something." Colm led me through the trees. "It'll take your mind off solving the world's problems for a minute."

"Just solving my own for starters would be great," I said, sulking as I was dragged behind Colm up molehills and around twisted root systems.

As soon as we ducked under a low-hanging branch, Colm stopped abruptly. I ran into his back, but he remained unmoved.

"Beautiful, isn't it?" Colm asked, making me step out from behind his shadow to see what I was supposed to be looking at.

We were standing in front of a lake. I did a double take at the expanse of water bordered by a rocky beach and a sea of thrushes and marsh weeds. My jaw dropped.

"I know, right?" Colm said. "It's breathtaking."

"When did you find this?" I asked, my eyes bouncing back and forth between the variety of elements in the lake. Another look and the size was more pond like, but it was much larger than I ever expected anything to be in the dreamscape. The trees were always thick and endless, but the perspective never allowed me to think of it in its entirety. It always presented itself like a false image loop on endless repeat.

Colm shrugged, shoving his hands into his pockets.

"I've never seen this before," I said.

"Really?" Colm turned to face me. "I thought you said you'd been visiting since you were little."

"I have been," I said in a hushed tone. "Don't forget it looks different at night. I don't even know if this part is here at night."

"Has to be, right?" Colm said.

"That's in the no friggin' clue column," I muttered darkly. "It's a really crowded column these days."

"So, how did you get here today? Not that I'm complaining." A smile pulled at his cheek. For the first time, I noticed he had a dimple.

I sighed heavily.

"No friggin' clue?" Colm asked. "Well, that's a shame. It'd be nice to see you more."

I stopped glaring at the marsh grass and turned to look at Colm instead.

"Why?" I asked bluntly. I bit the inside of my cheek as soon as it came out.

"Not sure," Colm said with a full smile. "It's nice to talk to someone."

"Bet you're wishing someone much nicer than me was able to visit." I snorted.

"Nah." Colm bumped my shoulder slightly. "Wouldn't be nearly as eventful."

"I am good for some party tricks," I replied in a dry voice. Looking out onto the lake, a wave of sadness came over me. "Yeah, I would definitely remember this."

"It'll give you an excuse to visit," Colm said. "Other than me, of course."

"Of course." A halting chuckle escaped me. Somehow I was feeling a little less doomsday about my possible death. I'd been convinced Colm was just stuck here as a daytime visitor because his consciousness was stuck between life and death. Now that I was here though, my logic felt weaker somehow.

My knees buckled underneath me, but Colm caught me and lowered me to the ground.

"Noah?" Colm's face was creased with worry.

"Sorry." I shook my head. I was feeling lightheaded.

"I think you're getting pulled back," Colm said. "Better not fight it."

I groaned, sticking my head between my knees to stop the lakeside from spinning.

"Whoever is piloting this sucks at the landing," I muttered nonsensically.

"I'll see you soon," Colm's voice said from too far away.

I felt a warm pressure on my head, but it was gone as soon as I registered it.

My palms stung. I could feel the scrapes on my knees as well, but I couldn't seem to open my eyes.

Slowly, I flexed my fingers, then my toes. Pins and needles lanced through my limbs, and finally I could feel the scratchy carpet against my cheek. It smelled like bleach and old socks. My nose crinkled, and I opened my eyes.

I was on my side on the floor of the practice room. Sean hovered over me.

"Are you okay?" Sean asked, his perpetual grumpy frown laced with concern.

"Your guitar is fine," I gurgled, wincing at the pain in my throat. My hand flopped toward where I'd set the guitar safely against the wall before I passed out.

"Have you eaten today?" Sean grilled me, taking my pulse and counting the beats to the ticking of his wristwatch.

"What kind of question is that?" I asked, trying to push him away so I could sit up.

Sean shoved me back down, keeping his focus on my pulse. "A necessary one. Get out." Sean bounced up from his heels. "Go grab dinner."

"I'm fine." I teetered to a sitting position. I had to pause, waiting for the pendulum in my head to stop swinging so erratically all over the place. My free hand went to my temple.

"Shut up and go eat," Sean said brusquely, "or you're never touching Sharon again."

"Who the hell's Sharon?" I muttered before I could catch my tongue.

Sean jabbed his thumb at the cherry red guitar, and my brain sluggishly caught up with his meaning.

"Fine," I muttered. "But I'm only going because I was about to go anyway."

Sean let out an annoyed sigh, offering his hand to me in an odd repeat of fate. I took it without saying anything, shoving past him through the door.

"You're banned for the next hour," Sean said. "I don't want to see you unless you're about to explode from eating so much at dinner."

"Sure thing, boss," I muttered. "Make sure no one steals my stuff."

Sean shut the door emphatically, checking the lock so I could see no one would get in.

He sighed again, waiting for me to get to the end of the hall. The lights buzzed on as I walked slowly to the staircase. I was mad at myself for dragging him into my mess, but I was secretly glad he'd been the one to find me. As much as he seemed to want to stay out of my drama, he was damn good at being there at the exact right time to turn it all around.

I trudged up the staircase one loud bang at a time. Just as I was turning onto the next landing, I glanced at the small windowpane in the door, seeing a flash of darkness right before the light dimmed. The jerk had enough heart to make sure I got up the stairs okay. I sighed, sending a silent apology to him for interrupting his practice time.

My phone buzzed again. Another email from Mags with a bunch of question marks. Succinct. I groaned as I rounded the final flight of stairs. I would have to have an audience for my dinner. I couldn't avoid Mags or the other Landing kids for very long. The smell of garlic bread lulled me into a false sense of security as I flung the door open. Maybe if I ate enough garlic, my dragon breath would scare them off. I hoped it would be that easy.

SEVENTEEN

"About damn time," Mags said as she sat down across from me.

I was dutifully shoving my face full of tortellini with only the occasional break for a piece of garlic bread. I could have chosen from the many varied healthy dishes, but today's episode left me feeling drained and empty. Only copious amount of dairy and simple carbohydrates could turn this day around.

"Sorry," I mumbled through a full mouth. "Didn't realize you were waiting for me."

"I put read receipts on my emails." Mags gave me a pointed look.

I answered with a shrug.

"We were worried about you," Adair said, frowning at Mags' pettiness. "How did your detention go?"

"Fine." I filled my empty mouth with another forkful of pasta.

"I've never heard of Ms. X giving detention," Adair continued. "I'm a little impressed."

"Why?" I said, any filter I'd previously attempted being irreparably broken by the past two hours.

"Oh, just that you seem unscathed," Mags said with a small smile. "Guess you're tougher than we thought."

"How's your ribcage?" I asked Adair, my tone flat.

"Fine, just a little bruised," Adair said. "Apparently getting beaten by Mags has made me invincible to surprise attacks."

"Hardly." Mags scoffed. Her attention was zeroed in on me. "Noah must not hit as hard as I do."

"No need to test that theory, thanks," Adair said with a fake chuckle. "You can get another volunteer for that."

I didn't even care enough to react to Mags' slight against me. I stabbed at the remaining tortellini in my bowl, ripping them savagely off my fork.

"Are you sure you're okay?" Adair asked, looking nervously at my four-pronged weapon.

Mags frowned at me again. "Yeah, you seem off," Mags said.

Adair winced, aware that two of the kids were no longer playing nice.

I looked up from my nearly empty bowl, my arms crossed and bracing my stabbing arm. I glanced between the two inquisitors and sighed. I was not up for this interaction right now.

"What makes you say that?" I asked, dropping my fork and abandoning what remained of my dinner.

The two remained still and silent. Not even a shrug.

"Do you even know me well enough to know if I'm acting quote unquote normal?" I said, finally speaking of the elephant in the room. "Maybe this is my natural disposition."

"If you were a cartoon, you would have a black thundercloud above your head," Mags said. "It doesn't take a genius to tell something's up."

"Is my dark cloud any of your business?" I shot back. "I didn't realize that was in the roommate agreement."

"If you would let us help," Mags said through gritted teeth, "I'm sure we could figure something out."

"You're assuming that it's a super special gifted problem." My voice was dripping with venom. "What if it's something as mundane as I had a fight with my mom?"

"You don't have one," Mags said back with equal animosity.

"Mags!" Adair said, his voice full of disapproval.

I inhaled deeply. "I don't know what kind of dossier you have on me, but I can assure you it's not complete nor accurate." My throat was burning again. "Stop trying to pretend like you know anything about me."

"If you would just let us help you, things would get better. Easier," Mags said. "Just stop being so arrogant!"

"You're one to talk. You say you can help, but can you? Really?" I said. "How can you help Adair? How can you help Evangeline? All you can do is predict the weather and tell me to bring an umbrella."

Adair let out a frustrated hiss, pinching the bridge of his nose. Mags' good eye was shining, and I could tell I'd hit a nerve.

"We're stronger together," Mags said, her voice strangled as she tried to contain her anger without shouting our business for the entire dining hall to hear. "You can't do this on your own."

"Watch me." I stood and grabbed my bowl. I chucked it so hard into the nearest bus bin that it cracked, which only made me growl in frustration.

I stormed past the table on my way back to the practice rooms. It was a shame I didn't have a punching bag in there. Right now, that seemed like the best way to let out steam.

Whispers followed me as I wove through the sea of half-filled tables of students attempting to grab a leisurely dinner. I ripped my phone from my pocket, finding I'd only been away from the practice rooms for forty minutes. Whatever. Sean was going to have to deal with it or get further entrenched in my drama.

I took great pleasure in making even more racket on my way down the stairs. The violence of the sound waves bouncing back at me buoyed my mood, convincing me the world was just as angry as I was. If there was something I hated more than illogical people, it was people thinking they knew me when they clearly didn't. The pretense alone made my skin crawl.

I hauled the door open and stormed down the hallway, unlocking the practice room savagely before Sean could even pop his head out to scold me for the ruckus. I slammed the door shut behind me, locking it and switching off the lights.

A banging came at the door, but I slid down against it, exhausted. My anger was extinguished with the light.

"Noah? Is that you?" Sean's voice called through the thick wood. It sounded like he was calling through a tunnel. Just enough sound made it through the door that I could hear him faintly.

He pounded again, and I answered with a pound of my own. My hand stung from the impact, but it was nice to hit something without damaging anything.

"One knock if you're okay, two if I should open the door," Sean called, extending an olive branch through the locked door.

I pounded once.

"Knock once if you ate," Sean said, "two knocks if you're going to pass out again."

I pounded three times.

"What the hell does that mean?" Sean called through the door. I could hear him grumbling under his breath.

"Go away," I shouted through the door.

"Fine, fine, but if you pass out in there, you're going to die alone," Sean warned, slamming his door behind him.

I sighed, sorry to take it out on him. I just couldn't handle anything anymore. I was beyond my limit.

EIGHTEEN

My brief foray into the daylit dreamscape had thrown off my internal clock. By the time I felt the pull of the dreamscape, I didn't have anywhere else to go except barricade myself in the practice room once more. Whenever I tried to push the timing, I always felt nauseated. I fought the pull long enough to stick my head out into the hall, checking to see if the light was still on in Sean's practice room.

I sighed in relief, seeing his light was the only one lit in the entire hall. As a signal to him, I turned my light on. I had a feeling he would try to check in on me before he left, but at least the light would sate his curiosity.

As soon as I locked the door behind me, the floor tilted beneath me. I managed to fall softly against the porous soundproof tiles lining the wall, letting gravity set me down like an oversized doll.

I blinked, and I was in the dreamscape again.

My heavy sigh disturbed the foggy tendrils that rushed in to wrap around my knees, but it was somehow less satisfying without the noise. I shoved my hands into my pockets and walked. Standing still was making silly thoughts run through my head, like how the dreamscape was much better when it was shared with Colm.

I tried to walk in the direction of the lake Colm had shown me only hours before.

When I climbed the same ridge of twisted roots a second time, only the endless forest greeted me.

I kicked at the fog, but after two kicks, I lost interest again.

A light blinked at me in the distance, once, twice, then it went dark. I pulled at the sides of my eyes, trying to determine the cause from where I was standing. I could see the different shimmering smudges of the other night visitors, but I'd never seen a light before.

I took off at a jog, refusing to blink so I wouldn't lose my destination to distraction. I slowed right before the spot I was convinced was the source of the light show. Several feet to my right was a night visitor, its loop in constant flux. Through the trees, I could count on two hands the number of night visitors. This was an older section that had filled up a long time ago, but I hadn't been paying enough attention back then to know exactly when. At least a few years.

The ground beneath my feet was black, the fog refusing to pass over the spot. The steady tide of the fog split around the spot as if a rock was blocking the flow.

Or a night visitor.

I spun around again, trying to remember which night visitor had been here. My thoughts spun around, but the search was ultimately fruitless. I crouched down to the spot the night visitor had been anchored. Unlike the rest of the dreamscape, the black patch on the ground looked scorched and was emitting heat.

Never in all my years in the dreamscape had I witnessed a night visitor being pulled from the landscape. My stomach turned as my fingertips traced the newly marked land. Was this normal? Or was something wrong?

I brushed my hand against my pant leg, trying to wipe away the nervous sweat I was convinced had pooled in my hand. My skin was crawling, and I had a sudden urge to run away from the spot. I backed up, tripping over my own feet in my haste.

Suddenly, the fog froze. I felt a boom erupt in the distance and clapped my hands to my ears in surprise. After so long without any noise, the vibrations struck me violently. My hands came away wet, and I realized I was bleeding.

Distracted by the red smear lines on my palms, I looked up to find the fog moving once more. This time, nothing stopped the rolling tide from swallowing up the space previously occupied by the night visitor.

I leapt back into the approximate spot, sticking my hand below the surface of the fog, feeling around for the scorched spot. My fingers bent back, proving my hand was against a hard surface, but nothing else seemed out of the ordinary.

My hand sliced through the fog as I punched the silent atmosphere. In less than a second, the fog flowed back as it was and I had nothing to show for my angry outburst. My feet were moving before I had a destination in mind. I couldn't storm around the dreamscape all night.

I needed a plan. Hell, I needed a hypothesis. Something I could prove was or was not happening.

My feet slowed as I passed a night visitor a little more closely than I'd intended. If I could help it, I always gave them a wide berth. Watching them die over and over again would do nothing for my anxiety tonight. In fact, I was sure it would shatter any resolve I'd managed to scrape together.

I sighed at the night visitor as its death loop started again. Marching on, I felt a ping of guilt as my eyes slid from theirs, leaving them to endure their horror alone.

The Elevated symbol popped into my mind unbidden.

My feet stuttered to a stop.

It couldn't possibly be that easy. I searched my mind back to this morning. How many notecards had I filled out for Ms. Xavier? Fifty? One hundred? I hadn't thought about the publisher as a way to sort relevance. That had been before Evangeline had shown me the symbol. Before I knew what I was supposed to be looking for.

I stuck my thumbnail in my mouth and crossed my arms. Shaking my head, I couldn't remember. Not for sure. Nothing specifically came to mind, but of all the volumes in Ms. Xavier's collection, I'm sure several matched the titles found in the snowflake room. What had the students called it? Winter?

My feet slowly traced an unseen path between two gnarly trees. As I filtered through what I could remember, they turned back around of their own accord when the path was blocked by the second of the two twisted trees.

The one drawback of the dreamscape was always that details seemed to blur the longer I was on the opposite side. I didn't forget, necessarily, but the answer seemed on the tip of my tongue. I could recite how I'd spent my day, even how many tortellini I'd shoved in my face before my appetite had been ruined. Something about more complex memories seemed to become watered down on the other side.

I shook my head again, hoping this time the answers would come.

Had the symbols been there? Or was I trying to force myself to remember them?

High up on my list of priorities when I awoke would be to talk to Ms. Xavier. If I was going to spend all this time sorting and cataloguing for her, I better figure out what for. Also, if the publisher really did have a connection to the Elevated, I would need access to as many different volumes as I could to try to decipher if their existence at the school had any particular relevance or if a graphic designer in the forties had decided that combination of lines was nifty.

The pessimist in me had a feeling the publisher knew exactly what he was doing.

My eyes caught a flash of red, and I froze.

Looking down, I realized the blood had dried on my hands. I tapped my jaw near my ear, but it was impossible to tell if I'd lost my hearing or if there just wasn't anything to hear. I glowered at my hands, wondering how I was supposed to get rid of the dried blood now. I rubbed them on my pants, deciding spit would be a last resort only.

I had an intense urge to return to the night visitor scorch mark. I felt a sick sense of dread fill my stomach, and my legs pumped back toward the site. While my mind had been searching for one thing, the reason the area seemed familiar floated to the surface of my subconscious.

Colm. The area with the scorch mark was where Colm's death loop existed. Or it had.

A shooting pain hit me in the stomach. Then a rapid series of tugs.

Not again, I thought to myself. Not now.

I needed to know. I needed to know if it had been Colm who had been pulled so suddenly from my dreamscape. I needed to know if I was too late.

The pain continued, but I was running full force. I didn't have time to stop.

My ankle caught on a root, and the momentum of my body caused me to pitch forward. I flung my arms out to brace my body for the impact. Just as my face breached the barrier of the fog, my field of vision went black and I was pulled back into consciousness.

NINETEEN

A pitiful groan escaped me as I came to in the practice room. My head felt like it was splitting in two, with a battle axe lodged helpfully in the gap. My fingers snapped to my ears, checking to see if the blood had followed me into the real world.

I squinted at my fingertips, holding them directly in front of my eyes.

To my annoyance, they were wet with blood.

My eyes snapped open fully, burning in the bright light of the practice room. I sat up, my fingers probing near my ears to find any tender spots. Other than some slight ringing, nothing else seemed off. I scowled at the drying flakes that fell into my collar as I rubbed at the trail. I was thankful it was only that much blood.

Until I realized I was sitting in something wet. Horrified, I looked down. Had I wet myself somehow when I was in the dreamscape? My entire backside was soaked, and the squelching sound that followed my butt as I leaned over to find the source made my nose crinkle in distaste.

Bracing my hand against my clothes, I pulled it away to find it was dark red.

Blood. Again.

My gag reflex kicked in as my head listed all the possible maladies that would cause blood loss to this extent. I tried to find the source of the blood. My eyes darted around, finding something to be extremely off.

The room I was in was a mirror image of mine. The piano was on the wrong wall. Everything else seemed identical, save for the guitar stands in the corner, one of which was empty.

The color drained from my face.

I was in Sean's practice room. I twisted around, finding the door wide open.

I stumbled to my feet, my pants sagging with the weight of blood they had soaked up. I felt the oversaturated fabric lose several beads of moisture. The slow parade of blood down my ankles to my boots clawed at my brain as my eyes tried to make sense of the scene in front of me.

Someone had disabled the air compressor so the door hung open, fluttering slightly at the mercy of the gusting air conditioning. In the gap of the doorway lay Sean's lifeless body, his face obscured in darkness in the hallway. The rips in his clothing and their mottled color rang alarm bells in my mind.

I closed the distance between us slowly, the lump in my throat blocking my irregular, ragged breathing.

I crouched down next to his head, my fingers tentatively searching his neck for a pulse. My brain was screaming at me not to bother. The size of the pool of blood that had saturated the carpet was as much an indication of Sean's health as his cool, rubbery neck. I pulled my hand back to my chest, cradling my arms to my chest.

The feeling left my body, leaving me tingling with pins and needles as my stomach hardened.

It was too much.

The lump that had begun in my throat dropped like a stone into my stomach, setting it on fire.

And I screamed.

All the anger I felt, the sadness, the confusion, was balled tightly into one fireball. I launched it as far as it would go.

I thought my throat would explode. Instead, my fear fueled the scream longer than I'd ever yelled in my life. I didn't know where the air was coming from, but the feelings didn't escape with the noise.

The lights along the hallways flickered on, the trails of light snaking through the whole floor and turning the somber scene into a center-stage production. In the brightness, I could see the contusions coloring Sean's pale skin. My scream turned into a keening shriek as soon as I saw the angle of his neck.

A blur rocketed into my field of view, giving my watery eyes something else to focus on than the sad state of my first real friend at Windermere. The blackness of the shadowy figure contrasted sharply with the eggshell white plaster wall.

A pair of green eyes locked onto mine, and the scream died on my lips.

I collapsed onto my knees, letting my sobs wrack my whole body. Ig circled the scene, taking in everything from every angle. His eyes flashed, and he was at my side. His paws delicately treaded around the saturated carpet, and he found a spot close to me safe for him to sit comfortably. I turned to meet his eyes, closing mine in defeat.

My nose went cold, and my eyes fluttered open to see Ig nose to nose with me. Even that small touch set me off again. I hated this cat. This cat hated me. Why was he trying to comfort me?

Ig pressed his check to mine, rubbing both sides equally. I reached out to touch him but froze when I saw how much blood was on my hands.

"Noah," a soft voice said.

I spooked, causing Ig to jump back out of harm's way.

Evangeline stood with a flashlight in one hand and her phone in the other. She was still fully dressed, even at this hour. Her wide-screened phone flashed an ungodly hour at me.

"What happened?" Evangeline said, her face averted from Sean's body. Her gaze was fierce, and I felt a deep sense of guilt.

"It wasn't me," I said in a hoarse voice. Tongues of rage flickered up from my stomach as my mind screamed at me, reminding me that we weren't the guilty ones. The past ten minutes flickered on a loop in my brain.

Evangeline's eyes narrowed, but all I could do was look back at Sean. Poor Sean.

"But it's my fault," I whispered to no one in particular. The indignation and guilt tussled for the forefront of my mind, but I felt so empty. The warmth of my anger that had fueled me moments before cooled into nothingness, and I felt stretched too thin. I was really in trouble this time.

Ig reappeared by my side, plopping his butt right in front of me, facing Evangeline. His chest puffed up, as if answering a threat. My eyes followed the swishing of his tail like the weight of a metronome. It lulled me into an odd sense of calm.

A sigh escaped Evangeline, and I felt her enter my personal space.

Fabric covered my shoulders, and I realized I was shivering. I pulled the coat closer, but it stretched awkwardly around me.

"Sorry," Evangeline said. "Here." A pair of shoes appeared in front of me beside a pair of stocking feet.

I looked up, confused.

"I doubt you want to trail blood across campus." She nudged them closer to me with her toe. "These socks are thick. I'll survive."

I realized belatedly that she'd given me her coat as well. Her petite frame looked like she would be blown away in the autumn breeze, and I felt a stab of guilt for getting blood all over it.

"We need to hurry before anyone else wakes up from that scream," Evangeline said in a steady voice.

I nodded, slowly rising to my feet. I slowly pulled my feet out of my boots, slipping into the waiting pair. My heels hung off the back pathetically, but I was able to balance on the balls of my feet just like I did with a pair of high heels.

Evangeline stepped forward, grabbing my elbow to steady me. I grabbed the boots and hugged them tightly to my chest.

"Why are you helping me?" I blurted out, my logical brain finally inching out the scared monkey brain that had taken over at the sight of Sean's body.

Evangeline met my gaze, her lips pursing slightly. "You're not the only one who didn't pick the right side," Evangeline said sadly, tugging lightly on my elbow. "Come on. We've gotta go."

"My bag," I said. "It's still in my room."

Evangeline tiptoed around Sean to my room, where the light had been turned off.

"Bastards," I muttered as Evangeline slipped in and out of the room, returning with my bag.

"Anything look off in there?" I asked through chattering teeth. The air conditioning was doing me no favors today.

"No," Evangeline said. "Did you leave the guitar against the wall?"

"Yeah," I said. "In the corner, right?"

Evangeline nodded.

"Okay, make sure it's locked. Technically, it's not my room," I said.

Evangeline tapped her temple knowingly, making sure to double check the lock. She shoved her hand in her pocket, unearthing a small packet of wet wipes. She grabbed the doorknob, giving it a good wipe down with the toilette.

"Hope that works." Evangeline tucked the wipe back into the folds of her cardigan. She grabbed my elbow loosely again, guiding me quickly down the hallway. "It's now officially a conspiracy, and I'd rather not take my chances."

"Thanks," I said.

We both winced at the clamor of the staircase but paused at the next level.

"Shortcut." Evangeline pulled me through the door toward the orchestra room.

I closed the jacket more tightly around my shoulders and didn't argue. I followed Evangeline down the hallway, taking the last door on the right. It was labeled as a custodian closet, but I saw a door on the far side of the room beyond the shelves of cleaning supplies and paper products. The door opened into a cramped stairwell, this time old, wooden, and rickety, just like the Landing.

Evangeline led the way, clicking her flashlight on to illuminate the claustrophobic space. The switchback surprised me, but I followed dutifully. She shoved the door with her shoulder, putting a fair bit of weight behind it. The door groaned open, and I took several steps into a dim echoing room before I felt her grab my elbow.

"Hang on a second." She turned back to the stairwell.

An indignant yowl echoed in the staircase, and Evangeline shoved something into my arms.

Ig's claws scratched at my arms, and I had to wiggle him around into a mutually respectable position against my chest and in between my blood soaked boots.

"Dummy," Evangeline scolded the cat, bumping herself against the door to close it. "This way."

It wasn't hard to follow Evangeline once I could see the glowing emergency exit sign. I could tell we were in the commercial kitchen behind the assembly line by the orange-lit shadows of the counters and army of hanging pans and utensils.

Ig purred against my chest even as he was bounced awkwardly from side to side while I navigated the half-lit course on my toes. I could only imagine what I must look like.

Evangeline held the door open for me, dodging past me to open the final one against the wind. I trotted down the small concrete steps, noting the Grecian urn planter turned cigarette butt graveyard. The door snapped shut behind us, and the back wall of the dining hall fell back into shadow.

"Where are we going?" I asked, keeping my voice low in the still brisk night. The wind cut through the jacket, causing my blood-soaked clothes to grow even heavier against the dropping temperature.

"I doubt we could get away with having you shower in your room," Evangeline said. "Someone just had to live on the seventh floor."

I snorted, causing Ig to pause his purring.

"There's an abandoned custodian's cabin that has a shower and a fireplace. I hope you're not attached to that outfit. It's going up in smoke as soon as you can get out of it." Evangeline jogged across the grass in her socks toward the woods.

I made sure I wasn't far behind. Ig resumed his purring, and all I could think about was his warmth and not the hours of internet scourging it had taken for me to find these limited edition leather biker boots.

Boots not bracelets, I chanted to myself as my feet hit the ground. I did not look good in orange.

TWENTY

The cabin was tucked behind a copse of trees just far enough behind the Landing that I couldn't see the rest of campus through the tree cover. The path was worn into the ground, but the overgrowth obscured the way for any creature taller than three feet. It was a true deer path.

Evangeline was able to duck easily, but with the added weight of Ig and my boots and single-handedly holding my jacket-turned-cape, my luck was not as good. I barreled through the brush more than I was able to avoid it, and the sting of branches kept my adrenaline high. I hoped I wasn't leaving an obvious trail, but the longer we stumbled along, the more the desperate need to get to the end came over me. I gave up on being careful in favor of forward momentum.

"How much farther?" I gasped, the looming shadow never seeming to come any closer the longer we stumbled.

"Almost there." Evangeline disappeared behind another switchback.

"Was the custodian intoxicated when he made this path? Good God," I grumbled into Ig's face.

He sneezed at me, unimpressed with my whining.

Emme DeWitt

After another five minutes of stumbling, a clearing opened up beyond a thick ring of trees. Finally, we had reached the cabin.

And it looked like the only thing keeping it upright was tradition.

The foundation sagged into the soft mound, half of the porch at a steep enough angle to discourage any foot traffic. The wood was soaked from years of rain and too few coats of sealant. One sigh from the inside and I was sure it would collapse.

I froze in the front yard, clutching at Ig until he yowled at me.

"Are we serious right now?" I called after Evangeline, whose pace had not slowed.

She waved at me from the porch before disappearing into the house. Ig yowled at me again, and I loosened my grip enough for him to wiggle free. Once his feet were on the ground, he shot after Evangeline into the cabin.

"Apparently we are serious right now," I grumbled to myself, trudging on my sore arches before I could think of ten better reasons not to enter the decrepit dwelling. Evangeline's shoes squished on the stairs, and I realized the blood had finally soaked through them from my clothes. I sighed miserably.

"Get in here before you drip all over the porch!" Evangeline said. "I'd prefer not to add arson to my list of felonies today."

I shuffled into the cabin without another word. The door creaked back on its hinges, closing with a soft sense of finality. I sighed into the room, my eyes roaming over the sheet-covered furniture and the dim light coming from the back.

"In here," Evangeline called.

I followed her voice toward the light, crowding the small doorway to an ancient bathroom. She waved me toward the bathtub. I stared at the butter yellow monstrosity, my body refusing to move.

Evangeline sighed, taking my elbow again and steering me to the tub, forcing me to step into it. I turned to face her.

"Wait here." She darted back into the cabin proper.

I frowned after her, clutching my boots more tightly to my chest. The metal buckles digging into my stomach kept me comfortably grounded in reality.

I looked around the bathroom, finding the wallpaper a horrifying parade of painted ducks.

Evangeline reappeared with a brown paper bag almost as tall as she was. She rolled the sides down, offering it out to me.

"Strip," Evangeline commanded, waving the yard waste bag at me.

"Excuse me?" I said.

"Everything you're wearing. In here." Evangeline made the bag dance merrily. "I'm going to toss it in the incinerator."

"Incinerator," I repeated numbly.

"Yeah, starting a fire in an abandoned building would be a big neon flashing sign saying criminal activity here." Evangeline shifted her weight impatiently. "Hurry up."

"You think it'll work?" I asked, suspicious at a plan I hadn't come up with myself. What if she hadn't thought through everything properly? My mind buzzed numbly at the horror.

"Incinerator starts cranking at five. At this rate, I'll have to run to the incinerator and hope for the best when I run to get you more clothes. Unless you'd rather not be fully clothed when they arrest you with a bag of evidence," Evangeline mused aloud. Her eyes trailed around the bathroom. "And you're right. Those ducks are creepy as hell."

I opened my mouth to question the rest of the plan, but Evangeline dropped the bag and walked out of the room.

"Wait!" I called after her, pausing only slightly to say goodbye to my boots before they were tossed into the bag. The cape coat was next and then the borrowed shoes. The soaked layers of clothes took more time to maneuver, but I was able to de-robe at record pace.

Until I realized I was fully in the buff with no towel, no clothes, and, to my dismay, no shower curtain.

"Uh, Evangeline," I called into the hallway. "You got a towel out there?"

"Depends," she shot back. "Do you need one?"

"Or something similar," I hurled back. "Also, you're going to have to come get this bag if you don't want my bloody footprints all over the cabin.

"Incoming!" Evangeline sprinted into the bathroom.

My arms jerked to cover myself a little belatedly, but Evangeline was laser focused on grabbing the bag and dropping a pile of something on the toilet.

The dark curtain of hair was still swinging to follow the rest of Evangeline out to the hall when she called back to me.

"There's your towel. I recommend a series of baths. If you make me come back and bleach the entire bathroom from top to bottom, you'll be in big trouble," she warned.

I stuck my tongue out in her direction.

"I'm going to ignore that. You have twenty minutes, and then you've got to be ready to go," Evangeline said.

"You bringing me something to wear?" I asked. "Or would you prefer for me to streak across campus."

"I'll see how I feel," Evangeline quipped, the crinkle of the paper bag disappearing.

The front door shut again, the vibrations shaking the whole house.

"At least I'll know if someone's coming," I muttered darkly to the ducks. They stared back at me with their darkly lined lashes. I grabbed for the faucet, wincing at the shriek of metal against metal.

Water gurgled from the pipes, and my hands cupped under the powerful flow to test the temperature. My eyes caught on the waterfall of pink turned red as my hands were the first to shed their coat of drying blood. I put a stopper in the tub, letting the tepid water creep up around my crouched frame.

Evangeline had been right about the series part of her bath recommendation. As I scrubbed the first several layers of skin cells off my entire body, I tried not to focus on the color of the bathwater until I could mostly see the yellow tint bouncing back at me.

A sliver remained of a bar of bright green soap that had melded itself to the corner of the tub. Before I could calculate the germs that could be living on the dusty old bar, I grabbed it, letting the suds catch the remaining streaks of blood. My hair hung limply down my back, the curls destroyed by the vicious rubbing I'd been doing to try to get all the blood out of their every nook and cranny.

I could only imagine the payback I would get

once my hair dried.

As I squeezed out the remaining water from my deflated mane, I let the water drain. I hoped gravity would pull any remaining evidence down the drain with it, but I knew Evangeline had been serious about the bleaching. I broke the remaining shard of soap into tiny pieces and shoved them down the drain as well. Better a forgotten piece of soap than a half-used one with blood splatter on it.

I sighed, standing in the tub. I let the cool air partially dry me. Even though Evangeline had left something for a towel, I didn't like the idea of sitting in a soaking wet towel. I dreamt of a warm fluffy bathrobe fresh from the dryer.

Instead, I got a moth-eaten blanket the color of expired oatmeal.

Careful not to slip on the bare floor, I stepped out of the tub and wrapped the oversized blanket around me like a burrito toga. I shuffled into the cabin proper and out of the line of sight of the prying duck eyes. Ig's green eyes greeted me.

Out of nowhere, the room started to spin. I crouched down, half falling, half leaning against the wall of the small hallway. The last thing I saw was a flash of green before the darkness took me again.

TWENTY-ONE

I popped back into my dreamscape for the third time in less than twenty-four hours.

I let out a frustrated scream, clawing at my hair.

"What the hell is happening to me?" I yelled into the void.

No one answered.

My foot lashed out at the fog but found it had nothing to kick up. My hands stilled in my hair, bracing against my temples as I surveyed what was in front of me.

It was an odd half-light, just like the dawn and dusk hours; the dreamscape seemed to be transitioning between shadow and light. I'd never been here at this time.

My hands dropped to my sides as I looked out across the landscape. Slowly the night visitors flickered out of existence. As the sky lightened, the fog I was so accustomed to seeing faded slowly into nothingness. The movement of the night visitors waved like a mirage, the light destroying any proof of their existence until the middle ground was just as clear as the sky.

A movement out of the corner of my eye caught my attention. Something was materializing.

Colm's broad shoulders appeared, leading the rest of his silhouette into existence. He smiled at me, eagerly closing the distance. My jaw dropped. I wondered if I looked that confident when I materialized into the nighttime dreamscape. A sarcastic voice in the recesses of my mind laughed, imagining me kicking and screaming instead. It wasn't wrong.

"What are you doing here?" Colm's blue eyes locked in on mine.

"Same old, same old," I replied lamely.

Colm cocked his head to the side, as if picking up on my distress. "What's wrong?" he asked, grabbing for my hand boldly.

I let my fingers slip out of his reach as soon as he'd caught them.

"Sean's dead," I blurted out, turning my face so I wouldn't see Colm's expression.

"What?" Colm asked. "Which Sean?"

"I don't know." My stomach dropped. "Practice Room Sean. I can't believe I don't even know what his last name is. I'm a horrible person."

"Hey." Colm laid his hand on my shoulder. "Just tell me what happened."

I shook my head, unable to stop once I started.

"I don't know. That's the problem." I itched to move my shoulder out from under Colm's hand. "I think it might have been me."

"Noah, I'm sure it was just an accident," he said. "You would never purposefully hurt someone."

A laugh escaped me, and I found the strength to pull my shoulder away from him.

"You don't know that." I met his worried gaze. "I don't even know that."

"You really don't seem like someone who just goes after people," he said. "Fine. You'd need a reason. A damn good reason. Do you have a good reason to hurt Sean?"

I snorted.

"To kill him, Colm. He's dead," I said, my frustration distorting my voice. "Sean is dead."

"What would be your end game?" Colm pushed me to answer. "What could killing Sean possibly do for you?"

"Nothing!" I shouted at him, my voice burning with anger. Tears filled my eyelids, and I kicked myself inwardly. "Killing him would be pointless!"

"To you, maybe." He stepped forward to press both his hands against my upper arms. "But not to someone else."

I let my mind take in the comforting pressure of Colm's steadying hands. Somehow, he was keeping me from exploding into a thousand pieces. I hated the comfort. I hated that I needed it.

I swallowed hard against the lump in my throat. After several tries and even more deep breaths, it wouldn't budge. When I was able to speak again, my voice burned.

"I hate this," I said.

Colm's face recoiled as if he'd been slapped.

I clapped my hand over my throat, my eyes burning an apology into his forehead.

"This?" he asked, his eyes darting around the dreamscape. "It's kind of awesome."

I shook my head.

"You're going to figure it out." A wide smile punctuated his simple platitude. "You're the only expert around here. If anyone's going to crack the case wide open, it'll be you."

I rolled my eyes at him, and his laugh filled the emptiness of the day-lit dreamscape.

"I don't think it's safe for you to be here," I said, breaking my silence. My throat still burned, and Colm winced at my words.

"How can I leave you now?" His hands squeezed me in reassurance. "I can help."

"I think you'll have to sit this one out." I flinched at his pained reaction. My hand gripped tighter around my throat. "See? I can't even control my own voice."

"I'm fine," he lied, a brave smile on his face.

"Shut up," I said dismissively, the words distorted with my banshee voice.

Colm's lips pressed shut. The look of surprise was comical, and I chuckled.

"Stop playing around," I gurgled.

Colm's brows furrowed, his mouth working to open again.

But it couldn't.

"Holy shit." My fingers reached out to touch his lips. They had been sealed shut.

I stepped back, keeping as much distance as I could from Colm.

"What did I do?" I whispered, the grating voice echoing back to my own ears, making me blanch with guilt.

Colm's arms hung in the air where my shoulders had been. His palms were out in a reassuring stance, like I was a skittish deer about to bolt.

He wasn't too far off. I felt like running as far away as I could. Guilt weighed down my feet, but my mind raced ahead.

"See? This is why you can't be here." I hugged my torso tightly. "Last night, I was convinced you were gone. Then, I woke up and Sean was dead instead. You can't be near me. You need to leave."

Colm stepped forward, his blue eyes pleading with me. I didn't know what he was trying to say, but I was thankful I could ignore it just as easily. I'd made up my mind, and I wouldn't have to hear any arguments about it.

I took a deep, steadying breath and counted to three.

"I'm sending you back," I told Colm, my eyes lingering on his locked lips as he fought to say something. "You can yell at me when we see each other next."

I stepped back a few more strides, shaking the loose nerves from my limbs.

My previous words had planted an idea in my mind. Testing my theory would either yield the result I expected or completely backfire in my face. I counted to three slowly, pushing all the possible negative side effects to the side in my mind.

On the count of three, I gathered all the breath I could hold and screamed my command.

"Go!"

The burning feeling in my throat grew the longer I held the scream. Eventually, as it had before, the scream took over far beyond what I could power on my own. Unfortunately, this meant I had an extended viewing of the effect my scream had on Colm.

He'd figured out what I was about to do as soon as I drew breath. He'd braced against the impact, but his mind was quickly overwhelmed. He dropped to his knee, his hands covering his ears, twisting away from the scream like he was fighting a gale force wind.

Slowly, he faded, just like the other night visitors had in the early morning light.

Colm's head jerked up when he was almost completely faded.

My scream was so loud in my own ears I couldn't hear anything else. As he slipped away, his essence unknitting itself from the dreamscape, his mouth was finally able to open again.

Colm's eyes met mine, and he let loose his own scream.

"Noah!" his lips read just as he blinked out of existence completely.

The ground shook as soon as the last of him disappeared. The dreamscape slammed the door, knocking the vacuum of energy back in my face. My scream died in my throat, and I dropped to the ground.

I rested my forehead against the brittle grass, trying to find the energy to get back up.

The realization that I'd successfully kicked Colm out of the day-lit dreamscape filled me with relief. Until the thought swung heavily the other way. I'd sent him away, but where had he ended up?

I sighed into the grass. I tried to push myself back up, but my balance lurched to the side, my senses overcome with one extreme bout of vertigo.

The ground cradled me as I collapsed onto my side, and the darkness took me.

TWENTY-TWO

I woke up on my back. This wouldn't have been out of the ordinary if I wasn't staring at an unfamiliar labyrinth of cracked and rotten plaster. My shoulder blades protested as they braced against an unforgiving hard surface. My butt tingled to life as well as I tried to take stock of my extremities. Nothing seemed broken or missing, but it did vaguely feel as if I'd been hit by a bus.

My head felt swollen and waterlogged. I sat up slowly, swaying as the pressure of a low-grade migraine threatened to pull me back down into the fetal position. I tucked my legs underneath me so the steadiness of my crossed legs would give me a solid foundation. My hands slid over the slick fabric of my favorite running tights.

I looked down, patting at my clothed limbs. My running tights led down to socks and running shoes. I could feel the tightness of a sports bra underneath my shirt and jacket. Even my hair was pulled back by my go-to headband.

"Finally," a voice sighed.

Evangeline stood with her arms crossed, one hand clutching a chipped ceramic mug to her chest.

"I was debating if I should wake you," Evangeline said. "My reflexes aren't that good, and I don't have time to get x-rays today."

"What time is it?" I asked, patting down my pockets for my phone.

Evangeline whistled at me, giving me enough of a heads up to catch my phone before it smacked me in the nose.

"Later than I'd like." Evangeline sighed.

I noticed Ig weaving around her ankles idly, and I flinched when I saw it was nearly seven.

"You need to get going ASAP."

"How did I..." I trailed off, patting myself down. The last thing I remembered before the dreamscape was passing out in the poorly wrapped mass of blanket Evangeline had left me.

"I knew playing with Barbies would pay off later in life," Evangeline mused. "Didn't realize I would be dressing unconscious bodies when I grew up, but I guess it could be worse."

"I'm not sure how," I grumbled, crossing my arms uncomfortably across my chest. The whole ordeal was unpleasant to think about.

"I should be the one complaining." Evangeline wielded her coffee mug at me. "You're the one who works out in skintight clothing. Could you choose something easier next time, like a sundress or a baggy sweater?"

"For running?" I asked, shooting Evangeline an amused look. "Sure, no problem. I'll get right on that."

Evangeline stuck her tongue out at me. Even Ig paused to give me an unimpressed look.

"Why am I in my running clothes?" I asked, crawling slowly to my feet. Waves of pain shot down my limbs from my tender head.

"You're going on an early morning run. That way, you coming from the woods isn't weird, and your desperate need for a cleansing shower isn't out of character." Evangeline grabbed her bag from the counter. "I already dropped off your bag in your room when I grabbed your clothes. Thank God Mags still snores like a lumberjack. I'm surprised you can sleep, even with two walls between you."

Ig led the way to the door, and Evangeline stopped to wait for me.

"Coming?"

"Why are you helping me?" I asked. "I barely know you."

Evangeline regarded me thoughtfully. "I'm a pretty good judge of character," she said. "I don't think about it too much. You needed help. So I helped."

"What's in it for you?" I asked. "No one's that selfless."

"You've heard the enemy of my enemy is my friend, right?" Evangeline said.

I nodded, a little taken aback at the old saying. Somehow, I only imagined gangsters living by such a code.

"That's the best explanation I can give you right now. Can you trust me?"

Evangeline held the door open for me. She stared back at me as I tried to parse out if it was trust I was feeling or some sort of guilt-ridden duty.

Her phone buzzed in her pocket, and she dropped her gaze to answer it.

"Yeah," Evangeline said into the phone, bracing the door against her back. "Trying. I'll see you in a bit."

During a long pause, Evangeline rolled her eyes at the monologue on the other side.

"If you don't hang up right now, how am I supposed to finish my errand?" Evangeline said. She glanced over to me, inclining her head outside into the woods.

She covered the microphone of her phone.

"You need a head start anyway," Evangeline said. "Do two loops of campus. Keep to the tree line. After you shower and change, I'll meet you on the porch. They're going to keep us in the dining hall once we enter based on the emergency plan. Don't talk to anyone if you can help it."

She tucked the phone back in place.

"Of course, I was listening," Evangeline argued into the phone, waving me out the door.

Ig vaulted down the stairs with me, racing me to the deer path back toward the Landing.

I followed his dark form, ducking around the overgrown brush along every turn. We burst out into the open just past the Landing, and Ig guided me along the tree line as Evangeline had instructed.

He launched himself back into the brush without warning. I stuttered to a stop, looking for him in the densely packed bushes and elderly trees. I couldn't see any sort of path, so I refused to follow him any farther. Picking up my pace, I glided along the tree line, keeping the deserted buildings in my periphery. Slowly, the tension in my head melted away as I found my stride.

The sleepy campus was just stirring as I neared my second loop, pleased to find my back soaked and my mind clear. I felt like I could go another several circuits, but the instructions from Evangeline had been clear. Today was not the day to buck sensible advice.

I still wasn't sure if I trusted her completely, but the events of the past few hours made it undeniably clear. I was going to need someone in my corner, watching my back. Adele had warned me as much, but I was a little late to be picky about who that person would be now that I was on my own.

My phone buzzed in my pocket, and I pulled it out before the third pulse.

It was Adele.

"It's like you're psychic," I said to my screen, accepting the video call as I closed the remaining distance between me and the Landing's front door.

"Yeah, my trouble meter has been going off all night," Adele snapped. "Why haven't you been answering your phone?"

"Must have been in a dead spot. The Wi-Fi's good, but it's not that good," I argued.

"Don't let it happen again," Adele bristled, crossing her arms. "I almost charged campus like a mad woman."

"Yeah, not a good idea," I replied. "Especially not today."

"Why?"

"Hey, can I call you back later?" I said, feeling a gaze on me. "I just finished my run and I need to shower. I'm meeting a friend to study."

"You just got there. And you don't run this late." Adele checked her watch. "What the hell is going on?"

"Talk to you later," I said in a falsely peppy voice. "Bye."

I disconnected the call with a savage tap and shoved the phone back into my pocket as I trotted up the stairs. The hairs tingled on the back of my neck, and I glanced back at the tree line as I leaned into the door. I couldn't see anyone, but I definitely felt like I was being watched.

The staircase was empty, but I could hear the

beginnings of morning life behind the closed doors of each landing. I took the stairs two at a time, trying to get into my room before anyone decided to make an early start and see me coming in at an ungodly weekend morning hour.

As I barreled through my bedroom door, grabbing my toiletry bag and robe, I snuck my phone out of its pocket. Something itched in the back of my mind. Evangeline had warned me of the inevitable campus lockdown that would come once Sean's body was discovered. I had a feeling the Wi-Fi would be shut off to ward off any crazy social media rumors.

I messaged Adele before locking myself in the bathroom.

Red line only, I typed. *The British are coming.* I hit send.

I turned off the Wi-Fi on my phone, letting it cycle uselessly trying to find a signal.

The message app Adele had built for our use was virtually untraceable, but to be safe, we used it only when we had no other option. By disabling my phone from the network, any messages I sent wouldn't be trickling through servers Adele didn't already have a direct line to. It would take the authorities much longer to produce a warrant for the private servers Adele maintained than whichever ones the school used. Plenty of time to hide anything incriminating.

I dropped my phone on the pile of black running clothes I'd piled on the pristine tile floor. I yanked the nozzle to scalding hot in the shower, creating a cloud of steam that quickly fogged over the wall of mirrors along the vanity counter. I inspected myself in the full-length mirror quickly, trying to make sure I hadn't missed any blood from earlier.

Grabbing my loofah from my tote, I stepped into the burning stream and didn't resurface until my skin was a raw, lobster red. Even then, I still didn't feel one hundred percent clean.

Sean's glassy-eyed stare floated up in my mind's eye. A full-body shiver wracked me in the muggy heat of the poorly vented room.

"Enough," I told myself in the blurry mirror.

It was time to stop being passive. If I was up against a chess grandmaster, I better open my eyes to the board. Colm was right. It might not be my end game, but that didn't mean I couldn't beat someone to theirs.

TWENTY-THREE

Evangeline was waiting for me on the front porch of the Landing. She checked her phone, sighing in annoyance.

"Fashionably late ended about fifteen minutes ago." She drew herself up to her full height.

I looked down at her, her bravado only reaching my shoulder.

"Sorry if I tried to look presentable," I said. "I had a bit of a shoe crisis."

We both looked down at my black high-ankle basketball shoes. Other than my boots and running shoes, I hadn't packed very many shoes in my carry on. The rest were in the boxes at home. It hadn't seemed important at the time.

"Did you do something to your hair?" Evangeline asked, peering around my shoulder.

"Had to do some damage control. Sorry it took a while." I stepped down a step so Evangeline and I were at the same eye level. The repair product I'd run through my curls caused them to tighten, making it nearly impossible to pull them into any sort of hair tie. I wasn't a fan of the crunchy texture, but the flip side was a mass of unruly hair that had people wondering if I licked electrical sockets for fun.

"I tried to imitate how you normally wear your hair on a run." Evangeline frowned. "What happened? Did I do something wrong?"

"When we have time, one day I'll explain to you what moisture can do to curls." A smile pulled at the corner of my mouth. "You did fine."

I set off for the dining hall, hearing Evangeline scurry after my long strides.

"So what's the play, boss?" I asked, feeling Evangeline slide into the spot on my right side naturally.

"Act dumb. Say as few words as possible." Evangeline shrugged. "It'll be easy for me. We've got about fifty feet until I shut down anyway."

I halted, causing Evangeline to slingshot past me before she floated back.

"What?" she asked, looking around for something.

"Words. More words." I rolled my wrist for her to continue.

"You've seen me in class." Evangeline shrugged. "I get to about five people comfortably, then it's downhill past that."

"Is it really social anxiety?" I asked, searching Evangeline's face for any twitch out of the ordinary. "Or is it something else?"

"Warmer." Evangeline cleared her throat. She shoved her hands in her jacket pockets, her legs dancing with impatience.

"And you're on which plane again? Relative?" I guessed.

Evangeline shook her head. "Colder."

I pursed my lips at her.

"Temporal?" I pulled the word out of the recesses of my mind. I tried to remember the other options from the diagram, but I was a little slow from exhaustion.

"Ice cold." Evangeline wrinkled her nose.

I let out a stream of air through my nose. "Sentient," I said, watching Evangeline pogo on the spot.

"Thank God. I'm freezing." Evangeline bounced around in the chill air. "I hate guessing games."

The sun was out finally, but her thin jacket was not as helpful as my quilted coat. I pulled it off around my messenger bag, throwing it around her shoulders.

"Focus," I said. "I need the full picture before you flake out."

"Fair enough," Evangeline said, her buzzing now relegated to minor fidgeting.

"Anything I can do to help with the overload?" I asked. A weight hit the bottom of my stomach. Maybe I would have to face the Inquisition on my own after all.

"I'll try and keep it together," Evangeline said. "But thanks. I'll try and step into the other room, as they say. Sometimes that's enough of a buffer for me to survive."

"How bad is it looking?" I nodded my head toward the dining hall.

Evangeline looked off to the side in contemplation. "They're still looking at the crime scene. Students are getting restless because their phones are being taken away and they can't leave. Some of them are still in their pajamas," Evangeline said. "Lots of nervous energy. Oh shit."

Evangeline ducked, grabbing me by my arm and dragging me toward the entrance.

"We gotta get in there now," Evangeline said. "Our window of opportunity is closing."

"What window?" I asked, but we were up the stairs and through the door before I could pull any more information from Evangeline.

As soon as she crossed through the entryway, it was like she walked into a wall.

She stiffened, her face going slack as her eyes darkened. Her forward momentum was halted, and I had to press against the small of her back for her autopilot to move her forward.

The buzz of the dining hall rose up around me as I guided Evangeline farther in. Police were stationed in all the doorways, even flanking the food assembly line. The dean was on the far end of the hall, her face partially obscured by a heavily decorated police officer with a pair of cords draped across his shoulder. He must be the one in charge.

Officers walked up to speak to the man briefly, his face turning to catch their whispers in his ear before returning to face the dean. She stood in perfect view of the entire hall, and her eyes slid from the police chief to mine.

The chief noticed the distraction and turned to find what had caught the dean's attention. While her face remained impassive, the slightest crease formed in the chief's forehead below the brim of his hat. I looked away from the dean, trying not to seem guilty by holding her gaze. Why should I dare lock gazes with her if I didn't have something to hide?

The bench nearest me was empty, the students having clustered farther into the mass of tables. The empty seats seemed like a buffer for whatever serious business was going on. Even the normal students seemed to sense the cloud of anxiety in the air and wanted nothing to do with it.

I led Evangeline to the empty bench and bent over to speak in her ear.

"Dean's looking at me. Stay here. I'm going to grab some food and coffee." I set my bag neatly on the ground next to Evangeline.

I ducked through the doors of the buffet line, the kitchen eerily silent as I piled some rolls and cold cuts onto a plate. A bolt of electricity shot down my spine. I had to remind myself to breathe evenly in and out. My hands shook slightly as I punched the buttons of the percolator. As soon as the coffees were ready, I balanced the plate precariously on my forearm, grabbed one of them in each hand, and used my back to push through the door and into the buzzing hive of students.

The door opened too easily, and I stumbled, sloshing coffee on my hand.

"You all right?" a uniformed officer asked, holding the door for me. I winced as my grip on the coffee cups slipped. Another officer stepped in and grabbed them, following me dutifully back to Evangeline, who had spaced out. I set the plate of food in front of her vacant eyes.

The officer from the door pressed his finger to his earpiece, frowning at the squawking voice. He pressed the microphone, muttering an affirmative to his chest. He caught the eye of the officer who had set the coffee cups down on the table next to where I'd set my plate.

"Miss, could you follow me please?" the first policeman said.

I glanced at Evangeline.

"Can it wait?" I asked him, my hand settling protectively on Evangeline's shoulder. "My friend has some really intense social anxiety. I don't want to leave her here by herself."

The officer relayed my request through his communication system, getting another series of squawks back.

"She doesn't look too good." The second officer glanced at his colleague from his observation of Evangeline. "Do you know if she's on any medication? Should we call a medic?"

"Bryant, stay with the girl," the first officer instructed, holding his arm out for me to follow. "We'll be right back."

The officer nodded, sitting down next to Evangeline and speaking in a soft voice. I hated to leave her, but it didn't take me long to figure out who had summoned me.

We walked down the side of the dining hall, attracting almost every pair of eyes. The buzzing of the students intensified, and I could see them whipping around in their seats to watch the procession.

No, I didn't look guilty at all.

The dean and the chief waited for us at the edge of the hall, and I counted primes in my head so my face wouldn't betray the flurry of panicked thoughts filtering through my mind. I strode calmly, being sure to hold my posture without seeming arrogant.

The officer kept a half step behind me, as if shadowing me should I choose to bolt. He paused as soon as we entered the inner circle of the chief and his assistant. The dean looked at me evenly.

"Good morning." I initiated the conversation as innocuously as I could.

"Ms. Young," the chief greeted me.

"Sir," I replied, reaching my hand out to shake his. I turned to acknowledge the dean with a nod. "Ma'am."

"Noah, why is Evangeline with you?" the dean asked directly. "I've never seen her attend meal times before."

"We have a project we're working on together," I lied effortlessly. "Originally, I was just going to grab some things to go, but it was too cold for her to stay outside. She left her jacket in the library."

I waved behind me.

"She's wearing mine right now," I said simply. "I promised her I'd be quick."

The dean peered around me, the crow's feet near her eyes deepening.

"I was unaware you shared any classes with Evangeline." The dean's eyes retracted to stare me down.

I swallowed, taking a breath before I answered too quickly.

"That would be my class, Annabeth," Ms. Xavier said from behind me.

The officer who had escorted me stepped aside to allow Ms. Xavier into the small circle, further obscuring me from my classmates' prying gazes. I reached up to scratch my nose in an attempt to hide the inch my jaw had dropped at Ms. Xavier's sudden appearance and seamless exposition of the lie I'd created.

"Teresa," the dean said in surprise. "What brings you out here on the weekend?"

"As Noah said, I'm overseeing a project," Ms. Xavier replied. Her eyes glanced around the circle. "What seems to be the problem?"

"Your syllabus was not approved with any projects." The dean dug in her heels. My finger moved to itch my eyebrow, blocking my amused expression from the group.

"My research project has taken a broader scope than I'd expected. Evangeline is my research assistant for one of her private study hours, and Noah is working off her detention debt to me by helping my assistant," Ms. Xavier said, a glint in her eyes.

I bit the inside of my cheek, hoping the pain would cloud my expression. Or at least skew it more toward neutral.

So that's what the notecards had been about.

"Detention in your first week, Ms. Young," the dean said, her tone icy. "I'm not impressed."

"I'm sure the situation has been remedied," Ms. Xavier said, speaking up on my behalf. "I don't foresee any future problems. Now that that's all cleared up, could I please have my assistants back? I'm afraid time is of the essence."

I turned to check in on Evangeline. Her pallor didn't look right, although the officer seemed like an attentive guardian.

"Evangeline isn't looking too good," I said out loud.

The chief shifted awkwardly, grabbing his utility belt uncomfortably.

"I'm afraid that isn't a possibility now, ma'am," the chief said to Ms. Xavier. "We're in the middle of an investigation."

"Oh?" Ms. Xavier crossed her arms expectantly.

"Yes, it's best everyone stay in the dining hall until my team has been able to determine it's safe to open campus again," the chief explained, earning him a flashing glare from the dean.

"Safe from what exactly?" Ms. Xavier said. "What exactly is going on, officer?"

"A boy has died," the chief replied, his gaze shifting to rest solely on me. "And your assistant seems to have been the last one seen with him alive."

TWENTY-FOUR

I had to give it to Ms. Xavier. She was a ball buster.

"What nonsense are you talking about?" Ms. Xavier said. "You're telling me a student is dead, and your idea of a thorough investigation is to parade a student in front of her peers based on one witness account."

"Teresa," the dean said sharply. "This is highly inappropriate."

"Yes, I'm glad you finally see that." Ms. Xavier looked back and forth between the chief and the dean.

"Ma'am, we just need to speak to Ms. Young to clear this all up," the chief said, his tone unconvincing.

"Oh, I bet," Ms. Xavier replied. "Is that before or after you build the witch's pyre out in the quad?"

"Teresa!" the dean said, her eyes glittering dangerously. "That is enough."

"Annabeth, you can play politics all you like. You've got a lot of people to please. I get it." Ms. Xavier kept her voice thin. Any moment, I expected the tight string of her narrative to snap. I wasn't the only one hanging on her every word. The officer next to me was trying to school his face, but his eyes were pinging back and forth between each volley just like mine.

The dean tried to argue, but Ms. Xavier put her hand out, freezing the dean's tongue.

"Let me finish," Ms. Xavier said. "If you're not going to look out for the students, I will. Noah is leaving with me. She's going to be in my office working on cataloging my research materials. If anyone needs to speak with her, you better unearth a parent of some sort for consent."

"Ms. Xavier," the chief said, the backpedaling he was about to perform evident on his overwhelmed face. "I'm sure we can all work together to resolve this matter civilly. As a witness, it is very important to hear from Noah what she saw last night. It's imperative to the investigation."

"Oh, she's a witness now?" Ms. Xavier replied.

"Of course," the chief said. "She's free to go as soon as she's given her statement."

"Who is it we're talking about exactly?" Ms. Xavier pressed. "I'm not impressed if your only lead comes from students finger pointing to get out of trouble."

"Sean Rector," the dean said. "Several students volunteered that they had seen Sean and Noah speak on multiple occasions."

"She's been here a week," Ms. Xavier retorted. "What qualifies as multiple occasions? Twice?"

"Ma'am, if we could hear from Ms. Young herself, I'm sure this would go faster," the chief offered, trying to toe the line between the warring glares from the dean and Ms. Xavier.

I hope she isn't planning on getting tenure, I thought. Standing up for me was going to have ramifications.

"I'm sorry, but I'm still getting to know people," I said to the chief. "The only Sean I remember is the one who carried around a guitar with him everywhere. He and I grabbed breakfast about the same time every morning. Is that who you're talking about?"

The chief looked to the dean, who nodded.

"Did you ever use the practice rooms in the basement?" the chief continued, making a short note in a small spiral notepad.

"I got lost down there one day trying to find my guitar class." I feigned intense thought. "I wasn't assigned a practice room, though. Sean told me once they were all assigned at the beginning of the year."

"That is correct." The dean bristled. "Are you sure you've never been down there otherwise?"

"What's the point if she doesn't have a practice room?" Ms. Xavier interrupted.

"Did you say Sean's dead?" I said, drawing the attention of Ms. Xavier. The dean was ready to shoot lightning bolts from her eyes.

"Yes, dear, I'm sorry to say," the chief replied.

I let the color drain from my face. Ms. Xavier reached out to steady me, laying a hand in between my shoulder blades.

"Noah, are you all right?" she asked, genuine concern softening her features.

"I—"

My throat closed up, and I couldn't finish my train of thought. I swallowed hard, trying to keep my emotions firmly behind a locked door. If I let any more out for effect, I wasn't sure I could rein them back in.

"I just talked to him last night," I managed, trying to give just enough information to satisfy the chief without giving anything else away. Evangeline had mentioned a master plan, but having improvised my part, I didn't want to get any more reckless without knowing what my part was supposed to be.

"When?" the chief pressed, eliciting a sharp look from Ms. Xavier.

"I saw him after dinner," I replied honestly. "We crossed paths after I had a fight with Mags. He asked if I was okay, but I didn't want to talk about it. He went back to practicing once he made sure I was okay. I didn't see him after that."

"You fought with who, sorry?" The chief scribbled in his notepad.

"Margaret O'Brien," Ms. Xavier offered happily, initiating a fresh stare down with the dean. "She's one of the dean's student assistants. I'm sure she'd be happy to confirm Noah's story."

"She also happens to be Ms. Young's roommate," the dean replied. "Ms. O'Brien would definitely be the one to confirm Ms. Young's story. Especially where she went after meeting Mr. Rector."

"Lovely," Ms. Xavier said. "Now that you have something better to do than hang Noah in the court of public opinion, we'll leave you to it. If you have any more questions for Noah, feel free to come to my office."

Ms. Xavier pressed her hand against my back, guiding me away from the interrogation squad and back toward Evangeline. I expected to be pulled back by the officer who had escorted me, but he stepped aside without a word. As soon as we approached Evangeline, the other officer stood, helping Evangeline stand next to him.

He handed her off to me with a polite nod, making sure Evangeline didn't trip over the bench as she climbed over the barrier. Once she was held up by my bracing arm, the officer returned to his partner.

A rush of whispers assaulted my ears with a pop, and I winced at the eyes glued to our backs.

"Keep walking, and make sure Evangeline doesn't fall," Ms. Xavier said through the side of her mouth.

I nodded, placing all my focus on Evangeline. I worried at her pallor, wishing we could have kept the interview shorter.

She'd known what was coming and had run straight into the fire anyway. The timing was impeccable with Ms. Xavier, and a wave of appreciation rolled through me. I had no idea how I would have survived without her.

Don't make me blush, I heard Evangeline say.

My eyes had been locked on her face, and she hadn't moved a muscle on her own. I shook my head, worried the stress had finally melted my brain.

"Noah? Everything okay?" Ms. Xavier held the door to the outside open for Evangeline and me.

"Yeah." I shook my head to clear the cobwebs. "I'm just tired."

"You're a horrible liar," Evangeline croaked, her color improving upon breathing in the fresh autumn air.

"I get by," I replied, relieved Evangeline was no longer in zombie mode. "Not holding my breath for an Oscar or anything."

"The amount of narrative chatter in your brain makes me wish it would melt," she retorted dryly, earning her a backward glance from Ms. Xavier.

I froze.

"When did I say that?" I frowned down at Evangeline.

She tapped the side of her head knowingly.

"Jailbreaks only work if you move away from the jail," Ms. Xavier called from several paces ahead of us. "And I, myself, am dying for a coffee."

"Ooo, coffee," Evangeline cooed, breaking away from me and jogging to catch up to Ms. Xavier. I watched the pair of them glide across the academic quad, while I was rooted to the cobblestones in shock.

What on earth was going on at this school?

TWENTY-FIVE

"So I've worked it out with the dean." Ms. Xavier leaned against the open office door. "You're going to keep a low profile until the investigation is over. Campus will be closed for the next few days, so stick to the office when you're not sleeping."

Ms. Xavier's phone had begun to ring as soon as we entered the safety of her office. The dean's timing was eerily on point. Evangeline and I had stayed in the hall until the conversation was over.

"For a jail break, this feels an awful lot like jail," I muttered out of the corner of my mouth. My phone tapped lightly as I spun it on rotation on top of the desk. The endless loop comforted me, even though it remained silent.

I really wanted to talk to Adele. I didn't know what I would say. So much had happened since I'd arrived at Windermere that I didn't even know where to start. When we were hopping states on the West Coast, I could go months without an episode with my voice. Meeting a night visitor in real life used to be an anomaly, but now I lived with a constant low-grade nausea alerting me to their proximity.

Avoiding the dining hall and the rest of campus for a few days didn't sound like such a bad thought after all.

Evangeline snorted.

"It sounds good now," she muttered, looking up from her attentive petting of Ig on the floor of the cluttered office. "Wait until it's long term."

"Hey, what did I say about digging around uninvited?" Ms. Xavier said, her eyes glancing at me purposefully.

"Sorry," Evangeline said, color rising to her cheeks.

"Both of you need to quit pouting." Ms. Xavier stood from her perch. "You've got plenty to do to keep you busy. No Elevated monkey business while I'm gone."

"Fine." Evangeline sighed, waving at Ms. Xavier as she disappeared down the hall.

I stared off after her.

"Did she just say Elevated?" I asked, my throat tightening.

"Yeah, best keep that between the three of us though." Evangeline looked down at Ig and back to me blatantly. "If we're under the radar, Ms. Xavier is in deep cover."

"I don't know how. Not sure how much you caught in the dining hall, but Ms. Xavier threw down the gauntlet with the dean," I said. "If I hadn't been accused of murder, I'm sure I would have enjoyed it a little more."

"Oh, it was just as dramatic in here." Evangeline tapped her temple. "The commentary from the police officer next to you almost broke me."

"Why is Ms. Xavier in deep cover? The dean doesn't seem the type to let anything slide on her watch," I said. "She must be someone important."

"The more you learn about the Elevated community, the more you'll notice it's a tight knit, almost incestuous bunch." Evangeline's fingers were still trailing through Ig's thick coat. "Everyone's always related to somebody. Ms. Xavier is posing as a relative to someone powerful. That person is too secretive to come forward to say anything though, so the assumption remains unchallenged."

"That's pretty brave of her," I said, my phone pausing in my hands as the gears of curiosity cranked with this new piece of information. "Seems a little Shakespearean."

"And reckless enough that she tries to remain as neutral as possible. If she doesn't make a fuss, the dean has no reason to look any further into her background," Evangeline said. "It's surprising the dean hasn't sought her out for her Elevated abilities sooner. That does make me nervous. Like the dean doesn't trust who Ms. Xavier says she is."

"Why all the cloak and dagger business?"

"Windermere is such a small slice of the Elevated pie, but it shows you what's going on. Shady, shady business," Evangeline said. "We're just trying to get a better understanding of what's going on and stop it before any other Elevated get hurt."

"By hurt do you mean dead? I feel like there's a lot of dead people popping up," I asked. "Sean wasn't Elevated though."

"True," Evangeline said. "But that didn't stop him from getting caught in the crosshairs."

"Because of me," I sighed. "Maybe banshees really are bad omens."

"We just have to stay under the radar a little while longer. Play the long game," Evangeline said, mostly to herself. "We'll get to the bottom of it."

Evangeline bit her lip, her hand pausing as she lost herself in thought.

I slid a pile of fresh notecards toward me, deciding to be productive during my house arrest. At least copying information was more gratifying than talking to myself. Ig sneezed, hopping down from Evangeline's lap to stretch. Even he was getting restless.

He jumped in surprise as Evangeline flew into motion. She leaned over and grabbed the nearest volume, snatching the highlighter from my hand. I tried to protest, but she threw me a mean look, begging me to shut up.

I heard a syncopated series of footsteps round the corner, and Ig shot out of the office in the opposite direction. My fingers found a pen in enough time to finish the notecard just as a shadow fell across the open doorway.

Evangeline looked up first from her fake skimming of a random chapter. Her eyes darted to mine a millisecond before the faces turned for me to recognize them.

Officers One and Two from earlier had found us.

I looked up from my work, cocking my head to the side in obvious surprise. The officers shared a look, and I waited for them to answer my nonverbal question.

"What's going on?" I asked, too impatient to have a war of wills with the police officers.

Evangeline's face darkened. Her eyes rolled back toward me.

"So much for a subpoena," Evangeline said dryly. "Apparently all it takes is some finger pointing to get suspected of wrongdoing around here."

The officers shifted uncomfortably. As much as they were just trying to do their jobs, I hated the showmanship being flaunted right now. Let me leave, only to pull me right back in.

"Ms. Young, if you would follow us, please." Officer One stepped into the cramped office.

"I would rather not." I pulled another book toward me.

"Ma'am?" Officer Two was giving me an out to change my answer.

"You heard me," I replied, enunciating each word. "I'm not going."

I flipped the cover of the book open, leafing to the copyright page to scribble down the information I needed. The officers watched me fill out an entire card without interruption.

"Are you going to watch me fill out every single card?" I asked the room.

"Ms. Young, please step outside," Officer Two said.

Evangeline snorted from the floor.

"This day keeps getting better," Evangeline said sarcastically to the small audience. "You might as well give up now. She's not going to budge."

"Evangeline, could you pass me the highlighter?" I asked, my hand reaching out without looking up from my notecard. "I need the orange one for this topic."

"Ms. Young, you need to come with us now," Officer One repeated.

I looked up, locking eyes with Evangeline.

"Why?" I asked, keeping my gaze firmly locked on Evangeline, hoping my mind reading comment from earlier wasn't too far off from the truth.

"You've been requested by the chief for further questioning. That's all you need to know." Officer One placed his hand on his belt.

Evangeline turned to look at the second officer, the one who had sat with her during my interrogation in the dining hall. She looked intently at him, her eyebrow rising in surprise after a moment of concentration.

Colm woke up this morning, Evangeline's voiced tinkled in my mind.

Her eyes slid from the officer to mine.

I bit down hard on the inside of my cheek, crossing my arms to cover my reaction to Evangeline's insight.

And he was screaming your name.

TWENTY-SIX

When I count to three, Evangeline said in my mind. *Run.*

I stood, seemingly to follow the instruction of the officers. They didn't question my sudden compliance but rather looked relieved that I was finally coming of my own accord. I tucked my phone in my back pocket, ready to sprint as soon as I got the go ahead.

"Where are you taking me?" I asked, inching out of the small office and past the officers.

"Straight to the dean's office. We should be able to escort you back as soon as they're done questioning you about what you saw last night," Officer Two volunteered.

I glanced back at Evangeline before I lost sight of her, and she flashed an okay sign with her fingers.

The jangling of the officer's belts gave me a good idea where they were in relation to me. I dragged my feet, making them slow their own pace so as not to crowd me. Their first mistake.

We finally made it to the stairs, and the grand decent began. Normally, I appreciated grand staircases, especially in older buildings. This time, I was cursing the slippery marble and curved descent. The lecture hall was directly across the base of the stairs, and we would have to pass by it before we could go out the main entryway to the quad.

An aerial map of campus popped into my head, and I stumbled on the stairs. I grabbed the handrail, steadying myself before the nearest officer could reach out to help.

"I'm fine." I tried to keep focused while Evangeline narrated the plan in my head. She lit up the route I was supposed to run. It wove through campus, doubling back to the infirmary that was directly across from the lecture hall entrance. I tapped the railing nervously, wondering if the plan would work.

One.

My foot hit the ground level. The officers were two stairs behind.

Two.

I sped up as the officers oriented themselves.

Three.

My legs pumped, getting several lengths ahead of the officers before they realized they had a runner.

A real runner.

I have to admit, I was a little disappointed. After only two minor maneuvers in the science building, I'd successfully lost my tail. Either they weren't trying, or I was getting more help than I was expecting.

The handlebar of the old emergency exit smacked loudly as I barreled through it and up a small flight of stairs back up to ground level. I slid along the edge of the outer wall, peering around the corner to make sure I wasn't running into an ambush.

The quad was deserted, and I sprinted for the door Evangeline had highlighted in my mind's eye. The sign in the lobby helpfully pointing me to the third floor for the infirmary. I laughed to myself, hoping I never needed an emergency. I didn't wait for the elevator, preferring the freedom of the stairs.

My shoes squeaked as I took a turn too fast, the noise echoing back at me in the tight stairwell. I paused at the top landing, pressing my ear to the cold metal door. The soft patter of voices leaked through the door, but I couldn't tell how many speakers there were.

I darted through the door, walking a normal pace as I scoped out the hallway. Oddly, I felt like I'd been teleported to a hospital. Each room had its own hospital bed, EKG monitors, and IV stands. Each stood dim and empty, pointing my feet toward the main desk at the juncture of the two hallways. Two nurses stood talking to one another, their voices light and playful.

A beam of artificial light trailed into the hall from the room closest to the nurses' station. I tried to go up on my toes and sneak into it without drawing the attention from the nurses, but I was unsuccessful. Just as I entered the shaft of light, the charge nurse behind the desk noticed me.

"Hey, you can't be here, honey," she called to me. Her grey eyes were kind but authoritative. When she waved me over to her, I had no choice but to comply.

"I'm sorry." I grabbed my hands in front of me. "I just…"

"Oh, are you the girlfriend?" the young nurse next to me asked. Her gap-toothed smile made me pause.

"Um." I reached my hand behind my neck.

"It's okay," the smiling nurse said conspiratorially. "I wouldn't be able to help myself either."

"The poor boy's been awake for two hours," the charge nurse grumbled. "Any more visitors and he'll pass out again."

"It's young love, Ruth." The younger nurse clutched her chart to her chest. "Let them live a little."

"If I promise to make it quick?" I asked, my eyes searching the charge nurse's eyes desperately. "I just want to see him. Make sure he's okay."

"If you make his heart monitor spike," she pointed threateningly between me and the dancing line on her monitor screen, "you're banned for good."

"Yes, ma'am," I said. "Two seconds, I promise."

I turned to go back toward the occupied room.

"You're a big softie, Ruth," the younger nurse cooed. "I knew you had it in you."

"Oh, I'm using it against him later when he refuses to take his medication," the charge nurse retorted. "It's strategy."

The younger nurse's twinkling laugh followed me into the room. My hand braced against the doorframe, and I knocked lightly, not wanting to scare him.

Colm lay slightly reclined in the bed, his face turned toward the window watching the sun dancing behind the cloud cover. His eyes flit to the door, returning to the window.

It took him a second, but he sat up, his face swinging back to stare at me in the doorway.

"Hey," I said, my eyes on the climbing heart rate monitor. "Long time no see."

"Noah," Colm said, his eyes pinging all over me, blinking over and over.

"Whoa, calm down." I stepped farther into the room. "I'm going to get kicked out if you go into cardiac arrest."

Colm frowned at me, then at the heart rate monitor. His bright blue eyes caught mine.

"You're really here," he said, half to himself.

"In the flesh," I replied. I held out my hands for proof. "I just can't believe you were here this whole time."

"What do you mean?" Colm asked.

"I feel a little guilty," I admitted, my thigh leaning against the foot of his bed. "If I'd known it was going to work or that you were hanging out on the other side, I would have done something about it sooner."

"You didn't know me before a couple days ago," Colm said. "Right?"

"It's complicated." I brushed off the awkward question. "I'm just really glad it turned out okay."

"Noah," Colm said, his voice dropping. His eyes locked in on mine intensely. "Is it true?"

"What?" I asked, confused at the jog in logic of the conversation.

"Sean," Colm said. "Is it true he was murdered? The police were in here earlier."

"What for? You were in a coma when it happened. I'm pretty sure that's the best alibi ever." I glanced at Colm's heart rate monitor. We were climbing into dangerous territory. "Can we talk about this later? I'm going to get kicked out in about thirty seconds."

"It's my fault," Colm said, a blush creeping up his neck.

"What is?" I asked.

"I sort of yelled your name. Earlier." Colm scratched the back of his head, refusing to make eye contact with me. "I tried to play it off, but I don't think they believed me."

I heard the squeak of rubber on laminate, and I knew Ruth was about to bust me for breaking my time limit.

"Did you say anything? I need to know. Now." I glanced behind me nervously.

"What would I have said?" Colm replied, rolling his eyes. "In my several months of comatose sleep, my brain conjured up a girl that actually exists in real life and she's the reason I woke up from this coma. I'd prefer not to be transferred to a mental hospital, thank you."

"So you denied knowing me?" I confirmed. The sneakers squeaked again, and I reached for Colm's hand in desperation.

"I played it off as two different words. You know. No. Ahhh." Colm squeezed my hand.

In real life, his warmth was even more comforting. I kicked myself mentally, scolding my brain for getting distracted.

"Okay, then, slight hiccup because I pretended to be your girlfriend to sneak in here," I muttered.

"You don't look anything like Aileen." Colm's eyes creased in amusement. "Not even remotely."

I pulled my hand from Colm's.

"Pretend not to know me. And pretend you're sleeping right now." I walked back toward the door. "It's safer that way."

"What are you talking about?" Colm was clearly ignoring my request to play asleep.

I waved him down, pleading with my eyes for him to just listen to me.

"I'll explain later," I mouthed at him. I turned to leave the room just as Ruth filled the doorway. She looked past me, a frown creasing her tired face. I turned around to find Colm's eyes shut, stirring just enough to toss his head to the other side of his pillow, obscuring his face.

Probably best. The boy didn't look like he could play a convincing possum to save his life.

"Time's up." Ruth ushered me out into the corridor. "Visiting hours don't even exist here."

"Thanks again," I said. "Just seeing him stir was so relieving."

"Off you go." Ruth escorted me to the elevator. "Back to the dorms. Lockdown is still in effect."

I nodded, letting the elevator doors shut in my face before I sank against the wall. The elevator hummed down automatically to the ground floor, and I took the alone time to rub my face vigorously.

Colm was awake.

Sean was dead.

The Elevated were everywhere, and I was upstream without a paddle.

"Up shit creek," I muttered to myself, waiting patiently for the elevator doors to open.

"I couldn't put it better myself," Mags said, her righteous smile greeting me on the other side of the doors.

She stood blocking the doors. I crossed my arms to mirror her stance, bending slightly to get in her face.

"You know you have to move so I can get off the elevator, right?" I said, wiping the smile off her face.

"The dean's asking for you," Mags bit back, storming off without me. "She doesn't like to be kept waiting."

I stepped off the elevator, sighing to the ceiling in frustration. I followed without another word, hoping if I trailed behind Mags far enough, I could limit her sassy remarks. If she wouldn't see it coming, I would probably have punched her when no one was looking. I thought hard about it as we crossed the courtyard and along the covered walkway leading toward the dean's office, planning to do it right outside the administrative building.

Mags slowed in front of me, twisting to scowl at me. A laugh escaped me, and I shoved past her into the administrative building. The door almost shut in her shocked face, and I smothered my smile as I had the last laugh.

TWENTY-SEVEN

I walked down the hallway, feeling Mags' hot breath on my neck. I shoved my shoulder into the door marked Dean's Office and walked up to the receptionist's desk.

The same woman from my first day sat in the chair, her ear permanently fixed to the phone lighting up on her desk as she transitioned between several lines, placing people on hold.

"You can't go in there," she called desperately as I walked past her. Her hand flapped at me to stop, but she chose to stay tethered to her desk rather than block my way.

My hand was on the doorknob, ready to twist as it opened in front of me.

Suddenly, I was face to face with Ms. Xavier, who raised her eyebrow at me. I looked behind her at the dean and the chief of police, who seemed displeased at my late arrival.

"I handled it," Ms. Xavier said. "Let's go."

Mags finally caught up to me, blocking me in between the receptionist's desk and Ms. Xavier.

"Well, this is kind of awkward." I glanced back at Mags. "I guess they didn't need me after all."

Ms. Xavier waved me back, and I dodged around Mags before she could catch my arm.

"Margaret," the dean called from within her office. "Come here."

Mags scowled at me, bumping me in the shoulder as she obeyed the dean without hesitation.

"Walk," Ms. Xavier said in my ear.

I moved, trying to get as far out of line of sight as was possible in the small reception room. As relieved as I was not to have to talk to the dean, the steel edge to Ms. Xavier's voice told me I wasn't free from rebuke just yet.

We kept up the fast pace in the hallway, and I kept my mouth shut.

"I've convinced them the murder and the coma boy waking up are not only unrelated to each other but unrelated to you," Ms. Xavier said through clenched teeth. "If you go anywhere near that boy again, I can't protect you."

"How did you know I visited Colm?" I asked under my breath, unsure if even mentioning it was against the treaty Ms. Xavier had bartered for on my behalf. "And what do you mean convince?"

"I'm trying to play the long game here, Noah." Ms. Xavier glanced over at me through the sides of her black-framed glasses while neatly dodging my questions. "You're important, but not that important if you can't help stirring up trouble."

"It's not my fault trouble finds me first," I argued. "If I could stay under the radar, believe me, that's exactly where I'd be."

"You have to take some responsibility for your actions," Ms. Xavier said. "You don't exist in a vacuum."

The admonishing words felt weird coming from anyone other than Adele. No other adult had cared enough to tell me to act right. As I watched Ms. Xavier stride across the courtyard, I realized she was probably the same age as Adele, give or take a few years. The same age my mother would be if she were still alive.

I followed Ms. Xavier back into the academic building, climbing the grand staircase carefully so as not to slip on the slick surface. The realization brought my mood down, and I counted the steps up the staircase to myself.

Ig waited for us at the top of the stairs.

"Go back to the office. Keep your head in the books until everything blows over," Ms. Xavier instructed me. "Next slip up, and you're on your own."

I nodded, my feet pointed toward the office.

"And Noah," Ms. Xavier said, making me pause. She looked at me, her head hanging slightly to the side. "The Elevated are given only the amount of power they can handle. The next time you doubt yourself, remember no one else can handle it like you can. You don't get to be perfect overnight."

"Is that the voice of experience?" I asked, curious to unwrap the mystery behind the young teacher. At the very least, I needed to learn her rebuff technique. Whatever her Elevation was, it kept me guessing.

Ms. Xavier laughed.

"If I knew at your age what I know now, let's just say the need to play the long game would be nonexistent," Ms. Xavier replied. "Now go fill Evangeline in before she explodes from curiosity."

I nodded, my feet already halfway to the office before I looked up again.

Evangeline scurried out from the office, hooking my elbow with hers.

"If my range were any better, you'd have a stalker for life. All the drama surrounding you is intense. It's like I'm living a telenovela." Evangeline pulled me into the office. She shoved me down onto my chair, boxing me in. "Spill."

"Wait, what do you mean by drama?" I said. "I was gone for an hour or less."

"The entire campus is buzzing. Particularly the dean's office," Evangeline said. "Normally, that place is a black hole and very annoying to crack into, but the emotions were all over the place today."

"Explain to me again how the Sentient plane works?" I bluffed, taking advantage of Evangeline's flightiness to sate my own curiosity. If I was going to be dishing about my mini adventure away from the confines of the office, I was going to get information in return. Ms. Xavier might be playing the long game, but I was just doing my best to stay in it and not get steamrolled.

"I read waves of consciousness from living things," Evangeline said, the words falling out of her mouth so quickly I had trouble understanding them until after my brain had decoded the individual words. "Mostly emotions, but sometimes thoughts and memories if the person broadcasts loudly enough. Kind of like you. You read like a billboard sign. Big, bright, and very catchy. Anyway, everyone's been having strong feelings wherever you go, even the dean's office which, like I said, is normally very dark and boring. Not today. Also, Colm. Wow. He's got some thoughts and feelings about you."

I reached out to steady Evangeline, worrying her hyper buzz would cause her to pass out from lack of oxygen.

"Whoa, how many cups of coffee did you have while I was gone?" I asked, counting the vending machine cups that filled the waste basket by the door. It was definitely in excess of ten.

"What else was I supposed to do while you were gone? Just sit here and take notes? With all that happening?" Evangeline's nose crinkled distastefully. "Even Ig was out making rounds. It was too quiet around here."

"Well, the lockdown has everyone else sequestered in their dorms. Except Mags," I said, my thoughts turning dark.

"Of course." Evangeline rolled her eyes. "Princess Margaret is always on snitch duty."

"Ms. Xavier mentioned she was the dean's student assistant," I said. "Is that true?"

"Yeah." Evangeline sighed. "She's been the dean's assistant since freshman year. We used to be friends, you know. Mags and I."

Evangeline looked past me, her eyes glazing over momentarily.

"Evangeline?" I waved my hand in front of her face.

She stuttered back to life, her cheeks blazing crimson. "Sorry." She shook the fogginess from her head. "I was too distracted by your drama across campus to put my barriers back in place. Someone took me by surprise."

"Back up." I tried to catch Evangeline's eye again so I knew she was with me. "Barriers?"

"It's the only way I stay somewhat sane," Evangeline replied. "I've had to build more since I first started hearing people. I still don't do well with crowds, but I can pay attention for short periods of time if I'm prepared."

Evangeline grabbed a lock of hair, twisting it idly around her fingers.

"I'm guessing somehow Mags was involved." I

caught the subtle pause in Evangeline's dancing fingertips to prove I was dead on with my leap. "Was that before or after Mags turned into a snitch?"

"Still a little foggy on that myself." Evangeline grabbed at her hand to still the nervous twitch. "All I know is one day we were friends, and the next we weren't. I got sent away after they found out I'd stopped taking my medication."

"And you think Mags sold you out," I continued, picking up the hint Evangeline had laid out for me.

"It had been her idea, too. We were both on some pretty heavy anti-psychotics, and she decided they were blocking our naturally given Elevation. I couldn't handle the constant barrage of feelings and thoughts though, and I got caught." Evangeline shrugged. "When I came back, Mags was the dean's number two and I could still barely handle eating meals in the dining hall with everyone else."

"That's messed up," I said.

Evangeline had sobered from the serious conversation, and I let her shoulders go since she'd stopped bouncing up and down. She slid her back down the wall, resuming her seat from earlier.

"Ms. Xavier was the one who got me practicing my barriers," Evangeline said with a sheepish grin. "She even gave me a metaphysics book that's helped me think of the energy waves in a better way."

"You get a manual? No fair," I joked, scuffing my shoe on the floor.

Evangeline chuckled. "Hang on, I have it if you really want to look at it." She rifled through her book bag and producing a weathered green hardcover.

I took it, dutifully flipping it open and thumbing through a few chapters. The paper was stiff and yellowing, and my fingers caught on the spine and cover where the title was stamped into the cardboard. Snapping it shut, I took one final glance at it before handing it back to Evangeline. At the last moment, I pulled it away, Evangeline's fingers grazing the cover.

"One sec." I ran my finger down the spine. My eyes locked on the bottom, tapping the spine where the publisher had stamped its emblem. I held it back out to Evangeline. "Look familiar?"

The Elevated symbol was stamped at the bottom of Evangeline's beloved metaphysics book.

"No way," Evangeline whispered, pulling the book toward her. "How did I miss that?"

"A bunch of books here have the same mark." I pulled out several to show Evangeline. "See? All different topics. It looks like a run-of-the-mill academic press, but I thought there might be something more."

Evangeline licked her fingers, flicking through her book for the copyright page. She lifted it up to her face, squinting to read the faded ink.

"Compass Rose Books. Boston, Mass.," Evangeline read aloud. "Boston's not very far at all."

"What's the year of publication on that one?" I asked, leafing through several of the nearest symbolled books for dates.

"Nineteen thirty-six." Evangeline let out a low whistle. "It's been a minute."

"All of these were published in the thirties and forties." I stuck my pen in my mouth for safe keeping as I grabbed another handful of books to check the date. "Is the Wi-Fi still down?"

"Let me check." Evangeline fished her phone out from the bottom of her bag. "Oh, would you look at that."

"Back on?"

"Back on."

"Can you find out if Compass Rose is still publishing books? It's a long shot, but we might as well try." I scribbled a note to myself on a spare note card.

"Uh, Noah," Evangeline said, her eyes bugging out behind the soft glow of her phone's screen.

"What?" I sorted the newly cataloged books into a fresh pile.

"Look." Evangeline shoved her phone in front of my face.

The webpage looked old but active. Compass Rose Books was scrawled across the top of the page, along with the Elevated symbol and a P.O. Box address located in Boston.

"Scroll to the bottom," Evangeline instructed, her impatience causing the screen to dance in her hand.

I snatched the phone from her grasp, tapping my finger on the screen to zoom in on the copyright notice on the bottom of the webpage.

"Copyright T.D. Xavier." I glanced up to mirror Evangeline's slack-jawed expression.

"Weird, huh?" Evangeline said densely.

"What was Ms. Xavier's Elevation, did you say?"

"I didn't say." Evangeline frowned. "Why? Does it matter?"

"What's the one she's pretending to have?" I asked more directly. "She's impersonating someone, right?"

"I'm not following." Evangeline squinted at me. "It's like Chinese to me right now."

"What's the opposite of death?" I said. "The opposite on my plane."

"Your balance is Regeneration. Technically, you're Entropy, but I'm following." Evangeline waved me on.

"So someone who has an Elevation in Regeneration does what, exactly?" I asked, my eyes drawn back to the webpage.

"Well, I suppose they would regenerate. I had a great uncle who could cut off a finger and have it grow back, but I always thought my abuela was just scaring me into eating my vegetables...oh my God, you're not serious!" Evangeline finally seemed to link the scattered thoughts in my brain together.

"Dead serious," I replied.

"Har har." Evangeline faked a knee slap. "It's funny because your Elevation is Entropy."

"Would you stop messing around? What happens if the dean finds out Ms. Xavier isn't actually immortal?" I asked. "That could end really, really badly."

"But why would the dean try to kill an immortal?" Evangeline countered. "That doesn't make any sense."

"If she thought Ms. Xavier wasn't an immortal, I'm pretty sure killing her would be on the top of the dean's priority list," I said. "Ms. Xavier must be looking for something in these books she needs to keep the ruse going."

"Like what?" Evangeline asked.

"If we knew that, we wouldn't need to be cataloging books older than your grandmother." I sighed. "I just wish we could narrow it down more easily."

"I wonder what possessed the real T.D. Xavier to publish books with our symbol on them," Evangeline said as she grabbed the marked spines from the piles within her reach. "The metaphysics book helped me a lot with creating barriers, but it's not like a how to guide for Empaths."

I stared at the growing number of books

Evangeline was stacking in front of herself. I crouched down next to it, scanning the various titles.

"Unless they *are* how to guides," I thought aloud.

"Okay, then, where's the how to be a good banshee handbook? It's bound to be in here somewhere," Evangeline said sarcastically, pulling more and more books closer to her. "We've got Shakespearean sonnets, topography for beginners, a history of European folktales, and echolocation in sea mammals."

Evangeline met my gaze as a lightbulb went off in my head.

"That is so cool," she whispered, handing over the zoology text. "It's not even fair."

TWENTY-EIGHT

I waited impatiently in the doorframe of Evangeline's private study carrel as she slowly packed her bag for class.

"We're going to be late if you continue crawling at a glacial pace." I checked my phone for the fifth time since I'd crossed the hall from my own marathon of private study hours.

"I'm savoring the last bit of emotional freedom I have for the next two hours, okay?" Evangeline threw over her shoulder, checking the buckles on her messenger bag for the second time.

"The last time I was this late to Ms. Xavier's class, I got detention," I said. "Can we not repeat the experience, please?"

"Just don't fall asleep." Evangeline shrugged her bag onto her petite shoulder.

"I didn't fall asleep, I blacked out," I muttered. "Are you ready now?"

"Yes, keep your pants on." Evangeline stuck her tongue out at me.

I returned the favor, letting her walk in front of me to set the pace. I forgot how quickly Evangeline could move when she felt like it.

"What would I do without your commentary?" Evangeline quipped. "So insightful."

"If you stayed out of my head like Ms. Xavier told you to, you wouldn't have to listen to it," I replied to her back. "I'm not censoring myself for you. Find a new research partner if you can't handle it."

"Three days in the trenches, and you think you're indispensable." Evangeline shook her head sadly from side to side. "Your ego really has no bounds, does it?"

I snorted, racing Evangeline down the stairs. When I burst through the door first, I pumped my fists in the air.

"Champion!" I faked a triumphant yell at half volume.

"Child," Evangeline muttered, her lip jutting out slightly. "And a cheater. Not fair at all."

I swung my bag around, walking backward so I could face Evangeline.

"You can beat me in our rematch later. It'll give you something to look forward to," I offered.

"I can hardly contain my excitement." A yawn escaped her and ruined her delivery.

I could tell when we were getting closer to the lecture hall by watching her facial expressions flatten out. The smile from moments ago solidified into a grimace, and I fell into step next to her as the steps of the hall rose in front of us.

"Maybe if you imagine everyone in their underwear, it won't be so bad," I suggested, aiming more for comic relief than practical solutions.

"Doesn't take much prodding to see them in their actual underwear," Evangeline said under her breath. "Believe me, I've tried to unsee that, and you just can't."

I covered my mouth with my hand, trying to hide the smile tugging at the corners of my mouth.

Even several days later, with promises from both the dean and the police that the investigation was ongoing for the perpetrator of Sean's attack, the looks I got from my fellow classmates made it clear a verdict had already been handed down in the court of public opinion.

My frog-march in front of the dining hall seemed to be the crowning piece of evidence, with hearsay from nosy onlookers of my tumultuous relationship with Sean (bordering on R-rated) and my alleged checkered past (a rumor of a rumor of a brief stint in juvenile hall) rounding out the obvious fact that I'd killed my classmate and seduced the chief of police into letting me off the hook.

Just hearing the rumors of my busy alter ego made me tired.

I glanced around, finding several underclassmen whispering at the base of the stairs. A small crowd had gathered, waiting for the doors to open for admission into Ms. Xavier's lecture. Without the between-class entertainment of Mags vs. Aileen, the students were growing restless as I stood patiently waiting at Evangeline's side.

A buzz began soon after we entered, but I ignored it. It was only after Evangeline nudged me purposefully that I pulled my head up from my idle inspection of my high top tennis shoes and looked out into the crowd. Aileen strode forward, leading a small mob of students behind her. I squinted at them, curious to find so many students coordinated enough to be this early to class.

This could not be a good thing.

Aileen stopped in front of me and signaled the rest of the gaggle of teenagers to stop.

"You," Aileen spat at me, "are not welcome here."

I looked around, wondering if Aileen had been speaking to someone else.

"Excuse me." I stepped forward to hide Evangeline partially behind my back. Whatever animosity was fueling the crowd, I was worried the focus would be redirected at her. Instinctively, I acted as a human buffer for Aileen's stupidity.

"I said, you need to leave." Aileen drew herself up to her full height. Even then, I still bent my head down to look at her.

"No, I need to go to class," I replied. "I don't know about you, but I actually care about things such as attendance and grades. Once I have my diploma, I will be more than happy to move on to greener pastures."

I glanced back, noting the door was still shut tight. Sighing, I turned back toward Aileen, whose face had inflated to a nice cherry red.

"I refuse to sit next to a murderer in class!" Aileen stomped her foot in indignation.

My eyebrow rose in mild amusement. "Me too, but until the police have brought Sean's attacker to justice, I guess we're all going to have to suffer," I said. I leaned in conspiratorially, stage whispering to Aileen. "Some of us will have to suffer more than others."

"As if playing around with Sean wasn't enough," Aileen growled, her rage spreading down her neck and ears, "you have to go around messing with my boyfriend, too. I won't let you ruin another life just so you can have your fun and spit him back out. He's a person, not a trophy."

My expression went blank.

"I'm not following," I said mildly. "Did you just accuse me of stealing your boyfriend? I didn't even know you had one."

Aileen was seething.

"Colm is off limits." Aileen's voice wavered with bravado. "You come near him again, and I'll make sure the charges stick this time."

"Listen, I think there's been a misunderstanding," I said. "I'm not stealing your boyfriend. I don't even know who you're talking about."

"Only the most handsome junior at Windermere," Honore said, her arms crossed across her chest.

"Star quarterback. Tragic accident. Was in a coma," Grace sneered, mirroring her sister's defensive stance.

"Until some little harlot went all Sleeping Beauty on him." Honore glanced knowingly back at Grace.

"Right after she went Maleficent on guitar boy," she reminded Honore. They shivered in disgust, fueling the rage leaking out of Aileen's every pore.

"You all need hobbies that don't include manufacturing gossip from rumors you also created yourself." I shook my head sadly. "And do yourselves a favor by picking up a book or twenty. Your plot could use some help."

The buzz of the horde flanking Aileen rose, and alarm bells rang in the back of my mind.

They didn't seem bold enough to actually do anything, but you should never underestimate the mob mentality. Just as I was debating making a run for the classroom door, the mob parted to reveal the man of the hour himself.

More than one jaw dropped as Colm walked through the tunnel of students, his bag slung loosely over his shoulders. He stopped beside Aileen, pausing to take in the ridiculous scene in its entirety.

He frowned at the crowd of students who had pressed in tightly to get a better look at the drama being played out in real time.

"What's going on? Has class been cancelled?" Colm looked around hopefully, seeing the door behind us shut.

"I wish it were that eventful." I sighed, drawing the heated gaze of Aileen again.

She latched onto his arm, and he took a step back to brace himself. A smile pulled at the corners of my mouth when he stiffened noticeably against the unwanted attention.

"I was just telling this stalker to leave you alone," Aileen cooed up at Colm.

His eyes darted to mine. "Who?"

Even though I'd been the one to tell him to pretend he didn't know me, the punch to my gut at his feigned ignorance still took me by surprise. I bit the inside of my cheek, hard.

"That's the girl who pretended to be me to visit you," Aileen snarled, hugging onto Colm tightly.

"Ah, that," I said, finally pretending to understand Aileen's earlier barbs. "The nurses just kind of shoved me in his room, thinking I was his girlfriend. I was actually looking for Evangeline. She had a little bit of a setback, what with the police and the dining hall and everything. A bit overwhelming."

Aileen sniffed at my excuse. My eyes slid to Colm's.

"Sorry, I didn't realize there had been a misunderstanding." I kept his blue eyes locked into mine. "I meant no trouble."

"I was asleep anyway." Colm shrugged. "It's not a big deal."

"It won't happen again," I assured him. "I'm glad you're awake though. Everyone seemed really worried about you."

"Thanks." Colm held back a sad smile. "Sorry to hear about Sean. I heard he was a friend of yours."

"Yeah, it's a shame," I said. "He was one of the few decent people here."

Aileen scoffed at me, her eyes moony over Colm.

"Yeah, and a good judge of character," Colm said, ignoring his clingy girlfriend. "If you passed his test, you're good in my book."

"Colm." Aileen bristled at his remark. "She's the one who killed him."

"Doubtful." Colm looked me over. "She has a lot of bark, but I'm not sure she has the heart to bite."

Finally, the door to the lecture hall flung open, and the students drifted toward the opening, streaking past us to get a decent seat. In the melee, I lost sight of Aileen and her twin minions as they fought to get to class on time. The warning bell tolled, and Evangeline and I were left to bring up the rear of the students.

A flash of blue caught my eyes, and Colm's face stared back at me from the bustle of students filing into rows. I smiled at him, and he smiled back before Aileen tugged him into his seat.

I turned to close the door behind me, pausing only briefly to find Evangeline making fake gagging noises in disgust.

Get a room, Evangeline's voice tinkled in my ears. I looked over at her grey-faced exterior and let it slide, focusing on the beginning of Ms. Xavier's lecture instead.

TWENTY-NINE

"Walk me through it again." Evangeline pinched the bridge of her nose tightly between her forefingers.

I glanced around, worried our conversation could be overheard through the glass of the private study carrel. Evangeline followed my gaze, picking up on my concern.

"There's no one here," Evangeline said for the third time, letting a sigh escape in her frustration. "They're all in class. Where you should be, technically."

"I was excused from the midterm since I started last week." I waved the excuse off. "Pay attention."

"I'm trying, but you're not doing a good enough job convincing yourself. I'm getting conflicting commentary on your hypothesis," Evangeline grumbled.

"Listen, all I'm saying is that the recent series of events makes it clearer than ever the Elevated community is fracturing apart," I repeated. "You said yourself that no one keeps records of Elevated people or Elevated-related people. While that may have been true in the past, that didn't stop T.D. Xavier from publishing books to help Elevated people. This was back, what, three or four generations ago?"

"I'm following," Evangeline chanted, keeping her eyes closed.

"Back in those days, Elevated people who weren't born into the great families had no idea what they had. Naturally, those generations would seek each other out in an attempt to unite the community and share their knowledge with one another," I continued.

"Still following," Evangeline said.

"The community grew too constrictive, even to the point of discarding some within the Elevated community. Again, the pendulum swings back, and this generation is fracturing apart again, trying to gain autonomy from the community trying to keep everyone together," I concluded.

"Not following," Evangeline said. "Where are the golden years? The ones when everyone gets along and grows and learns and loves?"

"We're talking about human nature here, not a Saturday morning cartoon," I said. "It's like a rebellion. The first rebellion was connecting everyone even though the previous generation thought it was a bad idea. The second rebellion is breaking apart the community the older generation thinks is necessary for survival."

"Wouldn't it be nice if everyone could get along though?" Evangeline asked, rubbing her eyes savagely. "Share information so everyone has it. They can learn or not based on their own abilities, and everyone benefits from Elevated people having control over their respective powers."

"You're assuming everyone has the same size slice from the pie of Elevated abilities," I countered. "You yourself have a bias against certain planes because of the assumption that their powers are not as vast or useful as yours."

"I never said that," Evangeline said.

"But you're thinking it," I replied. "Just like when everyone was fighting over me as soon as I got on campus because I'm on the Vitality plane. Do you think I would have gotten the red carpet treatment if I were on the Relativity plane?"

"I don't know. Teleporting could be damn useful," Evangeline muttered. "Or going back in time so I could take a nap. Also, very useful."

"I doubt that's how time travel works," I said seriously.

"Then they're doing it wrong," Evangeline said. "Or the least they could do would be research the different branches of the Elevated family trees. I'm dying to know who I get to blame for these lovely impressions."

"Didn't you say that the type of Elevation wasn't genetic? Just if you're a carrier?" I leafed back through my notes.

"Not usually, but some families have a natural affinity for certain planes. Mags used to brag that not a single person in her family ever strayed from the Temporal plane. Used to think that was cool," Evangeline muttered to herself. "At least before she went batshit crazy."

"Just because she's crazy doesn't mean she's wrong." I turned over page after page of notes until I found the note I'd been looking for. "Here, it says even carriers of the Elevated senses don't always manifest in full form. They can carry it on to their children, though, so it's possible to have two carriers birth a fully Elevated child."

"What's the point of this biology lesson again?" Evangeline rested her head on her pile of textbooks.

"We've been talking about it for so long, I've forgotten."

"My point is that even if you take the main families into consideration, there are still too many possibilities of Elevated kids being born into non-Elevated households. If enough generations snowball their energies together, you could ultimately have a super powerful, completely untrained Elevated person," I said.

"Or, conversely, a bunch of duds who will eventually push the Elevated lines into extinction by not breeding with other Elevated people to make Elevated babies," Evangeline said through a yawn. "It's a toss-up."

"I don't think the energy would just dissipate the weaker it got." I frowned at my notes. "Where's that physics book I had?"

"Oh, God, not the physics book," Evangeline howled. "I passed all my science classes early so I wouldn't have to deal with this."

"Hush." I waved my handful of notes at Evangeline's ruckus. "What's the rule about energy not being able to be destroyed, only transferred?"

"Conservation of energy." A sigh escaped her huddled mass. "I hate myself for knowing the answer."

"Five points for you," I replied.

"Yay," Evangeline said weakly into her notebook. "I'm a winner!"

"Something like that," I said under my breath.

"So your big grand point is that we need to track all the Elevated people back in time, cross reference all their baby making for generations to find possible Elevated kids who have no idea they're special little snowflakes caught in the middle of a family feud they never knew existed." Evangeline propped her head up on her hands.

"And warning them not to drink the Kool-Aid," I finished. "Essentially."

"Can I take a nap first?" Evangeline asked seriously. "That sounds like a lot of work."

"Why are you so tired? Didn't you have more coffee for lunch than actual food?" I asked, not understanding people's intense need for naps.

"Why are you so loud?" Evangeline said. "Just give me five minutes."

"Are you feeling okay?" I asked, sticking my hand out to feel Evangeline's forehead. "Maybe I should take you to the infirmary." Heat leaked from Evangeline's forehead, and I immediately thought low-grade fever.

"I don't get sick," Evangeline mumbled.

"Then why is your forehead hot enough to fry an egg on?" I reached into my bag for my stash of ibuprofen. "Humor me and take this. If you seem fine, I won't haul you to the infirmary for no reason."

"Just sleepy." A worry line creased her forehead.

"You didn't even pass your own lie detector test." I cracked open a fresh bottle of water and held out the ibuprofen. "Your body is literally rejecting its own lie. Drink up."

"Can't," Evangeline said. "Gotta sleep."

I stood up, crossing over to the opposite side of the table. I propped Evangeline upright, hoping she'd be awake enough to drink some water, but her head lolled to the side.

A bolt of panic shot down my spine.

"Evangeline!" I grabbed her face in my hand. "Can you hear me?"

"So loud," she muttered, her eyes rolling upward into her head.

"Stay with me, Evie," I said softly, hauling her petite frame into my arms.

My back hit the doorframe hard as I tried not to pin Evangeline's legs in my hurry to get into the hall. I winced but kept my focus on Evangeline. Her eyes rolled back in her head, but every other second, she kept coming to, as if she was beating whatever fever she was fighting, only to lose her grip on consciousness again.

A hiss of frustration leaked from Evangeline's mouth, and I frowned down at her, softening my footfalls in fear of jostling her too much. I looked around in the library, finding it eerily quiet once again. I couldn't see anyone, but the itch of eyes on me told a different story. The hairs on the back of my neck and forearms confirmed something amiss. I blinked my own eyes hard in quick succession. What was I missing?

As I neared the top of the stairs, I wondered if I should throw Evangeline over my shoulder in a fireman's carry or if my biceps would hold up the two stories down and across the courtyard. Regardless, I had to set Evangeline down to open the door. She crumpled forward like a doll, but I managed to catch her head before she smacked it against the floor.

My focus turned to the door, which was not cooperating as a fire escape door should. I jostled it hard, willing it to open. I traced the outline of the bar, trying to find the reason for it remaining locked. Just as I was about to weigh the option of breaking one of the fancy glass windows, Evangeline came to life beside me.

Her ragged inhalation spooked me, making me jump back in surprise.

When she was fully upright, a growl escaped her clenched teeth.

"Adair!" Evangeline hollered down the empty corridor.

My eyes darted behind me, waiting for him to walk around the end of a stack of books.

Evangeline let out a horrible scream.

THIRTY

"Coward!" Evangeline shrieked.

I crouched down beside her, placing my hand protectively on her rising shoulder. Her breathing was sporadic, as if she had just sprinted down the corridor instead of being carried by yours truly. A wild glint hardened her eyes, and any words I thought to say hardened in my throat. I could feel her anger shooting off her in tendrils of energy. The strength of it kept the hairs on my neck on end.

I wanted to wait to be sure she was back to normal, but she stumbled upright, lurching her shoulder out from underneath my hand. Her eyes bounced around the hallway in search of a ghost.

"Evie," I said quietly, not wanting to spook her. "What happened?"

"His party tricks have gotten better, I'll give him that," Evangeline muttered darkly. "I wonder how long he was in range."

"I thought you said no one was in the library?" I asked, biting the inside of my cheek immediately.

Evangeline's burning eyes swung to mine. "No one I could sense," she said, crossing her arms. "But I guess shields can work both ways. The audacity though.

A rude snort escaped Evangeline, and I couldn't help but smile. Somehow seeing her doll-like features creased in anger made it all the funnier.

Her dark doe eyes swung to meet mine again. I tried to stifle my smile but failed.

"I can hear you," Evangeline said, tapping her temple knowingly. "And as Adair knows, you don't want to get me angry. That's why he bolted."

"Are you sure?" I said. "He duped you once before."

"Yes, well, he's a little worse for wear since I sent him packing. I've been learning a few tricks myself," Evangeline said. "He should have practiced more on someone who couldn't see him coming."

"Did you see him coming?" I asked, leaning against the doorframe, now having no reason to rush through it.

"As soon as he was fully in my head, I caught him right away. I didn't notice him lulling me to sleep. It's not uncommon for me to nap around this time of day anyway." Evangeline shrugged. "Plus, it takes a lot more effort to pull someone below consciousness who isn't helping. Adair's powers work much better on those already under."

"So now that he's failed to pull you under, what's his next play?" I asked, watching Evangeline pace slowly in front of me.

"He's a lot better at shielding than I was expecting." She twisted a lock of hair around her finger. "I wasn't able to figure out quite why he was pulling me under, just something about him proving himself to someone. He seemed a little put out that he couldn't get you under."

"I don't sleep." I shrugged.

Evangeline paused in her pacing. "What?"

"I don't sleep," I repeated. "You said it yourself. You can tell I'm not conscious, but also not unconscious."

"Yeah, you turn murky." Evangeline twisted another strand of hair on another finger.

"So, if he can barely pull a fully awake person into unconsciousness, then he definitely bit off more than he could chew with me," I said. "Although I don't know why anyone would want to put me to sleep in the middle of the day. That in itself is super creepy."

"Agreed," Evangeline said, a shiver rippling through her entire body. "Dreamwalkers have always given me the heebie jeebies."

"I'm sure I'd be more worried if I weren't immune," I said, finally thankful my rotten sleeping arrangement finally had some sort of pay off.

"Oh, I don't think you're immune. Adair just hasn't cracked the code on you quite yet." Evangeline halted her pacing. "And if he's already been able to learn to shield since the fallout with Mags..."

She paled.

"What fallout with Mags? Did they have a fight?" I said. "They seemed quite close."

"No, my fallout with Mags. It was the beginning of winter term, last year," Evangeline said, her feet dragging slowly back toward the glass cubicle.

I trailed behind, not wanting to interrupt with the questions shooting out like fireworks in my brain. "We had been close friends for a while. I had some family issues that pulled me away from school quite a bit. Set me off more and more frequently, which snowballed into more and more frequent trips to the school psychologist. If missing school wasn't bad enough, the cocktail of antipsychotics kept me fuzzy at best. Mags thought I was weighing her down, so she cut me loose."

"That's a shitty thing for a friend to do when you were in a tough spot," I said, unable to hold my tongue. "So you were replaced by Adair?"

"Apparently." Evangeline sighed. "Mags always prefers someone a little lacking in her beta spot. I outgrew it, and I'm thinking Adair will outgrow her soon, too. I have a very bad feeling Adair wasn't showing his full hand."

Our feet stalled at the doorway of our cubicle.

"Or maybe he just did," Evangeline said, her jaw hanging slack.

Where there had been piles upon piles of books, notecards, and a nest of loose leaf papers, there was now an excellent view of the glossy shellacked cherry table, completely unmarred by any trace of the research we had been working so diligently on for over a week.

"I feel like I've been shot," I said, my hand on the ball of ice in my stomach. I was even starting to lose feeling in my fingers and toes. All of our hard work. Gone.

Evangeline walked slowly around the room, her eyes searching for any scrap of paper that might have been missed. She rifled through her bag on the floor, muttering to herself.

"Even took my sketchbook, the animals," I heard her growl into the depths of her bag.

I walked over to my bag.

"Of course." I sighed. "My composition notebook is gone, too. I'm not sure what they want with my attempts at songwriting, but it's a bit much."

"Oh," Evangeline said, mixing around the remnants of her personal artifacts carelessly. "Oh, not good."

"What?" I asked.

"I, uh, had another project I was working on." Evangeline cleared her throat. "That's gone, too."

"What do they want with your schoolwork? That seems excessive." I tossed the flap of my satchel back into place.

"No, not schoolwork. Banshee work," Evangeline said, her face contorting in guilt.

"Excuse me?"

"I had an impressions notebook for you specifically. Helps get all the details out," Evangeline said, her hands shaking wildly around her head. "But your impressions were a little too detailed. It was more like explicit words and screenshots compared to the waves of emotions I typically get. Especially about your banshee powers. And your dreamscape."

"And Colm." I kicked my chair violently.

Evangeline winced.

"How explicit are we talking?" I asked, gripping the high back of the chair to keep my energy focused there instead of denting the matching leg of the table.

"I know it well enough to be familiar with several of your night visitors, as you call them. I know you're by yourself when you're there and that you can't help getting pulled into it during certain times of the day," Evangeline said. Tendrils of dark hair snaked through her shaking fingertips.

"So you know enough to know what my weaknesses are, when they turn up, and my complete lack of control in changing any of them." My throat grew hot in anger. I shook my head. Now was not the time.

"And now they know, too," Evangeline said, finishing my thought out loud. Her hand flexed nervously.

"Do you know where Adair is now? I have a hard time believing he ghosted away with all those books and papers on his own," I growled.

"Oh, a novice on the Relative plane could have transported everything in ten seconds or less." Evangeline shrugged. "Let me see if he's gotten his shield back in place or not. It took a beating when I fought back."

Evangeline looked off in the distance. Anyone else would have thought she was lost in thought, but I knew enough now to know how far her range was in picking up emotions. Her zoned out concentration wasn't as irksome as Mags' had been, but seeing Evangeline retreat back into herself made me uncomfortable. She looked like a lobotomy victim.

"It'll go faster if you're quiet," Evangeline said, spooking me.

"Sorry," I muttered out loud, forgetting for a moment she meant the white noise of my thoughts.

"He's across the quad. Infirmary," Evangeline said, a line creasing her forehead. "He's shielded himself, but others are noticing him and pinging him like a wireless signal."

"What's he doing in the...goddammit!" I grabbed my bag as I sprinted out of the door.

Colm was let out for class and mealtimes but kept a room in the infirmary for overnight observation. The nurses were still uncertain at his miraculous recovery, preferring to keep on the cautious path rather than let him back in the dorms.

I yanked my phone from my back pocket, checking the time. The bells tolled the end of class as soon as my foot hit the stairs. As I rocketed down the cramped switchback, I hoped against hope that Aileen was dragging Colm down like an anchor. Keep him slow. Give me time to get there ahead of him to weed out the bump in the night before any lasting damage was done.

My shoulder caught on the doorframe, sending me reeling and throwing my balance off kilter. It slowed me down enough to propel my upper body forward too much, leaving my toes to catch on the cobblestones at my feet. I went down hard.

Eyes darted in my direction. Even a few laughs echoed around the courtyard at my expense. The crowd was growing denser with more students flowing from the building. I was up again before I could waste any more time. My hands stung, bouncing off blazers in an attempt to weave my way through the crowd. I didn't think I would make it in time.

I gasped when I broke through the final wall of bodies. The stairs in front of me were clear of any obstructions. What student wanted to go to the infirmary during free period? The hiss of the door cut through the empty space, warring for attention against the blood pumping through my head.

The elevator was stuck on the third floor, and I couldn't wait.

I flew up the stairs, finding myself in the same hallway I had a week ago. The déjà vu felt strong, and a growing sense of dread weighed me down as I marched toward Colm's room. A shadow passed over the vacant nurse's station, and my gut clenched.

Colm walked around the corner, his head down. The earbuds hung in stark contrast to his newly pressed blazer. He was alone. No Aileen. No Adair.

I released a sigh of relief. I had been worried for

nothing. I slowed my pace to match his, not wanting to fly at him and spook him. He would get to his room well before me. I could knock, pretending I hadn't been behind him the whole time. I could pretend to be there innocently and not to safeguard him against another Elevated person who saw him as a chess piece instead of a person.

Well, he was still a chess piece to me, but at least I cared enough to try to keep him out of it, if possible.

Colm didn't look up as he ducked into his room, and I began to count to ten before making my entrance.

Before I could even reach five, Colm's body keeled backward into the hall, his head hitting the linoleum with a sickening crunch.

"No!" I screamed, crashing to the ground next to Colm's lifeless limbs.

I pulled his head back slightly, checking for blood. My fingers came away clean, and I could tell a bump would be forming shortly. Luckily, Colm seemed otherwise unharmed from his fight with gravity.

My eyes slid to Colm's room, ready to give Adair a piece of my mind.

But the room was empty. Even the monitors in the background were black and lifeless.

You need to get out of there, a voice said in my head.

"He needs help," I whispered, glancing around the hallway for an answer to my not-so-silent prayer.

My eyes caught on an alarm box on the wall. I flipped the plastic casing up, pressing my palm on the button. Lights and horns blared to life, casting shadows in the hallway in between flashes of light. A door slammed, and I could hear sneakered feet smacking the floor at a run.

I walked backward, sending a volley of apologies toward Colm's eerily still body. The door to the stairwell hissed as it shut me away from the chaos. I kept my fingers braced on the bar, leaving enough room for one eye to peek through the crack unnoticed.

The nurses huddled around Colm, checking his vitals while assessing his injuries. They kept moving. He was still alive.

For now, the voice said. *At least for now*.

THIRTY-ONE

My fingertips clawed at the thin skin of my temples. The pressure was comforting, especially as a headache blossomed in my skull. I pressed my forehead against the cool metal of the stairwell door. The squawking of the alarm had been silenced, and any noise from Colm's room was too soft to pass the barrier of steel that hid me from the rest of the infirmary.

It's not your fault, Evangeline said in my head. A wave of sympathy pushed the headache to the corners of my mind temporarily, but the emotion felt slippery and fake. I had never felt that emotion so strongly before, and I wasn't really feeling it now. The feeling dissolved, and my mind fell back into analysis.

"If I'd been a little faster," I muttered against the door. "Or if I'd seen the move ahead of time. I could have done something."

He's safe with the nurses. Without Adair's special attentions, Colm will probably wake up soon. Trust me, Evangeline said. I could feel her desperation through the connection, and it was hard to believe she wasn't standing right next to me in the stairwell.

"I need to see him," I said. I pushed off from the door, slipping down the stairs as quickly and quietly as I could. No one knew I was here, and I would do my best to avoid any witnesses. I didn't need any added Aileen drama about sneaking in on her boyfriend again. Campus was still buzzing about my alleged involvement with Sean's death, even though the police presence on campus had dwindled back to pre-banshee levels. The rumor mill was stuck cycling between calls for my immediate arrest for the murder and gossip about whether my connection with Colm was friendly or a little too friendly. The storylines I'd overheard in the dining hall had better plots than most cable TV movies.

A question mark pinged in my mind, but I brushed it aside. Evangeline could wait to see about my plan, or she could pull the spoiler from the rapid thought web I was building for my next plan. As much as she claimed she was no mind reader, her impressions of thoughts I'd barely realized had been eerily accurate so far. Having Evangeline on my side against Adair, Mags, and what seemed like the entire Elevated community was a huge comfort. When Evangeline wasn't curled in the fetal position from an emotional overload, her Elevated abilities leveled the playing field. At least I hoped they did.

Going on the offensive required more attention to detail, so I thought of all the minutiae that had been gathering slowly in the recesses of my brain from my first moment on campus. I needed to be ready for every possible game plan.

The emergency exit door creaked as I opened it slightly. The exit dumped me into a side alleyway between looming brick academic buildings. Behind me led the way to the staff parking lot and a series of dumpsters.

My fingers trailed along the wall as my eyes darted toward the quad. The opening was sporadically overshadowed with passing students, and I had to hug the wall to remain unseen. I would have felt like a spy had the rough teeth of the brick wall not pilled my entire outfit into a large piece of velcro. The jagged stones opened up the scratches on my palms again, and the stinging of the open cuts pulled my focus back to task.

All clear, Evangeline hummed in my mind.

Without hesitation, I darted into the open courtyard, dashing across the quad and back toward the library before anyone noticed. For once, I didn't feel any eyes on my back as I ducked into the library and back up the stairs.

As I took them two by two, I realized the lightness of my bag. I had been carrying around several books lately, and their absence and the absence of my poorly penned melodies soured my mood considerably. One by one, everything I'd touched at Windermere was trickling through my fingertips.

Adele.

Mags.

Sean.

Colm.

I stopped short of entering Evangeline's assigned study room, finding it oddly empty. My head whipped around, searching for the slight dark-haired library gremlin who didn't get enough sun.

Har har har, Evangeline said in my head. Even her tone was dry. Her thought pushing was getting eerily realistic.

Why, thank you, Evangeline said, this time in her normal tone. *I'm filling in Ms. Xavier on our missing research. I'll be back shortly. Like you said,*

I'm only allowed to leave my dungeon for meal breaks and national holidays.

I scowled into the empty room, feeling stupid for worrying for no reason. Of course nothing had happened to Evangeline in the fifteen minutes I'd left her alone. Adair might be devious, but he only had his two legs to stand on. He couldn't be everyone's boogeyman at the same time.

The library felt as empty as it had before the massive plunder of research only minutes ago. No eyes seemed to be following me, but I still felt on edge. I walked past vacant stacks and empty tables, finding no apparent reason for my unease.

My feet took me to Winter automatically. If I had to start over, I knew where a plethora of new research materials was waiting. I crouched down, finding the old skeleton key tucked inside the tongue of my lone remaining pair of shoes. I patted myself on the back for not keeping the key in my bag, wondering if the pillager would have recognized it and stolen it along with my detailed, cross-referenced notes.

I slipped inside the old study before I lost my chance at anonymity. There was something highly satisfying about having a place completely to yourself. This wasn't some underrated French bistro in the commerce district. It was a literal treasure trove of forgotten Elevated knowledge.

The marked books still hung slightly suspended in the air from my first pass at the wall of shelves. The glint of foil waved to me from several spines, and I dropped my bag on the overstuffed couch to explore the shelves once more. The afternoon light fell on the bookcases differently today, and I zoned in on the odd infrequency of the foiled spines.

Evangeline and I had noticed the Elevated books were mainly printed between 1930 and 1950. The yellowing of the paper and the typeset was consistent, but the foil embossed covers caught my eye. Some glinted gold, seemingly never touched. Others had a more mottled look, as if the metal had tarnished over the years. Had those books been handled more? Or had they been stored poorly up until now?

My fingers ran down the spines, leaving the staggered books in place as I sorted through the multitude of possibilities. Amid all the details, I wanted to find a common thread. I just hoped it was relevant. I did not have time to waste on a fool's errand. Not right now, anyway.

A syncopated flutter of footsteps erupted down the curved hallway on the other side of the door. My fingers froze on a volume of Gorsky's *Theorem of Refraction in Echolocation* as a pair of voices joined the thundering footfalls. I held my breath, cringing at the thought of every sound in the private study echoing back out into the hallway and giving me away. But based on the argument erupting outside my door, no sound I made would even register.

"What did I tell you about drawing attention to yourself?" Mags scolded loudly. The reception was so clear, I flinched, imagining her standing immediately next to me.

"I handled it," Adair replied, his indifferent tone receiving a derisive snort from Mags.

"Yeah, at what cost? If you keep pushing her, she'll start pushing back," Mags growled. "She knows it's you. She won't trust you anymore."

"You're naive if you thought your approach would work," Adair said. "I had to do what I could. We're running out of time."

"It takes time to gain a person's trust," Mags said, her words choked. I could imagine her clenched teeth through the door. "Not everyone can be tortured into submission."

"I merely suggest possible outcomes to a subconscious mind. What they do with that information once they're awake is completely out of my control," Adair said. I could clearly hear the arrogance in his voice through the wall. Adair seemed to be believing his own lie.

"Your suggestions have an odd habit of emotionally damaging your victims," Mags shot back. "And who has to clean it up then?"

"Careful, Mags," Adair said. "Your inferiority complex is showing."

"I am not inferior because I don't throw my weight around like a petulant grizzly bear," Mags said. "Your brashness could damage the outcome of all the effort the Association has put in here at Windermere. Do you even know what it takes to corral this many Elevated kids into one place? How many years they've been waiting to bring everyone together?"

"If you want results, you have to take action," Adair said. "They wanted results. I took action. The details are irrelevant."

"The details include the daughter of the most powerful lawyer in New England and the youngest Deputy Chancellor in the history of the Association," Mags said. "The ramifications of not bringing her in could jeopardize the entire future of the Association. Do you really want a banshee to join the ranks of the unfaithful?"

"If you want Noah to join the team, by all means, bake her some cookies and roll out the welcome mat," Adair said. "One mention of her precious father, and she'll be too curious to say no. I'm just paving the way to make sure the answer she gives will be a no-brainer. There can be no distractions."

"Those distractions will point her in the opposite direction," Mags said. "I've seen it."

"Your range is lacking," Adair dismissed. "The only thing you can be sure of is tomorrow's weather."

I heard a strangled growl leak through the door. Silence followed, and the realization that Adair's words had struck true left me stunned.

"I have work to do," Adair said, a pair of footsteps walking further down the hall.

"You're wrong, Adair," Mags called down the hallway. Her voice shook with anger. "This is the beginning of the end."

THIRTY-TWO

Mags stormed off shortly after, and I felt the reverberations of another private room's thick door shut forcefully. I stuck my ear into a gap between the pulled-out books on the shelves to listen to the maple leaf room, Autumn. Muffled ambient noise echoed back, and I could tell someone was moving around. Apparently Mags and I were neighbors in more than one way.

Maybe it was because Adair was high on my shit list, but I felt a pang of sympathy for Mags. Being called out so bluntly for her lack of mastery on her Elevation by an alleged friend dug deeper than a passing comment from just about anyone else. I had clearly overestimated their friendship if Adair was so ready to toss Mags out as collateral damage in his misguided attempt to get to me.

My thumbnail pulled against the top line of my teeth as I unpacked the fight I'd just overheard.

As Evangeline had predicted, the recruitment game Mags was playing was not going well. I was intrigued they thought Adair could do a better job, but in the end, he would also fail miserably. If I hadn't been resolved before, the past ten minutes had me locked in to my decision. I was not going to join the rank of puppets, Elevated or otherwise. Aileen and Mags both had it wrong.

I would always go my own way.

My pocket buzzed. The sudden noise caused me to jam my finger hard into my nose as it slipped from its worrying spot. I cursed as the stinging sensation caused my eyes to water.

The formidable banshee, ladies and gentlemen. Skilled at predicting death and punching herself in the face simultaneously.

Adele's face popped up on my screen when I answered the video chat.

"Are you crying?" Adele asked, her face slack with shock.

"No," I moaned miserably, wiggling my nose and checking my fingertips for any traces of blood.

"Why are you crying?" Adele asked. "I didn't even know your tear ducts worked."

"I cry all the time when I sing," I said, rubbing the odd sensation from my nose. "Why are you calling?"

"I haven't heard from you in a few days. Not a single complaint or SOS," Adele said, waving her smart phone at me through her web cam. "I was taking bets on whether you were dead or kidnapped."

"Oh, I've been kidnapped a few times," I said, tucking my arms against my chest to prop up the phone more comfortably. "Got waterboarded. Not as relaxing as I anticipated."

"Oh, well, that's nice," Adele said, tucking her feet beneath her on her stool. "Any friends join in on the fun with you?"

"It's cute you think I have friends," I said.

Adele stuck out her tongue, and I returned the sentiment.

"Based on the phone calls I've been getting from administration, I figured you had at least one. Well, two," Adele said, pausing. Her grimace said it all.

"It wasn't my fault," I muttered quietly.

Adele sighed. "Anyway, everything's been taken care of. Unless you've managed to commit another felony since the last phone call I got." Adele's head craned expectantly toward the screen.

"What happened to innocent until proven guilty?" I shifted my weight against the couch back to relieve my sleeping foot. "And last time I checked, being a witness was not cause for indictment."

"How's the court of public opinion?" Adele rested her head on her knee. "Do I have to make a call? I hear parents have a lot more clout in private schools."

"You have to donate a lot a money if you want clout," I said. "And the court of public opinion is as useless as ever. There was a boy who got into an accident last semester. He'd been in a coma and just woke up. Luckily, he's drawn a lot of the attention from me."

I blushed slightly, not wanting to tell Adele he might be back in the coma as we spoke. Evangeline had promised he would be fine, but I would feel solely responsible if he slipped back under after Adair's visit.

"A boy?" Her eyes glinted with excitement.

"No," I said sternly. "Not like that. Factually, he is a boy. The end."

"Is one of the rumors that you're a boyfriend stealer?" Adele asked, her back stiff in anticipation. "How much girl drama is there? Like, cable TV movie level?"

"You are way too excited that I could be embroiled in a love triangle with a formerly comatose football player and the head cheerleader," I said dryly, my eyes sliding to the bookcase. I bit my lip. Could Mags hear my conversation through the wall?

"Is that what happened?" Adele squealed. "Let me get my popcorn. You need to start from the beginning."

"Hey," I said, dropping my voice. "I have to study. I'll fill you in later."

I winced slightly at the lie. It was my least favorite thing to do to Adele, but I didn't want to worry her with the truth.

"We are continuing this conversation later." Adele pointed her finger sternly at my screen. "You're not getting off the hook that easily."

"Oh, I know." A smile died on my lips. "I'll catch you up on everything soon. I promise."

"All right, go be brilliant," Adele said. "Have fun. Golden years and all that."

"Yeah, okay," I said, disconnecting the video chat. My face frowned back at me from the dim screen. I put my phone away, scowling at the time.

It had been too long since I'd heard from Evangeline. Errand or otherwise, the radio silence made me worry. She usually dropped in mentally after I thought about her. I wondered if it worked like someone calling out your name in real life.

Still nothing.

Evangeline didn't have a cell phone. Without knowing exactly where she was, which was usually in the library anyway, I had no way of contacting her. Today was not a good day to go missing.

I stood upright from the couch, suddenly convinced something horrible had happened. I marched to the door, pausing only to listen if anyone was in the hall. No sound bounced back, so I reached for the doorknob.

My hand flared with pain, and I pulled it into my chest reflexively. Cradling it, I could see the pink where the heat had seared my hand. Glaring at the handle, I approached it slowly. My hand hovered above the surface, but I couldn't feel any heat. I tried again, and the same pain flared.

I let a stream of curses fall out of my mouth, trying to shake the stabbing sensation that lit up my hand.

The old wooden door was cool to the touch everywhere else. I tucked my ear to it, trying to hear if anyone was on the other side.

"Noah," a voice said quietly on the other side. "Don't say anything."

I jumped in surprise. I had no peephole to see who it was, and the door muffled the voice just enough I couldn't quite place its familiar timbre. I pressed my ear back to the door.

"Evangeline is in the infirmary," the voice said. "She's fine. You need to stay here. It's not safe."

My lips began to form a question, but the voice cut me off.

"Shush," it said. "Just listen. She overexerted herself when she was trying to find someone at the end of her range. After a few days of rest, she'll be back to normal. It would be better if you lie low until she's back to one hundred percent. There's no time to teach you how to shield against any Elevated cerebral attacks. You're too vulnerable."

The urge to protest rose up within me, but I chewed on my lip instead.

Then what was I supposed to do?

"I'll make sure no one knows you're here," the voice said. "You'll have to trust me."

I waited for further instructions, but the voice was gone. The identity of the voice was on the tip of my tongue, and I growled in frustration that the name wasn't coming to me.

Bracing myself, I tried the door again. It didn't burn me, so I twisted it open a crack.

A dark form darted in, and the door shut itself against my will. I tried to pull it back open, but it was like trying to open a wall. A shadow fell across the ground, and I turned to see what the door had opened for.

There sat Ig, his green eyes hooded in bliss, hind leg high in the air as he cleaned himself peacefully in the center of the woven rug.

"Seriously?" I asked the room.

Ig paused with his licking, his eyes rolling to mine briefly before continuing.

A heavy sigh escaped me. I left my new personal bodyguard to finish his bath as I refocused on my new boredom breaker—figuring out the common link between Elevated books, preferably before any other Elevated hooligans walked away with my hidden stash.

THIRTY-THREE

Ig's bright green eyes twitched at my every move. I had piled all the marked books on the desk, much as Ms. Xavier had done with those in her office. Even with the sizable surface area of the behemoth of a desk, I had to make several columns on the floor as well. My fingers flicked lightly through the onion skin pages of a cartography book, while Ig's pupils bounced back and forth.

"Do you have anything to add, or are you just trying to be a nuisance?" I said aloud to him.

Ig's tail flicked once. He even gave me one of his slow blinks. My concentration kept breaking, thinking he was about to interject at any moment.

I snapped the book shut and set it to the side. My fingers steepled in front of my face, and I began what had become our habitual staring match. I hadn't been timing them, but I would estimate about once an hour, I couldn't handle the cat's intense scrutiny any longer, and I just had to give it back to him. At least for a few minutes.

"Are you going to at least fetch us dinner?" I said again, breaking the silence with the rhetorical question.

Ig blinked at me, his tail still.

"Thought not," I mumbled, pulling a new volume toward me. "How am I supposed to go out and get food unseen and then sneak back in? Huh? Riddle me that?"

I muttered to myself, wishing I had a human sounding board. Sure, Evangeline was a little difficult because her ability to understand my train of thought caused us to skip ahead, leaving some thoughts unfinished and rough. Adele would humor me with my manic thought webs, but she was always good at playing devil's advocate. Without them, I was left arguing myself to a cat. Somehow, it was more humiliating than I expected.

Ig's eyes flashed at me.

"If you're an Elevated psychic cat, I'm quitting right now," I warned him. "Humans are bad enough. I don't need to start exploring zoology as well."

Ig gave me another slow blink. I stuck my tongue out at him. The feeling was mutual.

"What I need is some sort of codex that will break the cypher of these ridiculous books," I said aloud. "There are too many variables to find the common link by hand. It's not even guaranteed we have all the volumes either."

Through the columns of books, I thought I saw Ig sigh in annoyance. He jumped down from his perch, finding a discarded notebook to sit on. I raised my eyebrow at him, questioning his seating choice when there were multiple comfortable couches and armchairs scattered around the room. Ig began to clean himself again, so I pulled my eyes away from him for privacy.

"It could be by date," I said to myself. "Or subject. The titles seem innocuous enough. Authors too. They could all be pseudonyms for all we know."

I grabbed a few of the volumes closest to me. I squinted at the random sample. Some of the embossed letters had foil, but not all. The material must have changed over time, however, because the wear and discoloration only showed on some of the older volumes. I opened several of them, checking the dates to see if that confirmed my hypothesis.

No. The tarnished ones had dates as late as 1980. An untouched gold leaf volume was dated 1936.

Well, that was a bust.

The gold leaf one caught my eye. *Sleep Disorders Among Young Adults: International Edition.*

I snorted, thinking immediately of Adair. I better hide this one well.

The next gold leaf volume I came across made my forehead crease. *The Complete Body Language Dictionary.* My fingers searched the nearest stack for all the gold leaf embossed books. The titles brought to mind either Adair or Evangeline immediately.

Influencing Influencers.

A History of Biphasic Sleep.

The Ultimate Dream Encyclopedia.

Aura Reading for Beginners.

My eyes slid to Ig. He sat at attention facing me, his eyes unblinking.

"Are you thinking what I'm thinking?" I asked.

His mouth opened wide in a yawn.

I snorted. "Apparently not."

I made quick work of reordering the piles. Standing up, the four separate piles still had a few columns on the floor, and the books were stacked to my shoulders. I paused, wishing for the tenth time this evening that Evangeline were here. I itched at the need I felt, but realistically her knowledge extended far past mine in the world of the Elevated. I needed her as a search engine to help me figure out where to go from here.

Ig finally vacated the discarded notebook in favor of a better spot. My eyes were drawn back to the bright green cover, which stuck out garishly against the prism of blues and silvers in the room. I walked over to pick it up, finding it filled with my poor attempts at Spanish. In the margins, I had doodled a few geometric patterns. It must have been an audio quiz. My eyes caught on the Elevated symbol. I must have drawn it subconsciously along with the triangles and geometric tile borders I had inked.

I tossed the notebook near my bag and returned to my piles. Grabbing the nearest book, my fingers traced the spine again. My thumb caught on the bottom, and I turned the volume over to see what it was.

The Elevated symbol stared back at me. I drew the symbol in the air, remembering Evangeline mentioning the Dawn of Eight story she had promised to tell me once I understood the planes a little better. Without context, she had warned, the story was doomsday at best and easy to dismiss.

My fingers tapped at the points. Eight points. Eight sides.

Evangeline's handwriting came to mind. Her sketch had been confiscated with the other research paraphernalia in the study cubicle, but I remembered her words.

"Relative, temporal, vitality, sentient," I mumbled. The four piles of books stood ominously on the desk and surrounding floor space. "Bingo."

I scooped the entire gold leaf pile to the ground and starting grabbing them one by one. Both Adair and Evangeline were Elevated on the Sentient plane. Using their duality of consciousness and unconsciousness, I sorted the books further into two piles. Evangeline's pile snagged on the edge of the circular rug that bordered the looming desk.

Using Evangeline's sketch as a map, I placed her pile across the desk from Adair's. My eyes pinged back and forth between the two piles I had separated, noticing that while the paper colors varied from cream to butter, the jackets were all the same. Evangeline's pile was a deep forest green, while Adair's was a deep midnight blue. Some were more faded than others, but the colors remained within a few shades.

"Fitting," I said, rubbing the mini bruises on my arms from the corners of the newly sorted piles of books.

I surveyed the remaining piles, realizing my ignorance was vaster than I had admitted. My eyes traced down the titles in each pile, trying to find any more obvious connections than the colors of the covers. While it had proven true for one Elevated plane, I needed something more substantial to link the others. The only other Elevation I had any familiarity with was my own. Nothing seemed to scream banshee at me, and I circled the table again.

Then a title caught my eye. I'd seen it before. Had it been in Ms. Xavier's piles?

Echolocation in Pacific Sea Mammals

My hand went to my throat. I doubted my scream had anything to do with sonar, but it was definitely more than normal human vocal sound waves. My eyes caught on a few more books in the same pile, and I pulled them so quickly, the tower slid slowly down, causing the remaining books to crash in a landslide on the floor.

A Choir of Wolves: Vocalization in North American Lupine Packs

10 Easy Steps to Training Your Dog

Dia De Los Muertos: A History

Death Masks in Tribal Communities

Grief and Loss: A Short Story Anthology

I clawed at all the books, the titles overwhelming me, the tarnished foil glittering at me against the ebony covers. I felt all the blood rush to my head.

And stupidly, my first instinct was to stand up.

My knees locked. I felt my weight shift back to my heels, and I was unable to rock back to balance myself. My shoulder crashed against the floor first, and the rest of my body followed in a heap.

I realized I was gasping. My chest fought hard against my crossed arms, trying desperately to rise to pull in enough air. Tears streamed from my eyes, and I felt an overwhelming sadness come over me.

Inwardly, I groaned.

If I'd known Winter was soundproof, I wouldn't have cared if a song overcame me.

But it wasn't soundproof. And if I sang, everyone would know exactly where I was hiding.

The heat of the song burned in my gut, trickling slowly up my throat like unruly bile. I sucked my lips in, biting down hard on them to avoid any sound escaping. I had to overcome this. I could not be ruled by the songs and their timeline. I needed to take control of my life.

As I lay on the floor, beating myself up mentally for getting too caught up in other things to work on controlling my own Elevation, I felt a bump on my lower back. I rolled over slightly so I was on my back.

Ig jumped onto my stomach, and the surprise impact caused me to cry out.

I smacked my hand back over my mouth, trying to stifle the few notes of the song that had leaked out. My throat constricted in rebellion, and the burning sensation intensified from my abdomen all the way up to my throat.

Then Ig began to knead my stomach.

I tried to brush him away, but my dominant hand was clenched tightly over my mouth. Ig continued to knead my stomach, and the heat spiked in agitation.

Stop! I screamed at him in my mind. My eyes bugged out in nonverbal meaning, but Ig ignored me. Soon, he was pouncing with his forelegs in harmony, and I wriggled underneath him to throw him off.

The song's pressure was building in my throat, and I couldn't hold it anymore.

"Stop!" I screamed, the edge to my voice making me cringe, but Ig froze. "Get off me. Now." Ig leapt off immediately. I sat up, bracing my weight against my arms.

The song still swirled in my throat, distorting my voice, just as it had in the dreamscape. I couldn't remember the last time I'd been able to speak during a song. My concentration was still on Ig, but I felt a sense of power I'd never felt before. The burning was bearable now, but I wasn't sure why.

It was still a horribly inconvenient time to let loose a song. Whoever was about to die would have to wait a little bit until I was in a safer space to let it out.

I moved into a crouch, standing up slowly. The song still swirled in my abdomen, but it was manageable. I took several steadying breaths through my nose, daring to let air hiss out of my mouth. Ig stared at me with rapt attention, still frozen from my scolding.

Slowly, I felt the burning in my throat lessen, the intensity trickling back into my stomach. I pushed it down until it felt like it was concentrated in a low and tight enough spot. Then I let it go. Any pressure I had used to force it down in my mind let it go.

The urge to sing disappeared immediately.

I stood awkwardly in the study, surrounded by an avalanche of books, my hands out to brace myself for the vertigo that had disappeared as soon as I'd released the song. My eyes fell on Ig, whose tail was flicking back and forth merrily.

"You're still an asshole," I said, my voice slightly hoarse. "Do that to me again, and I'll blast you with a banshee scream." Ig sneezed at me and disappeared out of sight.

My fingers hooked in my mouth, and I worried at the quicks of my nails. Even though I should be celebrating my small victory, I didn't know how long the song would stay buried. Or if I could repeat the exercise.

I shook out my hands, drawing them away from my mouth. My fingers reached for the nearest volume. Then another.

While my brain sorted through exactly what had just happened, I would mindlessly sort. Each decision I made, moving books into smaller and smaller piles, helped calm my jangling nerves. By the time the desk was clear, the books sorted and positioned on the round woven rug around the desk, I felt stable again.

My stomach growled.

Sighing, I grabbed my bag. Ig guarded the door as menacingly as a small black cat could.

"Move," I said. "I'm hungry. Even you don't want to fight me when I'm hungry."

Ig sneezed again, moving aside.

I twisted the doorknob quickly, leery of getting burned again. Nothing happened.

I swung my head out into the hall to check for signs of life but found the darkened hallway abandoned.

Ig darted out ahead of me, and I made sure the door shut behind me.

Then I heard voices.

"Ig!" I called out in a hoarse whisper. His head poked out from behind a stack of books, green eyes surveying me. "Come here."

He slunk over, his tail twitching. I crouched down and pulled the old skeleton key from my boot. I hooked it onto his collar, tucking it on the inside so it wouldn't be noticeable to anyone.

"Do me a favor and keep an eye on this for me," I said, looking sternly into his flashing eyes. "There's some very important stuff in there. Make sure not just anyone gets in, deal?"

Ig sneezed in my face, darting behind the nearest stack before I could straighten.

"For not being able to say anything, he sure says a lot," I muttered to myself, wiping the cat sneeze from my face. My stomach grumbled again, and I headed for the stairs.

Even though it was late, I was certain I could find something in the kitchens. I needed as many carbs as possible and definitely several cups of coffee to survive my new research project. I would get to the bottom of this whole Elevated thing even if it killed me, but preferably with a stomach full of bagels and coffee.

THIRTY-FOUR

My shoe hit solid ground, and I found myself on the main path. I shoved my hands in my armpits, trying to hold off the chill in the darkening fall air. I paused, taking a look at the evening sky, a muted blue violet streaked with clouds. I sighed, trying to let out any remaining tension to clear my mind. We had work to do tonight. My breath fogged in front of me, and I watched as it was slowly dispersed by the breeze.

I sighed again at my latest view, finding it cluttered with an unwanted visitor.

"No, Mags. Just, no," I said before she could open her mouth.

"You don't even know why I'm here!" she cried, her arms crossed in indignation. Could she possibly be sulking right now?

My eyes narrowed, daring her to continue. She fidgeted but then straightened her shoulders in a more commanding posture.

"We could've been friends, you know. Good friends," said Mags. "Even though it seems like you aren't the friend type."

"I have friends," I countered stupidly. I was losing feeling in my toes from the cold, and I was tired. The back of my mind where Evangeline's scold would have come through remained silent. She was still asleep, and I was on my own.

"They can't understand you like I do. Like we do," Mags said.

A chill ran up my spine, and I tried to sense the area around me. It was too dark, and the moonlight was blocked by another wisp of cloud. How many was "we?"

"Just because you and I have supernatural abilities does not mean we automatically sit at the same lunch table or are required to be bridesmaids in each other's weddings," I said, my jaw grinding my chattering teeth.

"Clearly." She sniffed. "It's just a shame, that's all. Doing it the hard way."

"Doing what the hard way?"

"Oh, we'll be friends. We'll be friends real soon," Mags said, tapping the Future eye temple. "You're just not going to like the interim."

"What are you even—"

Adair swung into view, and I saw his eyes flicker with silver before everything went black. The further I fell into darkness, the less I could feel the cold gravel beneath my limbs and the night air on my stinging cheek as I was lifted into the air.

"Dammit!" I screamed into the stillness of the dreamscape. I appeared in a crouched stance, and I took a moment to punch the ground furiously with all the frustration and humiliation I felt. As my energy drained and the punching slowed, I rested my forehead on the ground, my knees sliding to the forest floor in an attempt to brace the rest of my bodyweight.

"I don't have time for this," I whispered into the soil. "I really, really don't have time for this."

I sat back on my heels, staying low to the ground. I could collapse. I could throw the biggest tantrum known to man right here for as long as I wanted. No one would see. No one would care.

I growled, discarding the idea. No matter how much I wanted to shout "not fair" at the top of my lungs, it wouldn't change a thing. Resting my chin on my knees, I wrapped my arms around my hunkered body to comfort myself a little bit.

I had been duped a second time, and the sting was even worse. I imagine I might feel the same if I lived to be old enough to not control my bowels. The haunting fear of not being able to control one of the most basic instincts given to us. Adair was going to get his eardrums blown out the next time I woke up. He had way too much fun putting me under.

I smirked. Yet again, though, I was not where he wanted me to be. Sure, my physical body was unconscious and easily moved. I hoped they cared for my body and hooked it up to an IV. I wouldn't last long here without it. They wanted me; they didn't want me dead. However, they also wanted me in a controllable dimension, and that clearly was never going to happen.

Laughing aloud, I rejoiced in Adair's failure. I imagined him being berated by Mags for completely ruining their not-so-well-laid plans.

The sky above me matched the sky I had left, dark and clouded over. I felt the mists moving around and below my hips. In the distance, I saw the slight flickering of the night visitors at their posts. Looking around, I realized I didn't recognize this particular section of the dreamscape. It seemed cloudier than before, so I hoped against hope it was just because of that and not because it had expanded. Evangeline's range could expand all it wanted. I did not need more acres of dead people to watch.

Getting up slowly, I tried to look around in more detail. I had to have been here before. The lake had been new when Colm had been here. Was the landscape different according to the inhabitant? Not that I could ever test that theory.

An orb appeared in front of me. I sprang up, looking around. Nothing else changed. The visitors in the distance remained the same. The mist still crawled past my ankles. The orb pulsed, and I couldn't resist. I reached out my hand and touched it.

It felt cold and warm at the same time. It moved across my fingertips like wet clay being molded on a potter's wheel. Solid, or at least mostly so, but with the distinct feeling of having no particular set shape at all. The more I pressed into it, willing my hand to grip it, the more it moved away from my touch. It pulsed again, and I pulled my hand away, just in time for it to explode.

The wave of energy shot out like a supernova, cutting through me and streaking to the ends of the dreamscape. My vision was spotted and took several minutes to clear fully. I blinked and blinked again, willing what was before me to blink back out of existence.

It was Colm, but it wasn't.

Colm as a night visitor.

"No," I whispered. My hand reached out instinctively again, hovering at the bounds of the vision in motion. Colm's eyes were pained, but his face seemed determined. Somehow, that made it even worse. He looked exactly like he had in the classroom. He would die soon.

I walked around his visage slowly. For the first time, I was determined to know what his abstract death scene meant. I had to know because I had to stop it, even if it meant watching him die over and over and over again until I could solve this puzzle. His puzzle.

He indented himself, folding inward from all angles until he exploded, much like the orb had only minutes before. Or was it hours? The sky was still dark, and I continued to watch him die. Each time the reel started, I braced myself, watching Colm as he slowly became less of himself until he was gone.

Then, I remembered Harry. The middle-aged man I had seen since birth. He indented, too. What was the connection?

Once, I thought he'd had a heart attack, but Colm was too young for that. Some other traumatic event, maybe, like a car crash. That could crush any part of you multiple times over. But how could I stop a car accident? I had to think of something else. Please, let it be something else.

A bomb?

Never mind. Not like I could do well in stopping one of those either. It had to be something with enough force to impact its victim.

Impact.

Oh God.

My hands flew out involuntarily, and I tried to block what I knew would come in the next cycle. Instead, I stumbled into Colm's visage and froze. I had never walked through a night visitor. It seemed so disrespectful. Other than Colm's, I couldn't think of one that I'd touched with any intention either, but I was inside one.

A warmth grew in my stomach, just like when I was about to sing. Never once had I felt a song come on in the dreamscape. Made sense. No one else was here except for me. Why would I sing?

This time, I let it flow out of me. It was Colm's song after all. That knowledge hit the bottom of my stomach like a rock. I never wanted to hear a song for a friend, but it was there nonetheless. If I couldn't get out in time, this would be the last I would see of him. I needed to honor that.

So I sang.

And the weirdest thing happened as I sang. I could see him. Colm.

Wait, no. Where was he? I could see Aileen, and the nurse, and the Dean, and...

Oh my God. Oh shit. I was Colm.

I could see through his eyes. Was this real time? Too freaky, even for me. No. I would not be like Adair. I could not. I didn't want to test this boundary of my abilities. This wall could remain up and fully reinforced, thank you very much.

The scene changed. It had mist around the edges, the same kind that slowly crawled on the ground here. It was not a welcome sight. Did I do that?

The warmth that radiated up through my mouth continued, even stronger now. I was still singing, and I was starting to understand the reason why.

I was still in Colm's point of view. I saw only what he saw. I was disappointed I couldn't change vantage points, but I was not directing a movie, I was watching as Colm. More specifically, I was about to watch Colm die.

I could feel his emotions as if they were my own. I guess they kind of were. Fear. Anger. Duty. Duty to what? I couldn't see what he was trying to protect, just that there was something. There was no sound. I couldn't tell if he was speaking or if he was hearing something around him. Wrong use of the mute button, in my opinion.

I focused on what Colm was seeing and feeling. If those were going to be my only clues, I would have to work with that. I could see a nicely built desk. It looked familiar, but the angle was off.

Well, shit. It wasn't the infirmary. A sense of doom weighed heavily in my stomach as my throat burned. I was running out of song. We were following somebody. Was it Mags? I saw a flash of bright hair. Why were we following her?

I was frustrated—or maybe Colm was—when he tried to stop and figure out which room he needed. Mags grabbed him by the arm and led him to the furthest room, barging in without even so much as a knock.

And then everything went black.

THIRTY-FIVE

"Hello, Noah."

I spun around, trying to find the voice. I couldn't see anything but knew I was no longer in my dreamscape.

"You know what, Adair? I'm over this. I really am. You can't just yank around people's consciousness as you please," I said, finding I had folded my arms across my own body. Well, at least there was that.

"You'll understand. I know you will," he replied calmly. "You can't hide from logic."

"I'm not feeling particularly logical right now," I retorted. "Put me back in my body, and we'll see if I come around."

I could see him walk toward me, stopping a little distance away. He, too, was in full body, although the rest of my field of vision remained black, the spotlights on us reminding me of some avant-garde theatre show Adele and I had gone to once. I wondered if that's where Adair had found his taste for dramatic flair.

"I knew if I could get you alone, we could reason things out." Adair offered me a chair. The field shifted, and we were in a slightly muted grey space with a rectangular table and two chairs, all brushed metal.

"I think you watch too many crime dramas. Any reason we're in an interrogation room right now?" I said unpleasantly. I was going to get a headache with all these slight-of-hand tricks. I would not be the easiest person to win over if I was also battling a headache.

"Would you prefer something more comfortable?" Adair asked as he slid us into a deserted café.

"I preferred the interrogation room. At least it doesn't hold the pretense that I'm here voluntarily." The room shifted back, and I sat down before Adair could offer to pull out my chair. "So, what are we bargaining for? My freedom? My allegiance? To be honest, I'm not really a cup-half-full kind of girl, so I'd appreciate some candor. Think you can do that?"

"I'm confident you'll see the logic of our future partnership. Mags is skeptical, but since she's exhausted her resources, I've been allowed to try my hand. It's not just us two who have been wanting to get to know you. Surely you are aware?" Adair clasped his hands genially over his crossed legs.

I had assumed Adair was a Beta based on how little he talked around Mags and her general attitude of running the show. I straightened my posture, giving me some time to work around the man in the room who held all the power.

"Should I be flattered?"

"Of course. It goes beyond wanting to play with the shiny new toy."

"And here I was worried I wasn't going to be popular in high school. Glad that doesn't seem to be the case."

"This goes beyond high school, Noah. Honestly, do you think people like us just stay in the background, hoping for a quiet, normal life?" Adair's eyes shone with what I assumed to be a slight mania. How cliché that he seemed to be the perfect mad scientist in training.

"That has actually been my goal the entire time. I would swap my abilities with a normal person in the blink of an eye," I replied. "Of course, I could see how you can find good use for your talents. Shall I call you Mr. President now, or wait until you meet the age requirement?"

"President?" Adair laughed. "No. A little too limiting for my tastes. Once I find all the Elevated of our generation, we will find ourselves building a new world order. One that suits our talents, if you will."

"And for those, like me and Evangeline, who don't particularly feel like joining your new world order? What happens to us?"

"Oh, you'll come around."

"For argument's sake, Adair. Work with me. I need to know the endgame in order to play the game," I said. "Surely you can understand that."

"There are no other options."

"Of course there are."

"Well, I suppose we could just keep you here until you come around to reason."

"That's not really reason. That's some sick combination of blackmail and torture."

"Effective though."

"Okay, so I'm sensing my options are to join your league of villains, rot or go crazy in my dreamscape, or die. There's always death, you see, Adair. You can't forget who you're working with."

"The only option worth pursuing is mine. Of course, if that's still not enough, there are plenty of people you care about that we could use for motivation."

"See? And there you go with the blackmail again. You keep talking about logic, but I'm not hearing any."

"You want logic?" Adair said, bristling at my resistance. "Fine. Humans gravitate toward those they share a likeness with. Whether it's talent, identity, or aspiration, we all form groups. It's natural to want to band together with others who share your otherness. People who can help you. People who care about you and your whole self. We are those people."

"Evangeline's that person." I frowned. "Not you. Not Mags, and not even whoever you think is in charge of your little group. They don't care about you, they care about your abilities, just like all those normal people out there. I'm just a trophy for you to collect, and I refuse to go down easily."

I stood up from the chair.

"I will not be contained by your abilities. You can catch me and find me and put me back under as many times as you'd like. I won't go down without a fight. I'll be the thorn in your paw until you die of exhaustion. I'll be the nightmare you never saw coming."

"I'm not trying to control you, Noah." Adair sighed. "I'm trying to offer you freedom. True freedom. You can't get that anywhere else."

"I can and I will. Goodbye, Adair."

I turned, walking toward the grey wall I knew wasn't real. I passed right through it into darkness.

"I'll be back later, Noah, once you've had some time to see the merit of my deal. Don't take too long, or I'll be forced to motivate you." The voice seemed to echo around me, but I continued to walk, even though a small part of the back of my mind wanted to know how exactly I could walk in disembodied space. Adair had made the rules, not me, and I wasn't about to let one go to waste. Especially if I could find a door back to the waking world.

"I'll be coming for you, too, sweetheart. Don't wait up," I muttered. One liners aren't very good unless you can see the barb land. It didn't matter much. I just needed to find the way out, and fast. I began to think about a door, or hell, even a window.

Out of pure irony on my subconscious's part, a window appeared. The window was a twin of the one in Winter, and I reached out my fingers to trace around the somewhat familiar surface. I pushed on the frame after undoing the latches. It took all my willpower to budge it a crack. Not nearly enough space for a human. Frustrated at the millionth obstacle this week, I yelled. Releasing my anger, I felt my throat warm. The yell turned dissonant, and the window shattered.

I slapped my hand over my mouth. The warmth receded back down into my gut, and I counted prime numbers to make sure I wasn't losing my mind. I peeked at the frame, noticing it had moved enough to fit a human being. A Noah-shaped human being at least. Before I could overthink it, I climbed through the window to the other side, just as black as this one. Once I thought I was through, what little purchase I had fell out from under me, and I screamed, falling faster than any rollercoaster.

What are you doing making so much noise? a voice groaned in the back of my head.

Evangeline?! I thought back. *You're awake?*

Clearly. Although you're...not? How is this possible?

Shut up and let down your barriers.

What?

I have an idea. Just do it.

You do want me cognizant for this, don't you? I have a feeling I'm about to take another long nap if I lower my barriers right now.

Can you just trust me, please? We don't have time for this right now.

Fine. I expect a very thorough explanation.

Okay, just don't freak out.

This does not bode well.

Can you please concentrate on your barriers? I have, like, thirty seconds or less.

'Til what?

LOWER YOUR BARRIERS OR I SWEAR TO GOD.

Okay, okay, okay. Hold please.

A light opened up below me. The falling sensation had made me feel queasy, but I'd stopped screaming to concentrate on Evangeline's conversation. Plus, I didn't feel like finding out what would happen to a banshee who lost her voice. If that was even possible.

The light grew brighter the closer I came to it. The hole seemed to swallow me, and I was suspended in light for a brief moment until I hit the floor.

"Ow!" I grunted. "How does that even happen? I'm supposed to be asleep right now."

I looked up to find myself back in the infirmary, next to Evangeline's bed. Her face was perched above mine, her tongue sticking out as she tried to balance remaining on her bed with leaning over and poking me.

She couldn't. Her finger passed right through me, and a shiver ran down my spine.

"Woooowwwwww." Evangeline waved her hand back and forth through my crumpled mirage. "This. Is. So. Cool."

"Could you not?" I said, collecting my sprawled limbs and my remaining dignity from the floor. "It feels weird."

"You...look weird." Evangeline squinted. "I can kind of see you, but you have no color. I've been noticing the color thing more and more since you mentioned it. Very interesting stuff."

"Not remotely interesting lately. Did you know I was ambushed in broad daylight? How rude is that?"

Evangeline shook her head. "I kind of passed out. I can't read people when they're asleep. Usually." She frowned. "But..."

"This," I said, motioning to my ghostly frame, "does not count. This is left over from Adair. And kind of you, somehow. I just took advantage of his sloppy exit."

"So you're asleep?" Evangeline asked. "And you're...where exactly?"

"No idea. They took me somewhere, but I was stuck in my dreamscape a little early. Not sure how long I was out before Adair came to visit. How long has it been since you saw me in real life?"

"Like, two days." Evangeline bit her lip. "Maybe two and a half."

I sighed heavily. "On the bright side, campus probably just assumes I was arrested. Or possibly expelled since I'm a Boyfriend Stealer."

"Bright side?" Evangeline looked horrified.

"Well, normally I would find it amusing. I'm a little tired of crisis mode at the moment."

"I've been talking to Ms. Xavier. She knows our research has gone missing, so I could only give her the highlights of what we'd found. You're going to flip when you hear her thoughts on your rebellion theory," Evangeline said. "And she confirmed that the puppet master on campus is the dean. Kind of obvious when you think back to their little tiff when Ms. X was bailing us out."

I rubbed my hand over my face, trying to steel myself against the information overload about to happen. I didn't have time to complete the whole backstory of our fates when Colm was in immediate danger. I needed to focus on the present and worry about all the minutiae later.

"Okay, I was serious earlier about time being short. We can go over all this later. You need to find Colm and warn him. Like, now."

"Warn him about the dean?" Evangeline asked, sitting back in her bed.

"No. Yes. Well, she may be involved, but I don't know how dirty her hands get in these situations. She seems like a delegator to me. I mean that he's going to die."

"I'm sure he's aware. He just woke up from a coma, for Pete's sake."

"No, I mean again. He's going to die again, soon, for real this time. I saw him in my dreamscape. As a night visitor. You know, the mirages that reenact the person's death on constant loop?"

Realization dawned on Evangeline's face.

"Yeah, big problem. Because I'm like this," I said, gesturing roughly to my translucent body. What an inconvenient time to be a ghost. "So you need to do it."

Evangeline's face turned ashen. She shook her head vigorously. "Can't. Nope. Won't be able to help, sorry."

"Evangeline!"

"I'm stuck in here! And what am I supposed to say to him, huh?" Evangeline asked desperately. "Excuse me, the girl you made googly eyes at is a banshee and saw your death while she was comatose after she was attacked, but no worries, her best friend happens to be some messed-up medium who's come to warn you of some foggy details that may or may not save you from your imminent death?"

Evangeline took a deep breath.

"Maybe don't mention the banshee part," I suggested.

"How am I supposed to skip over that?"

"You know what? You're right. We sound crazy. I just don't know what else to do!"

"I know this is going to suck, but..." Evangeline held her hand out about where my shoulders would be. "I think you're going to have to wait. If the universe decides to give you a shot to save him, it will. And if not, you're going to have to let him go."

"Let him go?"

"Yeah. Everyone dies. Some people die young because they're meant to. What do you think you're going to do, save them all?"

Evangeline looked sympathetic, but the thought of letting Colm die so horrifically made me sick to my stomach. Surely I was meant to help. Why else would I have this stupid gift?

"I'll find another way." I stepped out of Evangeline's reach.

"What are you going to do?"

"Restrategize. You know me. I'll find a way." I mustered a slight grin, but Evangeline seemed skeptical. I wondered how well she could read me in this form. The answer was well enough to detect my bullshit.

"Let me rephrase. How do you plan on getting back to..." Evangeline waved her hand again. "Wherever."

"Easy," I said with a saucy grin. "You're going to kick me out."

"Sorry?"

"Put up your barriers again. Hard. Slam them so hard, not even a speck of dust could get in. The force should propel me back...wherever."

"I don't feel good about this," Evangeline warned.

"Trust me. Remember? And if I don't come back, I highly recommend messing with Adair until his brain melts. You know, my dying wish and all."

"Don't joke like that," Evangeline scolded. "But you've got a deal."

"Count of three?" I said, prepping Evangeline and steeling myself.

"Three."

"Two."

"One."

THIRTY-SIX

I opened my eyes, fully expecting to find silent mist nipping at my ankles and Colm silently collapsing into himself. Instead, I was staring into crystal blue eyes.

"Noah?" Colm said.

I gasped and sat up quickly. Colm had to jump from his seat on my bed to avoid knocking heads.

"You're fine." Colm braced my shoulders with his hands before I could go any farther. "Shhhh. You're safe. Everything's fine."

I barked a laugh, looking around the room. We were alone but probably not for long. Colm was in pajamas and a monogrammed bathrobe. School. We were still in the school infirmary. I sighed inwardly, glad we hadn't made it as far as my half vision. Colm moved his face in front of mine, trying to gain my attention.

"Relax," Colm said in an even softer voice.

I blinked at him, wondering if this was a dream or not. I'd been out of practice for so long, I was still unsure when I was awake and when Adair was putting thoughts in my head. Our prolonged eye contact made Colm blush, and he removed his hands from my shoulders quickly, as if they had started to burn.

"Where am I?" I asked, my voice breaking from disuse.

"Infirmary," Colm said, not taking his eyes off me, as if I were going to leap out of bed and through the door any moment.

My limbs felt like lead, and I wiggled my fingers and toes absently to shake out the pins and needles. Seemed real enough.

"You've been out for a while."

"Did I beat your record?" I asked dryly, my voice cracking on every other word. My hand found its way to my throat. Frowning, I looked to Colm, as if he had an explanation. Instead, he handed me a cup of water, and I downed it immediately.

"Nah. Although you might have created your own to beat for future coma patients. Number of minutes of straight screaming while sleeping. Nightmares?" Colm had lines on his forehead and around his pursed lips. Could he possibly have been worried? Over me?

"Something like that," I managed, relinquishing my empty cup. Colm set it aside and returned, inspecting my face.

"Are you sure you're okay?" he asked.

"I thought you said I was fine." I smiled.

"Well, you were loud enough three rooms away. I would hate to get one of your screams full in the face," Colm said, letting a chuckle slip through.

"Sorry about that," I said, unsure what to say. Adele never mentioned any screaming, but then again, I'd never sung in my dreams before. Was that where the screaming had come from?

"I actually got worried when you went quiet for so long. So I came to check." He scratched the back of his neck awkwardly.

"Thanks, then," I said. "For checking on me." *Even though you don't even know me. And you still have a girlfriend. And you look ridiculously good straight out of bed*, I thought.

"No problem," he said.

"Do you happen to know how I got here? What happened?" I asked innocently. I cringed inwardly at the fakeness, but Colm couldn't possibly know about Adair's abilities, and I didn't feel like blurting out some insane line about the boogeyman walking among us. I was not a fan of hug me jackets and padded rooms.

"You came in a couple days back," Colm said, looking at the wall as if trying to remember the details.

I took his distraction as an open invitation to stare at him, relishing his close proximity. It was weird how comfortable we seemed to be, even though we had both felt the awkward tension in the room.

"Your friends brought you in. Something about collapsing when you were studying? I'm sorry, I didn't really hear."

"Oh, wow. A couple days?" I was mentally hitting myself over the head. Evangeline had been right. I'd been under way too long.

"Yeah. And for most of it, you've been screaming. A couple times it almost sounded more like singing, but it was hard to hear through the walls. Sorry I can't be of more help."

He seemed sincere. It was hard for me to tell, and the beginnings of a migraine were coming on. I was not supposed to be awake right now. I still wasn't sure how I'd managed to wake up, but I had a feeling I should be thanking Evangeline.

I looked toward the window, but either the

blinds were shut or it was another concrete-block scenario. Surely it was dark by this point. My body was clearly averse to being topside this time of night. I swung my head around from the window to Colm instead.

"What time is it?" I nodded my head toward the dark window. Colm flicked his wrist, moving his heavy watch face upward.

"Uh, looking like three AM. Give or take," he said.

We've got incoming, I heard Evangeline say in the back of my mind.

Incoming? I blinked in surprise at my interrupted inner monologue. How long had Evangeline been listening?

Our favorite bump in the night is coming to check on you. Better get lover boy back in bed so he doesn't get zonked. That can't be good for a person's health.

My eyes must have gone out of focus while listening to Evangeline, and Colm reached out and held my chin, forcing my gaze to reconnect with his.

"Noah?"

"I'm fine. You should go back to bed," I said, trying to keep my tone light. I flashed a smile, but it fell away quickly in my distraction. Colm, unconvinced, held my chin firmly in his grasp.

"Is everything all right?"

In the building. Hurry!

"Oh yeah," I lied. "Fine." How was I supposed to get Colm to leave?

You suck at lying. He's taking the stairs. Thirty seconds or less.

Colm was still in front of me. This was not good. He wasn't leaving.

"Please," I said. "We're running out of time."

"Noah, are you sure everything's all right?" Colm asked, his hand dropping to the bed, accidentally bumping mine. "You're awake. Everything's fine."

"I wish," I muttered. My hand flexed nervously, and Colm laid his more solidly over mine.

Hold on tight, Evangeline said in my mind. *You're getting the express treatment.*

I felt a yank behind my belly button.

Then everything went black.

I opened my eyes in a swirling mist. My face was pressed against something hard, and I realized I was lying down in my dreamscape. I sighed, pushing upward.

Brushing myself off, I looked up and yelled in surprise.

"Why does this seem so familiar?" Colm asked, his eyes light and curious.

He looked around, and I covered my face with my hands, hiding my jaw hanging inches from the floor.

"You..." I started. How was I going to work this? "You've been here before."

"I think so," Colm said, striding through some of the trees. He touched them as he passed and rubbed his fingers together, perhaps checking to see if what he was feeling was real. He didn't seem to be freaking out. Yet.

"It was lighter," he said. "Last time, you know?"

I followed him hesitantly. "Yeah," I managed. My eyes were watching him without blinking. This was worse than the last time we had met in here.

"You were here, too," Colm said slowly, turning to face me. He smiled. "Weird."

"Yes," I confirmed. "Very weird."

"Whoa," Colm said. He had come upon a night visitor, something he had not seen before in his last escapade in my dreamscape. I held my breath, letting him explore before attempting to explain. As if I could explain what was really going on here. I'd like someone to explain it to me sometime.

Colm stretched his hand out slowly to the moving mirage. This was one of the tamer ones, which I was eternally thankful for. A woman, slight and hunched with age, shimmered slowly out of existence, part running water and part evaporating mist. She seemed calm though, so I'd always assumed her death was a natural one after a long, full life. I had named her Martha.

I slowly closed the distance between Colm, Martha, and myself. He seemed content in silent awe of the scene in front of him.

"This is so cool," he said, turning back to me, reminding me of an excited child who had just discovered an amazing new toy.

"There are more," I said quietly, nodding my head into the forest.

Colm looked toward the light smudges at standard intervals in the distance. "Really? I wonder who they are," he said.

"I'm not always sure," I admitted.

"That's right. You said you dream this often. Last time?" Colm said, tearing his gaze away long enough to look to me.

"Every night," I confirmed. "Although I did see you a few times during the day. When you were here, they weren't."

I indicated all the other night visitors in the distance.

"Then, this last time, when I was in the infirmary, they never left. A new one came," I said, dropping my voice. No, I shouldn't tell him about that. He can't see it.

"Awesome," Colm replied.

"Not really," I said, walking past him to an outcropping of rocks. I couldn't remember offhand where Colm's death image was, and I was not up for giving Colm the full tour. He didn't need to see anymore. He needed to go home.

"What are you talking about?" Colm said, following me to the rocks. He stood in front of me, taking my hand in his. I pulled it out gently, shaking my head.

"What's wrong?"

"We need to get you home," I said firmly, almost more to myself. "You don't belong here. I don't know what will happen if you stay."

"I'm fine," Colm said, taking my hand again and squeezing it in comfort, probably more for him than for me. This time, I let him keep my hand.

"Now," I argued. "But I really don't feel right about you being here. It was an accident. Evangeline was only supposed to pull me."

"Who's Evangeline? Noah, what are you talking about?" Colm asked. He rubbed his finger across my knuckles, and fire lanced through me. I pulled my hand away, unsettled by the sensation so close to my banshee warmth. Now was not the time, and this was not the place.

"Someone bad was about to come, and the safest thing would have been for you to return to your room. But there wasn't time," I said.

"Time for what?" Colm asked.

"To be more careful." I sighed. "You're stuck in here with me. Or at least until I can find a way out for you." I wasn't even sure if I would wake up in the morning or if Adair's nightly visit meant he had renewed whatever spell he had over my ability to awaken.

"We'll wake up together," Colm said with confidence and then blushed. "Well, not like that."

"You never know. You probably collapsed on top of me when we were pulled. Hopefully your sleeping self knows how to keep his hands to himself," I said, raising an eyebrow playfully at him.

"I'm sure he's being a perfect gentleman," Colm assured me. "We can blame my sleepwalking on your screaming. Can't get any good shuteye around you."

"It'll get better shortly," I said. "I promise."

"Pinky swear?" Colm joked, holding his finger out expectantly.

"Pinky swear," I said, rolling my eyes. "I need you to promise me something now." I was taking chances on whether he would remember, but I had to do everything I could. If he could recognize me at school from a few encounters in the dreamscape, I had high hopes this conversation would bleed over, too.

"Anything," Colm said.

"Don't trust Mags," I said sternly. "Seriously, Colm. I don't care what happens. Just stay as far away from her as possible. She's dangerous."

My mind was screaming about Adair, too, but if I said any more, I felt like I would have to explain. There wasn't enough time. My promise had to have impact.

"Okay," Colm said, searching my eyes, his own crinkled in concern. "I promise."

"Also, you have to promise me there are no hard feelings," I hedged, our pinkies still hooked together.

"About what?"

"About this," I said, gathering a full breath. I found the warmth traveling up my core and to my throat and thrust my hands out at the same time I released a scream.

Colm looked horrified, but only for an instant as he was thrown back into the mist before he disappeared completely, leaving me alone with Martha and my court of silent night visitors.

I felt a pang at the bottom of my stomach as soon as Colm disappeared. Now the dreamscape seemed lonelier than usual. Martha flickered quietly in the corner of my eye. Not quite the same.

My feet followed their own path, my mind heavy with worry for things far out of my control. I needed to stop reacting to all the cloak-and-dagger threats and go on the offensive. I was a banshee, dammit. I would not take this attack lying down.

I looked up and found myself in a mostly vacant area of my dreamscape. I couldn't remember the visitors I'd passed, so I couldn't orient myself to them. Not like this place had Google Maps anyway. I saw a night visitor along the edge of a copse of silent, dead trees and made my way toward it.

My legs locked up as recognition hit me.

It was Colm.

Cautiously, I edged toward the night visitor. It wasn't really Colm. Not the one I wanted to see by any means. He continuously folded in on himself, and the determined look on his face only left when he had no face at all. I bit the inside of my cheek.

Focus. I needed to focus.

Impacted, right? The working hypothesis had been a gunshot wound before I'd been ripped out of the vision. I needed to know more if I had any hope of stopping it.

I took a deep breath and exhaled to the point of

passing out. I was determined to finish the vision. Now that my personal connection with Colm was more than just a fantasy, I had warring arguments in my head as to whether or not I should see this. It might be painful to watch, but I knew I had to change whatever path I had directed Colm on. He was going to die because of me, so it seemed only right I would be the one to make sure that didn't happen. At any cost.

I shook out my hands to steady the trembling that had managed to escape from my agitation. *Think of it as a chess game*, I thought. *We need to know the opponent's endgame if we are to play any countermeasures.*

Chess. Not Colm, the caring musician with eyes the color of the ocean.

"Chess," I said out loud, gritting my teeth against the onslaught of new tingles tracing their way up my spine.

I clenched my fists and stepped forward, allowing the image of Colm's death to permeate my mind, welcoming it like an old friend.

THIRTY-SEVEN

I was following Colm and Mags down the halls of the infirmary again, only this time, something about Colm's posture was different. It seemed less trusting. Could my warning have worked?

The inside of my cheek was becoming raw from my self-reprimands. He was still following Mags, so the warning obviously wasn't good enough to dissuade him. Whatever his reason for still following Mags must be important enough for him to risk acting like an idiot.

Mags' hand was on the doorknob again, and I held my breath as it opened this time. No blackness followed.

We entered the room, which was like a mirror image of Evangeline's. Except it wasn't Evangeline who was in the bed.

It was me.

"Dammit," I said out loud to no one in particular. "Seriously?"

Colm ran forward, relief on his face. What was worse than being here, and why had he been so worried? Mags stayed behind, her hand still on the handle. Something flickered across her face, but I couldn't tell what. Her Future eye distorted a lot of her features, not that I was any good at reading them on a good day. I wished I could rewind the vision to study some of the details, but it ran full steam ahead, ignoring my desires.

"Is she okay?" Colm said, his voice sounding pinched, as if he had been worried. "Why is she in here?"

"She won't wake up." Mags shrugged. "Noah needed more attention than the school nurses could handle by themselves, so they moved her up to this secure floor. She's perfectly safe here."

"Liar," I muttered.

Mags' Future eye shifted toward me, which spooked me. She couldn't possibly be seeing me right now, could she? This was just a vision from who knows where. The Future eye shifted back into the room in general, and I brushed the hairs on my arm back down. Goosebumps could not be a good sign.

"I thought you said she just passed out from exhaustion. This doesn't look like exhaustion." Colm's desperate face was inches from my unconscious body. "She looks like...me."

"Your coma was induced by the doctors to regulate the swelling in your brain after a traumatic football injury," Mags said, the only tell for her agitation being the vice grip she held on the door handle. "And I hardly think you know what you looked like when you were under all those months."

"I don't expect you to understand out-of-body experiences," Colm said under his breath. "She might be here."

The Future eye swung back at me menacingly.

Luckily, Mags herself did not seem convinced.

"Look, we have to go," Mags replied. "I have to sneak you back out before anyone comes to check in on her."

Mags' good eye went to the clock on the wall, but she didn't seem in that much of a hurry. It was like she was waiting for something. Something like a predetermined time. My stomach dropped lower as I realized her lack of conviction about hurrying could mean only one thing.

"Bitch," I said, walking up to her face, staring down the Future eye with all the burning hatred I was feeling toward her right now.

The Future eye seemed to look back at me, boring into my core.

"If you let anything happen to him," I threatened, "and I do mean anything—it will all be your fault. One hundred percent of his blood will be on your hands. You are making the choice right now to lead him into a trap. And for what? He doesn't know anything. The worst you'll do is hurt yourself." And me, I added in a small voice.

The Future eye shifted away, but I touched her face, drawing its attention back to me. My hand seemed frozen, the pain of the coldness leaking through to me, but I held it there.

"Do not let this happen. If this is some ploy to win me over, I don't even have the time to tell you how wrong you're going to be when this backfires. Let him live. Me for him. Let him go, and I'll be your ally. You have my word," I said, my voice heavy with the warmth drawn up from my core. If she did anything stupid, I was ready to blast her Future eye with as much banshee noise as I had within me. It was not going to be pretty.

Mags stepped away from me, giving my spot a wide berth. Another expression flickered over her face, but all that remained was slight annoyance, which was pretty standard for her general demeanor.

"We really should go, Colm," Mags said a little more convincingly. "This floor is locked for a reason, and they take security very seriously. She's fine, but we're about to not be if we don't move it."

Colm shook his head slowly, his hand enveloping mine.

"I can't leave her. Not here, not alone like this," Colm said, his hip resting against mine as he sat on my bed.

"The hell you can't. I'm not going to be killed because of you and your sappy determination." Mags grabbed his shoulder. "Time to go."

"Go," Colm said, shaking Mags' hand off. "I'll be fine."

"Dammit, Noah," Mags muttered under her breath, only loud enough for me to hear.

My eyebrows shot up in surprise. Had she heard me? Did I change the vision with my promises?

Mags stepped in front of Colm's face, snapping her fingers to draw his attention from my sleeping body toward her.

"Hey," Mags said, her odd eyes even with Colm's. "I'm about to let you in on a secret. One I really shouldn't, but clearly, one that may save your life."

I held my breath.

"Noah here," Mags pointed directly at me, "is special. Special sort of like your out-of-body experience comment earlier."

Colm squinted his eyes, as if trying to read through Mags' sincerity.

"Well, I am, too. Special. There's a lot of special going on at Windermere, and it's really not safe for you to know any more details. I'm breaking so many rules even hinting at it, since you're not special. In that way," Mags qualified. "You know what I mean."

"Not really," Colm said, his tone even and honest.

"Ugh." Mags growled in frustration. "The baddies are coming, okay? Does that help? Special baddies. The evil villains, if you prefer. And if we're here, we're going to end up in beds right next to Noah, or worse." Mags flung her hands out, her face angled to emphasize what exactly she meant.

Colm's face darkened. "Then I really can't go. What if something happens to Noah? I couldn't live with myself," he admitted, his gaze shifting back toward me.

Mags' hands flew to her face and she released another frustrated growl. "If you don't leave with me right now," Mags said in a low tone, "I will be forced to endanger Noah."

Colm stood up, trying to guard my body from her threat. "Don't you dare touch her. She warned me about you," Colm said.

"You remember?" I whispered, stepping between him and Mags. I tried to catch his eyes, but he looked right through me and at Mags. If he remembered the warning, what else did he remember, and how?

"Yeah, well," Mags said. "I never said I was a good person. Clearly, trying to be is not working in my favor, so I'll have to rely on my tried-and-true methods. Get your ass out of this building now, or so help me you'll get reacquainted with your old friend, Coma Colm."

I frowned at her threat. Man, she was not very good at influencing strong personality types. And I thought my people skills were lackluster.

"Colm," I said, pushing as much energy as I could toward him, begging him to notice me and what I was trying to say. "Go. You need to go now.

Forget about me. You shouldn't be involved in any of this." I pushed at his chest, and this time, instead of ice picks attacking my hands, I felt a warmth nearing volcanic proportions.

Colm took a step back.

"Is it working?" I asked, turning around to the Future eye. It pulsed at me once, which I took as a yes.

I turned back toward Colm, and he wore a confused expression. He turned back toward my body, his fingertips brushing mine. "Noah?"

Mags looked at the clock and cursed. "We have a little time before it's too late, but I need to stress the word little," Mags said through her teeth. "Can we go now?"

Colm still looked a little unbalanced, as if unsure if what he was feeling was real. He looked down at his fingers and flexed them. I reached out, wanting to press against the barrier again, but I hesitated.

"Noah," Mags said, squinting at Colm's dazed expression. "We really really really have to go. I can't promise to keep him safe if we don't leave right now."

I swung back to the Future eye, my hand curling back to my side.

"The deal is void if he dies," I warned.

Mags nodded her head once, looking directly at me.

"Come on, boy scout," Mags said, grabbing Colm by the forearm and dragging him to the door. "We're about to miss our window, and your girlfriend can be really scary, even when she's just a vision."

"Girlfriend? Did she say she was my girlfriend?" Colm asked, turning the corner of the door.

I let out a laugh, thinking of the check yes if you like me notes we had passed around the classroom in grade school. It was so much more complicated than that.

I stayed in my room, listening for their feet retreating down the hall. I was curious, so I slowly approached the hospital bed. Evangeline and I, had we been awake, would be wearing matching pajamas. Somehow I was a little disappointed I couldn't run around with my bare ass cheeks flashing the staff.

My eyes were closed, and my hair was spread loosely around the pillow. Definitely a no-no when sleeping, but I guess there was very little possibility of tangling your hair with tossing and turning if you were stiff as a board. The monitors beeped quietly in the background, proving I was still alive at some near distant time in the future.

Then I heard gunshots.

Even out of body, the vibrations punched me in the gut, one after another.

My head whipped around to follow the noise. The monitors in the background were freaking out, but I was out of the room and running down the hall before I could even blink.

I found the staircase I had used for Colm's second floor visits. I pounded down them, cursing that my vision body couldn't just float through walls and blink into rooms on a whim. Damn physics slowing me down.

The landing came too soon, though, and I was not prepared.

Colm lay slumped against the wall, a pool of blood growing larger as he struggled to sit up, struggled to say something.

"Colm!" I yelled, falling to my knees next to him. I counted the holes. Four in the chest. I frantically tried to press down to staunch the bleeding. My touch did no good. My hands remained clean as the blood fled its host's body.

I looked around for help and saw two security guards on the landing below, one talking calmly into the radio strapped to his shoulder. The other, although bigger, was having a hard time restraining a blur of arms and legs.

"Intruder subdued," guard number one said lazily into his radio. "Gonna need maintenance in Stairwell Four."

"Don't. Touch. Me!" Mags screamed, bucking and twisting in the grip of the second guard.

"Also gonna need a psych team stat. We've got a witness," the guard continued. "Says she's with the program. ID not found."

"Roger," the radio squawked back.

I pulled my horrified eyes back to Colm, whose breathing was shallow.

"Colm?" I whispered, my hands still moving from wound to wound, trying to do something to stop the inevitable. "Oh my God. No. This can't be happening."

"Noah," Colm whispered, his head turning in search of my voice.

"No," I said firmly. "No, this is not how you're going to die. I fixed it. You can't go!"

The stairwell door opened below us, and I heard a new voice enter the din of Mags' screams and the radio static.

"I can't follow you if you die," I said, the lump in my throat making my voice sound froggy. "You have to stay here. You have to stay alive."

"What happened to the plan?" Mags screamed behind me, her rage cutting through my last moments with Colm. The words pinged dully on the back of my mind.

"I should be asking you the same thing," the voice replied coolly. "The dean will not be pleased. This was not what you promised."

"You don't know a damn thing, Adair," Mags said, spitting more venom at him than I'd ever heard her use on him before. "You don't know what you've just done."

"I seem to be doing a lot lately. I don't appreciate picking up your slack," Adair said brutally. "Getting my hands dirty is tiresome."

"First Sean, and now Colm," Mags roared. "And what do you have to show for it? Any closer to scaring Noah straight?"

"She'll come around. She just needs some isolation away from the meddlers," Adair replied. "I've got everything under control."

"The hell you do!" Mags shouted, kicking out a new wave of anger and striking one of the guards.

I looked back to see the Future eye as it whizzed in my direction and pulsed. Once. A pause, then once more. I couldn't have gotten a bigger hint if Mags had brought her very own flashing neon sign.

So the show had been for me.

They had set me up to take the fall for Sean, but I had wriggled my way out of that one. With both Colm and Evangeline subdued, and Ms. Xavier trying to keep a low profile, only Adele would care to look for me. Even so, she was no match for the several Elevated masterminds that wanted me cooperative. I was at their mercy now.

"Go let her cool off," Adair said to the guard. "She's in my way."

Emme DeWitt

"Yes, sir," the guard replied, dragging Mags still kicking and screaming out into the adjacent hallway.

My eyes, locked on Colm as the light drained from his eyes, flickered as a dark shadow entered my peripheral vision. My thumb brushed away the blood trailing down Colm's neck, but the stain remained.

"Don't you dare touch him," I growled at Adair, unsure if he would be able to hear me.

Adair approached, undeterred, bending over to peer into Colm's dying eyes.

"If you had just died the first time, Colm, you wouldn't have gone through so much pain. I tried to save you from it a few months ago, but you just wouldn't cooperate. Now, I get to clean up your mess," Adair said, lifting his hand to cover Colm's face. "I am not a fan of messes."

"I said, don't touch him, asshole." The lump in my throat dissolved with the fire streaming up from my core. "One finger on him and I will become the scariest nightmare you never saw coming."

Adair, deaf to my threats, began pulling Colm apart from his consciousness. I could practically see Colm's soul being pulled through his skin, and I screamed.

Colm jerked, his soul shrinking back into its dying shell. Adair frowned.

My eyes flashed in an epiphany, and I gathered as much rage and air in my diaphragm as possible.

Adair leaned in closer. Colm's eyes had shut in the failed attempt. Adair's fingers jabbed into Colm's neck, and I could see the disappointment on Adair's face grow darker and darker. His plaything had died prematurely.

Just as the flicker of a pout began to form on Adair's face, I lost it.

My agony burst from my mouth, shredding my throat, mixing with the fiery trail of tears marching angrily down my cheeks. I felt my hair blow back and rise, crackling with electricity. I screamed so loudly, Adair jumped back, falling down the stairs in a mass of elbows and knees.

I planted myself in front of Colm's body, daring the crumpled body of a former friend to touch the only human I had truly cared about more than even myself. Adair remained huddled, bracing himself against the cacophony of noise I was forcing upon him.

Slowly, my mind became heavy. The scene around me blurred like a watercolor painting blended with too much water. The colors, shapes, and noises muddled into a grey scene darkening slowly into black, but I was still screaming. I took a deep breath when it all became too dark to see. Too dark to know if I was still me or if I was trapped once again in a nightmare.

Then I felt a flicker of sensation on my fingers.

Footsteps.

The beeping of a monitor.

A series of rumbling crashes. Was there a thunderstorm outside?

My eyes searched in the darkness for something, anything. Slowly, my fingers moved. Twitching first, then a few bends. I still couldn't see anything, and the noises were muffled now.

I felt a punch to my gut. No.

Colm.

And I screamed.

EPILOGUE

I convulsed on my bed like a crash cart victim. My eyes flew open, and I braced myself against the high thread count sheets, pursing my lips and forcing my accelerated breathing through my nose.

Count to ten. Easy in, silent out. Lower your heart rate before they notice, I heard in the back of my head. *Elevated levels like that will get you medication that fills your head with cotton balls that itch more than you ever thought possible.*

My pajama top was twisted up, baring my torso to the cool room. It stuck everywhere else, giving me goosebumps in the heavy gusts of air conditioning. I was losing feeling in my foot, so I squinted through the darkness, noticing the sheets were coiled like a boa constrictor around my entire right leg, providing ample evidence of this evening's nightmare.

Perfect. Situation new normal.

I tried to straighten my top, the only manageable thing to do in a darkness so complete I often forgot which way was up and which way was down. I still felt too exposed, but there wasn't much else I could do.

Much better, the voice said, commenting on my normalized breathing. *Now quit fidgeting. They'll notice you're awake. They'll put you under worse*

next time if they know you can break out of the
nightmares on your own.

*They're idiots if they think I need any help with
nightmares*, I flung back, sending the heavy sigh I so
desperately wanted to release into the stillness of my
room.

Don't let them figure that out, the voice said in
mild amusement. *You're the only interesting one to
talk to in here. I'd hate to have to resort to
conversing with Uriah. He still thinks I'm some
demon taking over his brain.*

Gee, thanks, I said.

You're welcome, the voice replied.

Tell me, how are you not dreaming right now?

*Oh, I don't sleep much. I find it
counterproductive to my sanity. Not much of it left,
so I'm trying not to squander what's left. You'll have
to let me know if it's working.*

Not sure I'm the best person for that, I replied
with another internal sigh. *I can't even tell what's a
dream anymore.*

*Come on, now. That's not the fighting spirit I
know. You've got to think outside the box. Or
outside of outside the box. You know what? Forget
there ever was a box. That should help.*

*How am I supposed to forget the box we're
trapped in? That's the stupidest advice I've ever
gotten.*

*Maybe, but you'll figure something out. You've
got so much to work with, it's really a surprise
you're even still in here with us wackos. I would've
expected a break out weeks ago.*

*Sorry to disappoint. Why aren't you coming up
with an escape plan?*

I defer to the experts, in most things. You're also better equipped. You know, being a people person and all.

I laughed internally, a smile leaking onto my face. *Is that what we're calling it?*

Well, it's not wrong. Do you want to get out of here or what? the voice said, posing an excellent question.

If I did get out, what would I do? Where would I go? There were a multitude of options and infinite possibilities in not only getting there, but also figuring out where there was. I couldn't just think of the right now. I needed a master plan. Preferably one concocted after a good night's sleep, whenever that was going to happen.

So, what's the plan? I asked, half to myself and half to my conversation buddy.

I don't know, Evangeline. You tell me.

COMING SOON

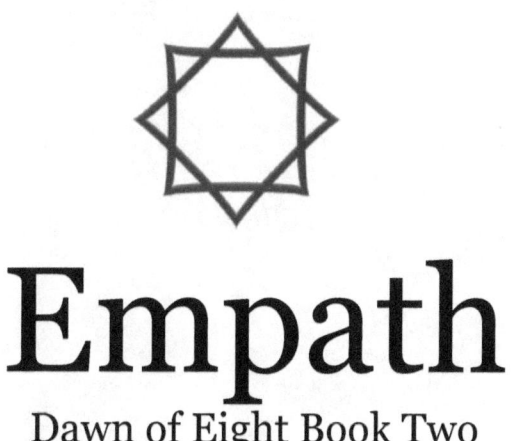

Empath

Dawn of Eight Book Two

Winter 2016